The wind was cold enough to bite through his borrowed overcoat.

But Jesse couldn't seem to feel anything but warmth as he looked down into Erin's warm blue eyes and slightly parted lips. Between her fall and the rush to board the train, her raven hair had loosened from its pins. Now wisps of dark curls blew against her delicate cheek. His fingers itched to find out if the locks were as soft as they looked.

He cleared his throat instead.

"You always need this much help?" he asked. "You all right?"

She lowered her eyes, her dark lashes fanning her pink cheeks and gathering fluffy white snowflakes. "It has been a particularly harrowing morning. But I'm quite all right, thanks to you. I believe you can release me now."

When she looked back up, those expressive eyes showed everything she was feeling. Embarrassment, a hint of wariness, attraction.

No, that moment when their eyes had met on the train platform hadn't been a fluke.

Books by Lacy Williams

Love Inspired Historical

Marrying Miss Marshal
The Homesteader's Sweetheart
Counterfeit Cowboy

LACY WILLIAMS

is a wife and mom from Oklahoma. Her first novel won ACFW's Genesis Award while it was still unpublished. She has loved romance books and movies from a young age and promises readers happy endings guaranteed in all her stories. Lacy combines her love of dogs with her passion for literacy by volunteering with her therapy dog, Mr. Bingley, in a local Kids Reading to Dogs program.

Lacy loves to hear from readers. You can email her at lacyjwilliams@gmail.com. She also posts short stories and does giveaways at her website, www.lacywilliams.net, and you can follow her on Facebook (lacywilliamsbooks) or Twitter @lacy_williams.

LACY
WILLIAMS

Counterfeit Cowboy

Love Inspired

Recycling programs for this product may not exist in your area.

ISBN-13: 978-0-373-82946-0

COUNTERFEIT COWBOY

This edition published by arrangement with Love Inspired Books.

www.LoveInspiredBooks.com

Printed in U.S.A.

If someone takes your cloak, do not stop him from taking your tunic. Give to everyone who asks you, and if anyone takes what belongs to you, do not demand it back.

—*Luke* 6:29–30

Be merciful, just as your Father is merciful.

—*Luke* 6:36

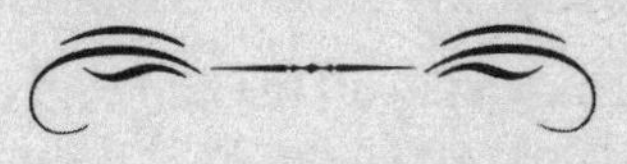

To my dad, who has had the courage to change his life, not once, but many times. I love you, Daddy.

To my mom, the glue in our family.
You are precious to me.

Acknowledgments

Endless thanks to Luke, who works so hard to make my dreams come true.

A huge thank-you to all the babysitters without whom this book would not exist: Gammy, Nana, Grandmother, Aunt Abby and Donna. And a special thanks to our "live-in nanny" Aunt Pingie for the extra time you spent with the kids!

With thanks to all my family and friends for your continued support and encouragement.

Regina, Mischelle and Denice, thank you so much for your critiques that helped make this a better story!

And as always, with extreme gratefulness to my editor, Emily Rodmell, whose guidance and editorial work is invaluable.

Chapter One

December 1890—Boston, Massachusetts

"You'd best hurry, miss. The train's leaving now."

A loud whistle drowned out her thanks, so Erin O'Grady simply smiled at the man behind the ticket counter and turned to the companion at her elbow.

"Are you certain this trip is all right with your father?" he asked.

The query from the man beside her was one of the two reasons she wouldn't consider marrying Patrick MacKenna—her dear friend was far too concerned about her father's opinion. And Erin wanted the freedom her father refused to give her. At nineteen, she'd never been away from home on her own. Until now.

The second reason was that she'd known Patrick since he'd worn short pants and there was no attraction between them. But he was her closest friend, as evidenced by the fact that he'd brought her to the train station this morning. And he'd never lied to her, not like her father had.

"By the way, you look horrible," he continued. "Where did you get that awful dress anyway?"

Sometimes her friend could be a little too honest.

"One of the maids let me borrow it." The housedress in question was drab brown and did nothing for Erin's figure. It was inches too long, and Erin had stepped on the front hem several times in the short time since she'd donned it this morning before leaving her father's house.

But the dress served an important purpose. If her father managed to figure out she was leaving Boston by herself and sent someone to fetch her, they'd never recognize Erin in the ugly dress. She hadn't recognized herself when she'd used the looking glass to pin her hair up.

She couldn't wait to get far enough away from Boston to change into the traveling dress she'd packed.

Erin accepted her valise from Pat and checked over his shoulder. She was gratified to see he'd entrusted her other luggage to one of the porters.

"Are you certain this is what you want to do?" Pat asked.

"I'll be fine." It wasn't quite the answer she knew he wanted, but it was all she could give him. She only hoped it was true, was still raw from the confrontation with her father several days ago. Her anticipation for the trip was muted by the familial discord.

Ignoring the worried crease between Pat's auburn brows, she bent to retrieve the packages she'd bought for her brother and his family on her way to the train station. Christmas gifts that she hadn't had time to stow in the trunk that would make the trip with her. She bobbled the armful as she straightened, and Pat steadied her with a hand to her elbow.

"I'll be sure to tell Da you tried to dissuade me from going."

Patrick blanched, his freckles standing out against his pale cheeks. "But—"

"I'll be fine," she repeated, fervently praying that it was true. She'd never done anything like this before.

The train's whistle blew again and she stood on tiptoe to buss his cheek, then turned to the crowded platform.

She was on her way to Wyoming. On her own.

Two days out of Boston's Deer Island House of Corrections and all Jesse Baker could hear was the ring of his stepfather's voice.

You'll never amount to anything—never be more than a petty thief.

He remembered the disgusted look that had accompanied the shouted words as if it had happened yesterday instead of nearly a decade ago when he'd been a boy of fifteen.

He wasn't a thief. People *gave* him their money, once he persuaded them to his line of thought. A confidence man wasn't a thief, even if he'd been sentenced to five years for swindling.

Although he wasn't exactly a con man any longer. He'd been out of the game for five years, while he'd been in prison. Two days of making his own decisions had muddied the waters he thought were so clear upon his release. He hadn't had any intention of returning to his life of tricks and schemes—he'd intended to find honest work if he could.

But a visit to the family of Jim Kenner, his former cell mate, had changed everything. He'd promised to bring Jim's brother home to Boston, and he'd hoped that would relieve his guilt.

Now he needed money to get to Chicago. To fulfill his promise made to Jim as he'd died. And he needed to leave now, today. There was no time to get an honest job and save up the funds it would take to buy a train ticket. Even though his mother was still alive, he didn't ask her for help. She wouldn't have forgiven him, not even after all these years.

Jesse blinked away those thoughts. He needed to concentrate, needed to find a lemon—someone who would give him the money he needed.

He scanned the crowd on the platform, some people headed for trains and others disembarking. Men in suits, families with children, porters juggling luggage… There! He spotted the perfect woman, across the platform.

She was tall, wearing a dress with an oversized bustle. White gloves up to her elbows. An ostentatious hat complete with a garish purple feather covered her perfectly coifed hair.

She was obviously made of money. And seemed to be alone. The perfect target.

Jesse began moving through the crowd, already spinning a story in his head. *My sister's eloped with an unscrupulous man. Need to get to Chicago to stop the wedding.* Or maybe, *I've got a sick aunt and need to visit before she dies.* The best stories always evoked sympathy. And the truth was too convoluted—and who would believe a man fresh out of prison?

What he really needed to do was figure out a way to incorporate his borrowed clothing into the story. Jim's sister, the only person who'd shown him any kindness since his release two days ago, was a laundress and had given him the clothing that someone had left behind. The denims, woolen shirt, leather overcoat, boots and Stetson had turned Jesse into a cowboy. Albeit with boots that pinched his toes a little and a hat that felt uncomfortable after going without for such a long period of time.

What would a cowboy be doing in Boston?

He kept the ugly plume in sight as he followed her through the thicker part of the crowd. Someone bumped into him and for a second Jesse was back in the prison yard amid crooks with burly shoulders and cold eyes. He shook himself into the present. This wasn't prison. But what were all these people doing here?

Then all the packages and cheerful faces began to make sense. It was only a few days until Christmas.

Jesse hated Christmas.

He shoved the emotion down into the blackness inside. *Don't get distracted. Just focus on getting to Chicago.*

But then he nearly stumbled on top of a young woman in a brown dress crossing his path. For a moment he froze as everything else around him faded and he met her startling blue eyes.

Then she turned to rush toward another departing train and the moment was broken.

He couldn't help glancing over his shoulder and saw that an unsavory-looking character followed the girl a few paces back. He knew the look on the man's face—

predatory, focused. As if he were chasing the girl and not merely a fellow passenger who happened to be going in the same direction. He doubted the girl was even aware of the man a few steps behind her.

Don't lose focus. Jesse fought the distraction again and forced his eyes back to that feather as it bobbed above other passengers' heads.

But the young woman had reminded him of his little sister, Helen—who he hadn't seen in a decade—and Jesse couldn't just ignore that this girl was in danger. Maybe in danger just of losing her wallet, but his time in prison had taught him there were many evil-minded men who would do much worse to a young woman alone.

Jesse changed direction in time to see the unscrupulous man's shoulder connect with the girl, sending her sprawling. On the crowded platform, it could've been an accident, but Jesse knew it wasn't. He twisted and elbowed his way past several people toward the girl who scrambled to gather several brown-wrapped packages scattered at her feet.

Jesse glared at the man who'd knocked her down, and the fellow hurried away. Jesse knew the other man had hoped no one would stop for the girl, making her more vulnerable.

"You all right, miss?" Jesse asked, squatting and reaching out to help her gather her packages. She was older than he'd first thought, maybe twenty. And prettier, too, with long sweeping lashes against her cheeks and a button nose. But her plain dress and shapeless coat showed Jesse she wasn't anyone that could help him get to Chicago.

She barely glanced up at him, just a flash of those bright blue eyes. "Yes—"

The hiss of a train's brake releasing interrupted her. "I mean, no. That's my train!"

She speared him with a frantic gaze as she reached for the two small packages he held and darted toward the nearest train—one that had already started to depart.

He could see she was never going to make it.

A glance behind him revealed the woman in the feathered hat was long gone.

He still needed a way to get to Chicago. Surely there were other wealthy people in this crowd, someone who could be convinced to turn over their money to Jesse.

But that girl… As he watched, she bumped into someone else and nearly fell again.

Jesse knew she wasn't someone who could help him. But she obviously needed looking after.

He'd come out of prison intending to start a new, honest life. Was this a test to see if he could put someone else's needs above his own motives?

The maid's ill-fitting dress was going to keep Erin from boarding her train. Carrying all her packages, she didn't have a free hand to hike up the front of the skirt, and she nearly tripped on it again. The train was picking up speed!

She couldn't have come all this way not to make it onto the train. She couldn't—wouldn't—give up!

And then the cowboy was there, propelling her forward with his large hand under her elbow.

"Need a hand, miss?"

"Yes. Thank you," she panted, glancing at him only long enough to get a picture of molasses-brown eyes and hair just a shade too long, curling beneath the brim of his hat.

She had no idea how he was going to get her onto the moving train. They were nearly there, the steps of the train car looming…

Snow blew in from the outside gap between train and station. The sharp wind threatened to tangle Erin's skirt around her legs. She fought forward, feet pounding loudly with the cowboy's boots. They were running out of platform.

The cowboy ran so fast and pulled her with him until Erin felt as if she was almost flying.

"Ready to jump for it?" the cowboy asked. Wind whipped her hair out of its pins and into her eyes, but she could still see his rakish grin, as if he were enjoying their flight to board the train.

Erin opened her mouth to let him know that an O'Grady would never do something so commonplace as jump—if she could get the words past her burning throat—but her feet tangled in her skirt and she stumbled, coming precariously close to falling onto the tracks. The smell of heated metal filled her nostrils—

A strong arm clamped around her waist and hauled her against a muscled chest. Then her feet left the ground entirely, and she was bodily dragged onto the train car's steps. With a jolt and huff as his boots clanged onto the step, the cowboy gripped a handle on the outer wall as they sped out of the station and into the open air.

They'd made it!

Chapter Two

It had been a gamble.

Jesse knew there was a chance he'd be thrown off this train at the next stop for boarding without a ticket. But something inside him had pushed him to help the girl he now held loosely by the waist. Her scent, something sweet that smelled more expensive than he expected, swirled around him on the icy wind.

It was cold enough to bite through his borrowed overcoat, but he couldn't seem to feel anything but warmth as he looked down into her bright blue eyes and slightly parted lips. Between her fall and the rush to board the train, her raven hair had loosened from its pins. Now wisps of dark curls blew against her delicate cheek. His fingers itched to find out if the locks were as soft as they looked.

He cleared his throat instead. It had been a long time since he'd been close to a woman like this.

"You always need this much help?" he asked. "You all right?"

She lowered her eyes, her dark lashes fanning pinking cheeks and gathering fluffy white snowflakes. "It's been a particularly harrowing morning. But I'm quite all right, thanks to you. I believe you can release me now."

When she looked back up, those expressive eyes showed everything she was feeling. Embarrassment, a hint of wariness, attraction.

No, that moment when their eyes had met on the train platform hadn't been a fluke. She'd felt it, too. He was sure of it.

For a moment, Jesse forgot all about Chicago and the promise he'd made to Jim Kenner about taking care of his family. He wanted only to sit next to the pretty girl on the train and discover everything about her—including if she could genuinely care for a guy like him, one who'd made innumerable mistakes.

He had his doubts, and they were based on the facts of his past.

She readjusted her armful of packages and her action served to put a few needed inches between them. He released her, letting his arms fall to his sides.

He was careful to stay behind her as they crossed the small vestibule outside the train car proper, in case she slipped or stumbled again.

After being confined to a small cell most days, the scenery rushing past threatened to make him sick. Good thing there wasn't anything in his stomach.

He held the vestibule door, gripping it tightly. Her shoulder brushed the lapel of his jacket as she passed, the sweet, flowery scent of her hair spiking in his nose above the dust and grit swirling around them. As they entered, she smiled up at him. "I suppose it must be true what they say about cowboys and Western courtesy."

He'd nearly forgotten about the outfit Jim's sister had

given him. He didn't correct her misconception, only followed her into the train car.

The door opened and closed behind them but he only glanced away from his companion long enough to see someone short and slight of stature—maybe a child moving from one train car to another?

The softness under his feet was his first clue maybe he was in the wrong place. Jesse looked up and realized they'd entered a fancy sleeping car. He'd never been on a train before, but the opulence here told him the ride wasn't going to be cheap. From the gilded chandeliers swaying overhead to the velvet-upholstered seats to the plush carpet runner, all of it bespoke the expense of riding in this car. It even smelled like money—clean and with a slight scent of coffee.

Had his companion meant to be on *this* train car? She didn't look as if she could afford it.

He wondered how long until the conductor came through. Probably not long, so he needed to work quickly. He glanced around the nearly full car, trying to see if there was someone alone he could approach, trying to spin a story that would gain him sympathy. *Lost my wallet.* It might work.

With only a few empty seats, the girl moved toward a pair of vacant benches nearest the door—where she would get a blast of cold air each time more passengers boarded, no doubt. Jesse followed close behind and took the seat across from her, his eyes still skimming the other passengers.

She spoke as she settled in the empty seat, dropping her packages beside her. "Thank you for your assistance. Mr.…?"

He spoke absently. “Jesse Baker.”

“I’m Erin O’Grady.” There was only a slight hesitation before she extended one dainty hand across the space between their seats.

His hand engulfed hers when he took it. Jesse was surprised at its softness. He glanced at her again, at the simple dress beneath her coat, one fitting for a working-class girl. But her hand didn’t feel callused like a working girl’s hand should…

Petite and curvaceous, with her soft Irish lilt and sparkling eyes… Looking at her, a strange hard knot formed behind his sternum.

Someone plopped down beside him, jarring his shoulder.

“And I’m Pete.” The voice came from near his elbow, and Jesse was astounded when a street urchin smiled winningly up at him—complete with stained, too-short pants, white shirt turned gray and tattered sweater. No coat. His unwashed face, gaunt figure and hands with dirt-encrusted nails completed the picture.

Jesse was further astonished when the boy yanked his thumb in Jesse’s direction. “I’m his brother.”

Opening his mouth to protest that Jesse had never seen the kid before now, the conductor banged into the cabin with a whirl of cold air, stalling him.

“Tickets!” the uniformed man barked.

Some of Erin O’Grady’s packages wobbled and fell onto the floor. She bent to pick them up, and the kid leaned close to Jesse, providing a whiff of unwashed body. “I saw you snitch a wallet offa that man in the station.”

Jesse had to laugh, albeit incredulously, at the kid's audacity. "I did not."

"Then what's that?" The kid pointed to Jesse's lap and Jesse was surprised that a leather billfold peeked out from between his side and his coat.

The kid's knee bounced up and down, belying his confident manner.

Jesse picked it up. He'd never seen it before. The light finger must have planted it there. "This isn't mine—"

"You might wanna put it away then. Here comes the conductor."

Jesse looked up sharply, but the man had stopped just across the aisle, his back to where Jesse, Erin and the kid sat.

"I need ta get outta town, and we're gonna pretend like we're brothers, otherwise the conductor's gonna find that wallet and a couple others in your coat pocket," the little pickpocket said. His little face was so serious Jesse didn't doubt he'd do what he said.

Jesse glanced covertly at Miss O'Grady, but she was bent over, head nearly touching the floor. Apparently, her package had slid underneath the seat. Between the two of them, they were the least nicely dressed in the train car. Why had the kid approached them?

"I don't even have enough money to buy one ticket—" Jesse started. He didn't need trouble. What he needed to do was get to Chicago, but that was looking less and less likely.

The conductor turned, eyes assessing their group, and Jesse stopped speaking.

The kid beside him cleared his throat and Jesse knew he didn't have a choice but to go along with what the boy wanted, not if he planned to stay on the train. He'd go along for now.

Erin straightened up with an "Aha!" waving a small wrapped package successfully.

"Tickets," the uniformed man grunted. His foot tapped, as if he was impatient to move forward in the car.

Erin quickly proffered a slip of paper. Her ticket.

When the conductor looked to Jesse pointedly, he cleared his throat. "I'm afraid I boarded the train in a bit of a hurry." This was where it was going to get interesting. "Didn't have time to get to the ticket window."

"Extra charge," the man grunted, appearing nonplussed and digging into his vest pocket. "Where to?"

"Well, Chicago. But, sir, I can't afford—"

The kid cleared his throat from next to Jesse. He cut his eyes to Erin and the conductor, then gave a little quirk of his eyebrows as if silently asking Jesse *What are you going to do?*

Shame, leftover from his time in prison, drew Jesse's shoulders tight.

"Please," Erin interrupted with a soft touch on Jesse's arm. It made him jump.

He couldn't remember the last time someone had touched him kindly. The guards had grabbed, pushed, shoved; no one had touched him with gentleness since Catherine and he didn't want to think about her or her betrayal.

"I'd like to pay their fares." Erin dug around in her carpetbag and came up with a small leather pouch. It tinkled when she opened it, and Jesse saw a wad of cash inside. What was she doing with that much dough?

"No—" Jesse started to protest. Someone like her with that kind of money—it had to be some kind of inheritance and he didn't want to take it from her, only from someone who could afford it. He'd never taken from someone who couldn't afford to lose a little.

"Please, I insist. I wouldn't have made it onto this train without your help."

The conductor huffed his impatience, and with a look at the kid, Jesse shrugged. Maybe he could find a way to pay her back before they parted company.

Jesse was on his way to Chicago. In much nicer fashion than he'd imagined when he'd come to the train station this morning. Maybe it was a sign for him that his plans to build a new life would come to fruition.

After all, he wouldn't have any bad memories following him around in Chicago, not like Boston.

As the conductor moved off, Jesse settled back into the seat, finally taking off his slicker because it was pleasantly warm in the train car.

The kid sat beside him, and Jesse spared a thought to wonder why he'd approached Jesse and Erin. What purpose did he have, blackmailing Jesse into taking him to Chicago? What did he really want?

Jesse sat back and watched as the two chatted. He'd learned the value of watching and biding his time during his stint in prison. Not that the practice had helped him escape when another prisoner had come after him with a knife…

"What you got all those packages for?" the kid asked.

Erin continued arranging the stack of brown-wrapped packages she'd carried onto the train. "They're gifts for my brother and his family. That's who I'm visiting in Wyoming."

"All of 'em?" The incredulous question seemed to burst out of the boy.

Erin nodded.

Jesse waited for her to tell the boy to be quiet and leave her alone. He didn't understand why she was still talking to the kid, who'd quickly proved an annoyance to Jesse. Maybe she felt sorry for him.

"My brother and his wife recently had a baby," she told the kid patiently. "And I haven't met her yet." Her expression turned inward for a moment, as if she regretted what she'd just said.

One thing was clear. This brother and his family were important to her.

Jesse tried not to think about his own family. His ma, who he hadn't seen in a decade and who had likely disowned him. Or his brother Daniel, who he'd been responsible for and had failed completely.

Erin had felt Jesse Baker flinch when she'd touched his arm. He hadn't reacted in any other way, but she knew she'd felt his arm jerk away when she'd lightly touched him.

The question was why.

She was naturally curious, and drawn to the man who'd helped her. He was certainly handsome, with chiseled features beneath his Stetson and those arresting brown eyes. She guessed he was five or six years older than her, in his mid-twenties; although the lines around his eyes seemed to indicate he had led a harder life than she...

A muscle in his jaw ticked and he seemed to be glaring at Pete, who paid him no mind as he glanced around the train car. The poor condition of the boy's clothing seemed to indicate he'd lived a harder life than Erin, as well. Her heart pinched as she remembered many faces just like his, faces she was leaving behind.

"So…what's in Chicago?" she asked to distract herself from thoughts better left in Boston.

"A new start," came Jesse's reply. He shifted his feet, his boot brushing against the tip of her shoe. Muted conversations from other passengers weren't audible enough to break into their conversation, offering them a bit of privacy even in the well-populated train car.

"Really? You're giving up being a cowboy?"

He looked down at himself, as if assessing the woolen shirt and denims he wore. Shook his head slightly. Looked away, as if he didn't want to answer.

Well. She looked to Pete and smiled, if a little thinly. Certainly, Jesse didn't owe her any explanations, but this would be a long trip with a quiet companion… "And you're going with your brother. What about your other family?"

"Ain't got much family left. Our parents died off. I was living with my aunt 'n' uncle when my brother, Jesse here, came to get me—"

Jesse nudged Pete with his elbow, breaking off the boy's sentence. "I'd been away from home…for a while."

"Well, that explains the disparity—" She paused and chose another word when Pete began to look confused. "The difference in your clothing. You don't really look as if you belong together."

Jesse shot a long look at the boy sitting next to him. Pete returned it in kind. Erin didn't know what communication they'd exchanged silently, but whatever it was, the message didn't make either one particularly happy.

"But you're bringing your brother to live with you? That's quite compassionate of you, Mr. Baker."

His eyebrows drew into a slight questioning frown as he looked at her for a long moment.

"Yeah, real compassionate," said Pete with a cuff of Jesse's arm that seemed to bring him out of his stare. He shook his head.

Erin encompassed them both with a smile. "Family is important," she said softly with a little twinge for what she'd left behind in Boston. She shored up her smile, determined not to let what had happened with her father ruin her trip. "Especially this time of year."

Pete's expression remained blank.

"Christmas?" she offered tentatively. "The joy of Jesus's birth should be shared with those we love."

The boy's nose wrinkled. Did he know the Christmas story? Erin had to wonder and, if his clothing was any indication of his home situation, she guessed he might not.

What would it be like to go through life without having the Savior's love as comfort? She didn't want to imagine the bleakness she would have endured without that hope during her lonely childhood…

She opened her mouth to say something—she didn't know what—only to find Jesse considering her thoughtfully, his brown eyes almost seeming to take her measure. Heat climbed in her cheeks. Perhaps he thought she was sticking her nose in where she shouldn't.

Then an attendant approached, and the tension between them was broken. The uniformed man recited the menu for the midday meal included in the ticket price as he installed a plank table between the two facing seats. Ingenious.

Her companions allowed Erin to make her selection first, then made their own. When Pete asked for a cup of coffee, she nearly inserted that he shouldn't have any, but Jesse glowered at him and told the waiter to bring him a glass of milk.

"And no potatoes," Jesse added as the man moved away. Curiosity piqued, Erin was going to ask him about the unusual request but he'd twisted to face his brother.

"You ever been on a train before?" The inflection in Jesse's voice made him sound suspicious, rather than curious.

"Oh, yeah. Lotsa times—" Pete stopped midsentence, as if thinking better of his statement. He glanced warily at his older brother. "I mean, once. Mam took me to see, um…a friend of hers in New York. Before she passed."

Something about his statement didn't ring true. The two brothers continued to consider each other, almost fiercely. Silence stretched awkwardly, and Erin could hear the clinking of other passengers' silverware against their plates and the low hum of other conversations. She shifted in her seat.

And then the attendant returned, bearing two plates of beefsteak for the men, one with no potatoes gracing its plate, and Erin's split pea soup.

The steam tickled her nose as she bowed her head and said a silent blessing over her food. When she raised her head and lifted her spoon she found Jesse's eyes on her, an incredulous look on his features as if he'd never seen such a thing done before.

He looked away quickly, and she followed his gaze to Pete, who was stuffing his mouth so full that his cheeks puffed out. The boy's plate was already considerably emptied.

"Kid—" Jesse started speaking, a warning tone in his voice. Before he could say more, Pete's face turned green.

"Is he all right?"

Before she could get the entire question out, Jesse launched into the aisle, dragging Pete by the elbow, but it was too late. Pete lurched once, couldn't seem to get his footing, and then lost the contents of his stomach on the edge of the seat and floor.

He continued to heave as Jesse hauled him down the aisle toward the washroom until Erin lost sight of them.

Jesse pushed the kid into the men's washroom, just in time for another round of retching. Jesse kept the door mostly shut. He had an iron gut, especially after the things he'd seen in prison. The sharp scent of the kid's sick didn't bother him a bit, even in the close confines of the small hallway outside the washroom, but he didn't want the other passengers to see or hear the kid expelling his lunch.

He'd almost felt a little sorry for the knucklehead. The kid's arm in Jesse's grasp had been slight, and there wasn't much of him to have to haul to the washroom. He was obviously on his own, and not doing too well at it. Jesse wondered about the wallet the kid had tried to foist off on him. It hadn't occurred to Jesse to check and see if there was anything in it. It could've been empty—a ruse to get Jesse to help the kid with a ticket.

The kid was proving to be a pain. Jesse wanted to get to Chicago without much fuss, and making a scene like this wasn't in his plans.

Jesse wondered if his seatmate would notice if the kid didn't come back with him. Maybe Jesse could put him off at the next stop?

Although it didn't sit quite right with him to leave a sick kid on his own. Even if the kid had already caused Jesse a heap of trouble by blackmailing him into a train ticket. If Jesse could figure what the kid wanted, maybe he could get rid of him.

"What happened?" asked a soft voice from Jesse's elbow and he turned to find Erin O'Grady standing near. She was even more rumpled than she'd been after their wild flight to board the train. And there was a suspicious stain at the hem of her dress.

"The kid ate too fast is all," Jesse explained, turning toward her and using his shoulders to block her from the sight behind him.

A moan came from the washroom. The train rocked and because they stood so close, she swayed forward and Jesse got a whiff of her sweet smell.

"Shouldn't you go in and help him?"

"Hmm? Oh." Jesse started to respond that the two of them wouldn't fit in the small washroom.

Either that or give up the ruse and tell her the kid wasn't really his brother, but she expelled an exasperated little huff and used his elbow to twist him out of the way. She pushed into the tiny washroom, her skirt brushing against Jesse's legs, and slid her arm around the kid's shoulders, helping him slump against the wall.

Jesse watched through the half-open door as Erin took a handkerchief out of her pocket and wet it with fresh water from the pitcher, then used it to dab sweat from Pete's pale brow. She spoke soft nonsense words to him, kept gentling him with touches and fingers combing through his hair.

Jesse was momentarily glad for the kid, even if he himself had never received such gentle treatment.

His clearest memory was of his father—his real father—talking to him man to man. That was about as close as the man got to gentle. Jesse had respected him so much. But those memories brought thoughts of Daniel, and those thoughts were trouble.

A moment later, Erin moved out into the narrow aisle with Jesse, again coming closer than he expected. Water splashed inside the washroom.

"Have you embraced him?" The vehemence in her question surprised him, as did her flashing eyes. "There's nothing to him but skin and bones. Why, I think he's practically starving. I imagine that's why he couldn't keep the food down. He probably hasn't eaten in days."

Jesse opened his mouth to tell her the kid wasn't really his concern, starving or not. Now that the conductor was gone, he had no reason to continue this farce. Before he could speak, she poked him right in the chest with her finger.

"It's a good thing you've done, coming back to Boston for him. He needs a champion like you." Her eyes flared with such admiration that he stood dumbfounded while she helped the kid out of the washroom and back toward their seats, leaving Jesse to follow.

She was the first person other than Jim in a very long while to look at him as if he might be worth something.

But what would she think if she knew the truth about how he'd failed as his real brother's champion?

Chapter Three

In the privacy of the women's lavatory, Erin changed out of the soiled, drab housedress and into her traveling gown, feeling more like herself. And a little relieved to be out of the smelly dress.

Ensconced in the tiny, overwarm room with barely space to move, Erin studied her image in the water-speckled mirror as she tucked her dark hair back into a proper chignon.

She touched her fingers to her hot cheeks. In the looking glass, they were rosier than usual. Was it because of the stifling warmth of the lavatory or due to the presence of her two unlikely companions?

She hazarded a guess that it was the latter.

There was something curious about the two brothers. They didn't resemble each other, but she'd known other siblings who looked nothing alike. Possibly they were half brothers. She didn't know. But something about Pete's rough edges touched her heart. Just like the kids at St. Michael's Hospital, where she often visited to encourage the sick children.

What she felt for Pete's older brother was much different. The moment their eyes had connected on the train platform, her heart had fluttered wildly like a sparrow taking flight. She was drawn to him in a way she hadn't been to anyone in a long time. Not even Fin in those first few days she'd been caught up in the romance of knowing him, before she had discovered he was in her father's pocket.

Erin was accustomed to flirtations, but the men of her acquaintance were usually subtle and charming. And very aware of her wealthy father's watchful eye at whatever event they happened to be attending.

Jesse was nothing like the polished, poised gentlemen she knew. And yet, something indefinable drew her to him.

But she didn't trust herself, not after what had nearly happened with her father and his protégé, Fin O'Leary. Her friend Patrick hadn't understood the depth of the betrayal, but she couldn't forget it. It was why she had left.

However, she was aware that she and her two companions would only be together a short time. Perhaps she could befriend Jesse and his younger brother without worrying about getting too involved.

What could happen in a matter of two days?

"You just gonna sit there?" Pete asked, a hint of defensive belligerence in his tone. The kid still looked a little green, but less as if he was going to fall out of the seat at any moment. The attendant had removed the remains of their lunch and put the table away, and Erin had escaped to the ladies' washroom.

Jesse's stomach still rumbled since he hadn't gotten

to eat anything, which did nothing for his temper. He'd snitched a roll from a bakery down the street from the train station, but that was all he'd had in the last two days since he'd been released from Deer Island. Smells of coffee and cooked meat lingered, reminding him just what he'd missed out on by helping the kid.

Without the chattering Erin there to make conversation, Jesse was more aware of the discussions of other passengers. He wondered how many of them had noticed and been upset by the scene the kid had caused.

Jesse was still contemplating putting the boy off at the next stop.

He still questioned why he'd agreed to the boy's absurd demand in the first place. Was it because of the resemblance between the boy and Jesse's deceased brother, Daniel? Some shred of compassion the prison guards hadn't beaten out of him?

When Jesse ignored his question, Pete slid across to Erin's seat and began rummaging through her satchel, muttering to himself. "Book, book, book, pencils. What is this?"

He held up a pair of field glasses, pinched awkwardly between forefinger and thumb.

"What are you doing?" Jesse demanded.

"She left her bag right here on the seat. Serves her right if someone steals from her," the boy muttered.

"She paid for your train ticket," Jesse reminded him. "And now you're going to steal from her?"

He couldn't imagine she had left the money pouch in the bag, not if she was as intelligent as she seemed to be, but Jesse could see the fine quality of the belongings Pete was strewing across the seat. He wondered if she'd splurged part of her inheritance on the nice things, because the dress she'd worn before sure didn't match up with her things.

"Put it back, why don't you?" he asked, but made it more like a command. "All of it."

The kid glared at him. "You gonna make me?"

"I might." It wouldn't take much, not with the kid still looking nauseous. "Why'd you pick me, anyway? You could've sat down next to anyone and blackmailed them into buying you a ticket."

For a moment, the kid's eyes appraised Jesse shrewdly. "You're like me," he said simply.

Jesse recoiled at the statement. How did the kid know Jesse had had early lessons in the art of pickpocketing, that he'd done much of his growing up on the streets of Boston? He'd been careful to cultivate a different image once he'd grown into being a con man. Even now, dressed in a cowboy's garb, how did the kid know that Jesse wasn't what he seemed?

"Put her stuff back," Jesse warned again sharply, wanting the conversation to end.

The kid grumbled, but to Jesse's relief he began putting the things back in the satchel, a little haphazardly.

Jesse glanced up again to the aisle where Erin had disappeared a moment ago. He let his eyes unfocus, remembering the admiration plain on her face when she'd commended him for taking care of his fake brother. When was the last time someone had looked at him like that?

Catherine didn't count, because in the end she'd been running her own swindle scheme on him. Maybe his mother, when he'd been much younger?

But Erin O'Grady had looked at him as if he'd done something admirable, and for a moment, he wished it were true, that he was a good man who'd come to the aid of a brother in need. Wished he was already the man he wanted to be.

Jesse shook those thoughts away before they could suck him down into the pit of his own guilt and shame. He forced himself to think only of Erin's lovely bright blue eyes, and the way they were framed by her sooty lashes.

Distracted by thoughts of the way her eyes crinkled at the corners when she smiled, Jesse found himself staring into those very eyes, but the woman who approached wasn't Erin.

Or was it?

The dark blue traveling dress was of finest quality and accented her fair skin. Her hair had been corralled into a pretty knot behind her head.

It *was* Erin, only a fancier Erin, one who looked a lot more like the lady with the feathered hat than the woman who'd left them a moment ago. Someone to target. Was this the real Erin?

"Wow," Pete murmured from Jesse's side, but Jesse couldn't tear his gaze from the girl coming toward them, padding on slippered feet and holding on to the seat backs to keep her balance.

She smiled tentatively, her eyes questioning. He shook himself out of his distraction, looking away as she swept into her seat with a rustle of heavy skirts, the scent of clean laundry whisking in along with her.

"Are you feeling all right now?" she addressed Pete,

adjusting her skirt. The voluminous material brushed against Jesse's shin.

"Mmm-hmm." The boy seemed as discomfited as Jesse felt, his eyes wide. They'd both watched a woman from the lower class, like them, leave, and now a princess had returned in her place.

"When they serve the evening meal, you should try something lighter. Perhaps some soup. It might go easier on your stomach."

The kid shrugged.

"Are you all right?"

It took Jesse a moment to realize she was speaking to him. He found himself shrugging like the kid and cleared his throat. "Yes. You look…nice." *Nice* didn't do justice to the way she looked with her hair put up like that and the dress complementing her creamy skin. It even made her eyes look bluer.

She lowered her eyes for a moment, those dark lashes fanning her cheeks. "It's a bit different than the dress I was wearing before."

"I'll say," Pete commented, not knowing or not seeming to care that his remark sounded rude.

A pink glow filled her cheeks. "The dress I had on before was borrowed from a…friend."

Some friend. The dress had obviously belonged to someone well below her station.

"Were you in disguise?" Pete asked.

Erin's slight flush deepened, turning her cheeks scarlet. "I didn't want anyone to recognize me at the train station and stop me from leaving."

And suddenly Jesse recognized her type. She *was* the same as the other rich girls he'd met before. She did what she wanted. Didn't care about the consequences. Was self-centered.

He could find a way to separate her from that fat purse he'd glimpsed before, if he needed to.

Jesse raised his brows teasingly, his natural charm returning as his equilibrium did. "Miss Erin O'Grady, did you run away from home?"

Erin hiked her chin and worked to make her voice cool. How had he guessed that she'd wanted to escape before her father found out? "My father didn't know about the trip but I certainly don't need his permission. I'm of age."

Jesse looked at her, skepticism in his eyes, though a teasing, flirting gleam was buried deeper. "How old are you?"

"I'm nineteen," she said firmly.

He smiled and something shifted in the pit of her stomach. Attraction sparked between them, but she was suddenly wary of his admiring gaze.

The conductor banged into the car, bringing with him a burst of cold air that sent a shiver down her spine. Pete's eyes shifted to the aisle and back to the window as the uniformed man passed by, probably on some errand or to check more tickets.

"I thought I'd read for a little while." She forced her eyes to remain on Pete. "Would you like to read along with me?"

She pulled her Bible from the satchel, its familiar leather cover against her palm a comfort. She gestured to the seat next to her. Pete watched her, but shook his head. "No, thanks."

"I read fairly slowly. I'm sure you can keep up if you sit here next to me."

Pete glanced at the man next to him and then lowered his chin, speaking to his lap. "I cain't read."

Was he ashamed for his brother to know that about him? A pang of pity speared Erin. "Well, I'm sure your brother will make arrangements for you to attend school when you get to Chicago."

The two males shared a speaking glance.

"But for now," Erin continued, "I can just read to you." She repeated her gesture to the seat next to her. "Come on. I won't bite."

Pete dutifully moved next to her, shoving her parcels aside. His small, bony shoulder pressed into her arm, and she was astonished again at how very thin he was.

She had to swallow a lump in her throat and clear her throat before she spoke again. She opened her Bible to the beginning of Matthew. This would be a good opportunity to share with him the real meaning of Christmas. "Let's start here," she began. "'The book of the generation of Jesus Christ, the son of David, the son of Abraham, Abraham begat Isaac; and Isaac begat Jacob; and Jacob begat Judas and his brethren—'"

The familiar verses brought memories of family Christmases. And a mild guilt that she would not spend Christmas with her parents this year.

Her distraction led her to see Pete fidget from the corner of her eye.

"Hmm. Maybe that isn't the most interesting place to begin." She flipped forward several pages. "Let's try here instead," she continued. "'And it came to pass in those days, that there went out a decree from Caesar

Augustus that all the world should be taxed. And all went to be taxed, every one into his own city. And Joseph also went up from Galilee, out of the city of Nazareth, into Judaea, unto the city of David, which is called Bethlehem—'"

"Why?"

Erin glanced up at Pete's interruption.

"Why would he do that?" the boy asked. "Go to his hometown to be taxed?"

"Well, because it was the law," she explained.

The boy's brows wrinkled so much it was almost comical. "But…" He trailed off, and Erin could see there was something more that he wanted to say.

"We must always obey the laws," she said gently, thinking that perhaps the family he had come from mightn't have taught him the right way of things. "They're meant for our protection."

Pete opened his mouth, then closed it again. A choking cough came from the man across from them, but when Erin turned her gaze in Jesse's direction, he appeared serious with a hand covering his mouth.

Erin glanced between them but finally Pete crossed his arms and slumped back in the seat. She took that as a sign to go on and continued where she'd left off.

"'—to be taxed with Mary his espoused wife, being great with child.

"'And so it was, that, while they were there, the days were accomplished that she should be delivered. And she brought forth her firstborn son, and wrapped him in swaddling clothes, and laid him in a manger; because there was no room for them in the inn.'"

Now Pete's interest showed again because he sat forward. "What's that mean, a manger?"

"Ask your brother," she said, nodding in Jesse's direction. For a moment, a look of utter panic crossed his features.

"It's…ah…something to…feed the animals in?"

His answer sounded more like a question, but she nodded anyway. "Yes, that's it exactly." She smiled warmly at Pete, a little concerned about his brother's answer, but she went on anyway. "I suppose they probably looked a bit different back then than they do now, but I imagine it was like a trough that might hold hay or dried grasses."

"So they slept in the barn?"

"Something like that. It doesn't say exactly." She smiled gently at him, encouraged by his interest. A look across to Jesse saw him watching the boy curiously.

"I'm sure your brother has spent the night in the barn before," she said, wanting to draw the brothers together.

"Or worse places," Jesse murmured.

When she questioned him with a glance, he only smiled enigmatically.

What an interesting couple of companions she had to travel with. They were a nice distraction from what she'd left behind. She just needed to keep reminding herself that her departure had a purpose.

Chapter Four

"I need another blanket."

Jesse was really beginning to regret allowing the kid to blackmail him into sticking around. He'd captured Erin's attention throughout the evening meal, and while Jesse wasn't jealous per se, he felt he needed to get to know her better in order to talk her out of some of the contents of her purse before they reached Chicago. *If* he decided to do it. He'd gone back and forth all night, considered how he'd planned to live on the straight and narrow once he'd gotten out of prison. And how he needed money to start his new life. He still hadn't decided one way or the other.

"No, you don't," Jesse replied firmly, standing in the aisle to take off his boots. The car had been transformed into sleeping berths shortly after supper. Now the passengers' conversations faded into soft murmurs as they readied for bed.

"But I'm cold."

Jesse stowed his boots at the foot of the upper berth, steadying himself with one hand against it as the train rocked. He glared at the boy huddling in the lower berth with a blanket already wrapped around his shoulders.

"Miss O'Grady's not around to hear your whining so just be quiet." She'd gone to visit the women's washroom as soon as the attendant began setting their berths.

"I'm not lying," the boy said defiantly, his chin jerking high. "I'm cold. Can't you ask the man for another blanket?"

"Here." Jesse shoved the blanket from his own berth into the boy's arms, tired of listening to him complain. Besides, it was plenty warm in the train car, and he'd slept in worse conditions during his incarceration.

"Just go to sleep." He jerked the curtain closed over Pete's berth.

Other than the few minutes earlier that afternoon, he hadn't had time alone with the boy to figure out Pete's motivation for blackmailing him. If the kid had stolen a wallet from someone, he should've had enough funds for a train ticket. But perhaps the conductor would've been suspicious if the boy was traveling alone?

Jesse's patience was used up; he wasn't going to ask the boy now. He hoped to get a few hours of shut-eye before he tried again to gain Erin O'Grady's trust. And maybe her wallet.

And here she came down the aisle toward him now, her dark hair loose and flowing around her shoulders, her eyelashes spiked together and face pink as if she'd just scrubbed it.

Jesse gulped. It was true he hadn't been around women at all in the past five years, but awareness for this particular woman hit him like a fist to the solar plexus. What was it about her? He'd been attracted to plenty of women before, but nothing like this.

Sensing his scrutiny, she looked up and those bright blue eyes seemed to connect with him somehow. A becoming flush crept into her cheeks.

"It's a little unnerving sleeping in a car with mixed company," she whispered. "Although I understand it's commonplace."

He looked down at his sock feet. He didn't know much about fancy manners, but it probably wasn't proper in mixed company. He couldn't imagine getting his boots off in the small space inside the sleeping berth.

"I suppose," she went on as she drew closer, "having a sleeping berth is a little better than being in one of the passenger cars. Not that I would mind," she hurried to say. "I don't think there is a sleeping car between Omaha and Cheyenne, but I'm sure I'll be fine in a passenger car… I'm blabbering. Sorry."

She stopped long enough to take a breath, her eyes guileless as she peered up at him. Darkness had fallen outside and with the lamps turned low, she'd drawn close enough that Jesse felt her warm exhale on his chin.

"Is there anything I can do for you?" he asked.

"No, I'm all right. I'm just… I haven't been away from home, at least not alone, and…" Her voice trailed off.

She should know better than to tell a stranger—someone who might intend her harm—that she was afraid. She seemed to trust Jesse already, which meant he'd have a good chance of success tomorrow if he wanted to part her from her wallet.

He reached out and touched her wrist, the coolness

of her skin a shock. He didn't know if he meant to offer comfort, but part of him wanted to draw her closer.

Jesse was brought out of his reverie by a softly cleared throat. The attendant stood slightly behind them in the aisle.

"Water, miss? Sir?"

Jesse blinked and noticed the uniformed man had the water pail in hand, offering the dipper to them. Erin took a small drink, then handed the dipper to Jesse, their hands brushing in the exchange. He sipped from the metal dipper, aware that her lips had just touched the same place.

The attendant moved away and she shifted as awareness crackled between them.

"Good night," she whispered, sliding into the berth opposite Pete's. She quickly pulled the curtain closed, leaving him to climb into his own berth above the boy's.

"Good night," he answered softly.

Erin lay in the stuffy, confined space, acutely conscious that she was separated from the other passengers only by a simple curtain.

She was half-afraid that she might roll out of the berth in her sleep and end up in a heap on the floor. She was used to her large, comfortable four-poster bed, with its clean, sweet-smelling sheets.

The cot inside the berth was lumpy and the air stale and for a moment she wished she'd never left the comforts of home. And then she thought of the lies and machinations her father had perpetrated to try to keep her from following her heart and knew she'd willingly suffer this discomfort and much more.

It wasn't as if she'd wanted to elope with someone inappropriate or attend an opera he didn't approve of. No, she'd wanted something more simple, more important.

Her mother was a benefactor for several charities, one of which was a hospital, St. Michael's, that served the indigent. Erin had accompanied her mother on a tour of the facility and stopped to talk to a small boy confined to a stark, white hospital bed.

After being frail and sickly much of her childhood, Erin had a special affinity for that child and several others that she'd met. She'd come back often, sometimes daily. The doctors and nurses welcomed her as she visited with the children and sometimes enlisted her help in smaller chores like changing bed linens or helping at mealtime.

And when her father had found out about her time at the hospital, he'd been furious with the hospital for allowing it. He'd discouraged her from returning, but Erin had tried to express how much it meant to her to help those who'd been just like her.

How well she knew the loneliness of being bedridden for long periods of time. Her only companion had often been a hired nurse. And her birds, the ones she'd watched for hours outside the large windows in her upstairs bedroom. That's where her love for bird-watching had begun.

But her father hadn't understood her passion for the hospital children. Instead, he'd filled her social calendar with teas, parties, and then a beau that he'd encouraged her to see socially.

When Erin had found out that her father had paid Fin O'Leary a sum to take up her time in order to keep her away from the hospital, her temper had sparked. Why should her father run her life, choose which activities were worthy of her time?

But she'd bided her time for nearly a week. Or maybe it had taken her that long to gather her courage for the trip to visit her brother for Christmas.

She wouldn't regret coming on this trip, even if she was stuck in a tiny, airless berth for the night.

Erin allowed her thoughts to turn to her two unexpected companions, hoping the distraction would allow relief from thoughts of being enclosed in this tight space.

They seemed more like strangers than brothers, although a sharp sibling rivalry did seem to exist between them.

Pete tried to put off a confident, uncaring air, but she could see beneath his outer veneer that there was a lost little boy inside.

And while Jesse didn't seem inclined to coddle him, she'd sensed the older brother's concern when Pete had gotten sick at the noon meal.

What kind of family starved a nephew or a cousin…? She hadn't gotten the family relationships straight during that first conversation with Pete, but regardless, the boy was family and shouldn't have been missing meals.

It was good that Jesse had come for him, even if the brothers weren't close. And what had Jesse said about his destination of Chicago? He hoped to find a fresh start there. Perhaps it could be a fresh start for *both* brothers.

She shouldn't allow herself to care so much about

Jesse Baker's plans. But she found she couldn't help herself.

She knew they'd part ways in Chicago. She would spend one more day in his presence and that was it.

Erin knew she'd been sheltered. Only introduced to men her father deemed appropriate. She was expected to marry someone her father approved. She should ignore the sparks she felt for Jesse. Even now her heart pounded the same rhythm as the train's *clack-clacking* as she thought about Jesse.

But what if…God had put her on *this* train, to meet *this* man?

What if she wasn't supposed to ignore the connection between them?

And *that* thought wasn't going to relax her enough to allow her to sleep.

It seemed a very long time until the noise from the other passengers, the scuffling and quiet voices, settled to only the *clack, clack, clickety-clack* of the rails. Even longer until her heart calmed.

After five years sleeping in close confines among other inmates, Jesse was used to the noises of the night. Snores, gasps, groans, creaks.

Even the small, claustrophobic space didn't faze him, though he couldn't straighten his legs all the way and if he sat up, he was likely to give himself a concussion.

It was the girl sleeping in the berth across the way that bothered him enough to keep him awake.

Something had ignited between them, and it was as surprising as it was strong. But he didn't josh himself that they moved in the same social circles. She was from the upper echelon of Boston society. He wasn't.

She thought he was a cowboy, because he'd never corrected her initial assumption. That occupation was still well below her social strata, but it was loads better than the truth about him.

He'd been raised in a small tenement apartment, lived on the streets, been in jail. Was responsible for his brother's death. Daniel wouldn't have gotten sick and might've been able to see a doctor if he hadn't been living on the streets with Jesse. Jesse was trying to earn penance for Jim's death with this trip to Chicago. Jim Kenner, who'd been sure of his salvation, even though he'd been a crook like Jesse. Sure enough to take the knife meant for Jesse.

And Jesse was trying to figure a way to relieve Erin of the contents of her purse. Maybe.

He felt a little twinge of guilt about it. He wasn't sure if he would call himself reformed. Before Jim's death, he had been questioning what his cell mate seemed so all-fired sure Jesse should believe. About God and the Bible.

Jim was the kind of man that would stuff his opinions down a person's throat until they were liable to choke.

But some of what he'd said had started to make sense to Jesse.

And then he'd died, saving Jesse's life. A debt Jesse couldn't repay, and one he didn't want.

Maybe the pinch of guilt was because Erin had been so kind to both Pete and himself. She was wealthy, like many of the other women Jesse had approached in the past. But she didn't act like it. She spoke to the two of them as if they were friends, not merely acquaintances who had attached themselves to her.

She was special.

He'd thought Catherine was special. Not only was she someone like him, but she'd *wanted* him. At least, she'd pretended to, but it had all been a calculated betrayal. A double-cross. He'd thought he'd loved her, but she'd never loved him and had swindled his heart.

Could he even trust Erin O'Grady? Experience had taught him to trust no one. He could only rely on himself.

He couldn't stop his thoughts from whirling. Tried to focus them into a way to get Erin's cash for himself, but a plan never coalesced.

Then, because he was still awake long after he should've been sleeping, he heard fabric rustling and a soft clunk like two shoes hitting the floor. Was someone up and about? He peeked out the curtain without opening it, and saw Erin sneaking away from her berth. What was she doing?

He waited a moment, and then followed her. Without his boots, his sock feet didn't make any noise on the carpeted floor. Erin hesitated near the outer door. He reached out for her.

"What are you doing?" Jesse asked softly, realizing he'd startled Erin when she jumped.

"Jesse!" she hissed. "You scared the life out of me."

"What are you doing?" he repeated.

"I heard a noise. I thought it might've been Pete, sneaking out of his berth."

Jesse turned to the lower berth where Pete had been

and pulled back the curtain. Sure enough, the boy was gone.

"Where would he have gone?" she asked softly.

Jesse shrugged, although he had some idea that the boy would be hunting for easy pickings...wallets, purses, watches, anything of value that sleeping passengers hadn't secured adequately.

For a brief second, he considered telling her Pete wasn't his responsibility, but Erin was already moving toward the door. "Should we notify the conductor?" she asked over her shoulder.

And he realized that's the direction she'd been heading in the first place. He caught up to her and halted her with a hand at her elbow. "Were you just going to go off by yourself? At night?"

He saw the answer in her expression.

"You were. What if an unsavory character were to come upon you?"

She couldn't know he considered himself in that category.

But she looked up at him with those innocent eyes.

Soft yellow light flashed on her face in a pattern. The moon shining through a narrow window, he realized. It gave her smooth skin a golden glaze. She looked up at him with luminous blue eyes turned silver and he found himself leaning closer, his focus on her lips...

A draft of cold air brushed the back of his neck and pushed Erin's unbound locks against his jaw and her skirt against his legs, breaking the moment.

And the conductor came through the open door, clutching Pete's arm and dragging the boy behind him.

Chapter Five

"He was sneaking around the next car over," the conductor said, mouth set in a stern line.

Erin stepped back, ready to allow Jesse to deal with his brother.

She was still trying to catch her breath from the way Jesse had looked at her. They'd been standing so close together, his hand warm at her elbow. For a second, she thought he'd been going to lean down and kiss her…

Now Jesse stood silent while Pete stared defiantly between the conductor and his brother.

"I was hungry," the boy said belligerently.

Jesse looked skeptical.

"Can't have passengers wandering about in the night," the conductor said, a disapproving frown on his face.

A muscle in Jesse's cheek jumped. "I'll make sure he doesn't wander off again."

As Erin watched, they seemed to have one of their mysterious silent conversations again.

"Pete and I will switch bunks. That way if he tries to sneak down, I'll hear it."

Jesse's solution seemed to pacify the conductor, but Pete remained upset with arms crossed.

Erin knew it wasn't her business how Jesse disciplined his brother; if it had been her father, his temper would've already gone off and he'd be blasting her ears with his shouts.

But Jesse simply waited for the conductor to retreat, not saying anything.

Not wishing to interfere, and still shaky from the almost-kiss, Erin slipped into her berth and pulled the curtain so she could no longer see the two brothers.

But she could listen, and she did.

"Did you take anything?" Jesse's voice was low, but even over the *clickety-clack* of the train on the rails, she could still clearly hear his words.

"If I did, I would've lost it between that passenger car and here," came Pete's grumbled response.

The cryptic words didn't make much sense to Erin. If Pete had been hungry and found some food, why would he have gotten rid of it? The brothers didn't say more, which was a surprise, because Erin fully expected Jesse to lecture his brother or threaten to "tan his hide" or whatever the Western equivalent of a thrashing was for wandering off in the night.

But Jesse said only, "Get in the bunk." He muttered something else too low for her to hear, even though he was probably standing in the aisle right outside her own berth.

She bit her lip and stared at the thin line of light that crept into her berth between the curtain and wall. It was obvious the brothers didn't get along. Maybe they didn't know how to relate to each other, after being apart for so long. Maybe she could help them get to know each other better tomorrow. Perhaps a good deed like that would make up for the visits with the children she would miss while she was in Wyoming.

The long day of travel finally caught up to her, and she succumbed to sleep.

After removing the two blankets from Pete's lower bunk and shoving them into the upper berth with the kid, Jesse settled into the bottom bunk. Or attempted to.

He was furious.

It was obvious the kid had gone on a stealing spree, thinking that passengers wouldn't notice if their wallet had disappeared while they slept.

At least the kid had had the good sense to get rid of any evidence—anything of monetary value—before the conductor had dragged him back to his "brother."

Part of Jesse admired the kid's brains. It actually wasn't a bad plan, lifting valuables in the night, if Pete had planned to get off the train early in the morning before he could be caught red-handed.

But his actions could have gotten Jesse in trouble. He was trying to live right—mostly. What would Erin think if he allowed Pete to steal from other passengers and she found out about it?

Thinking about Erin muddied the waters. He'd almost kissed her, standing in the aisle of a moving railcar. What had he been thinking? He hadn't, that much was clear. He'd been caught up in the moment, in her beauty.

Forgotten she was a potential mark.

In the morning, he would start gaining her full trust, so that if he needed that wallet he could get it.

No matter if he would rather have the kiss.

Between the late-night adventures and the little sleep she got in the confined, stuffy berth, Erin woke bleary-eyed and groggy when the attendant informed her he needed to make up the bed.

She stumbled to the women's lavatory, blinking against the bright morning light, only to find the corridor packed with other women waiting. And when she finally took a turn in the small closet, there was only a splash of tepid water in the pitcher.

By the time she reached her seat, transformed back to a bench instead of the bed, Erin was flustered and overheated. A glance at a sullen Pete and tight-lipped Jesse proclaimed that today's travel might not be as pleasant as yesterday had been.

"Good morning," she ventured softly.

She got a nod and partial smile from the older brother and a grunt from the younger.

The pungent smell of coffee roused her further. Perhaps once she had some food, she would feel more like herself.

Breakfast was a quiet affair, with Pete stuffing his face—thankfully, he didn't make himself sick this time—and Jesse pushing all the fried potatoes on his plate to one side.

The table hadn't been removed yet when Pete excused himself to use the washroom.

"Come right back," Jesse warned him, and they exchanged another one of those unreadable conversations before the boy nodded tightly and went off.

"I'm sorry about the trouble last night," Jesse said, finally looking her full in the face. He looked tired and worn this morning. About like she felt.

"It was kind of you to be up looking for him," Jesse said, then quirked his lips. "Even if you shouldn't have been going off alone in the dark."

She pointed her fork at him, tines forward, an unladylike and flirtatious action that would have appalled her mother. "I'm old enough to look after myself."

He shook his head, a small smile playing about his lips. With his chin covered in reddish morning stubble, the moment felt more intimate than it probably should've, teasing each other over breakfast.

"You're remarkably patient with him," Erin said, attempting to turn the conversation in a safer direction. She sipped her coffee, the brew hot against her lips.

Jesse hiked his brows, wrinkling his forehead as if in disbelief.

"You *are,*" Erin said with a little laugh because he didn't even know how lucky Pete was to have his older brother. "If what happened last night had happened with my father, he would've lost his temper. He probably would've woken the whole car with his shouts."

Jesse's eyes darkened and he leaned forward, though the table still separated them. "Did your father…hurt you in some way? Is that why you left home?"

She was almost as shocked by the venom in his tone as by the absurdity of his words. "Of course not."

He only stared at her with those hooded, unreadable brown eyes, so she went on.

"My father has never laid a finger on me. He might bluster and shout, but he would never be violent with me."

Jesse sat back in his seat, considering her.

"To be honest, he is much more likely to try to manipulate me to do what he wants," she whispered, looking down at the hands now clenched in her lap.

Jesse pretended a casual interest in what Erin said. It was the hardest lie he'd ever spun.

For a moment, he'd thought her father had hurt her, and the anger that had rushed through him, drowning out the sounds of other passengers and tinkling silverware, had taken him by surprise.

He was afraid his unthinking words had revealed how he was beginning to feel about her. Thankfully, she hadn't seemed to notice, and she'd denied that her father had done such a thing.

She contemplated him thoughtfully, the tines of her fork indenting her full lower lip as she paused, her bright, expressive eyes showing that she wanted to understand him.

"What do you mean? Manipulates you?" he asked.

"We had a disagreement several weeks ago and, ever since then, he's been arranging things to keep me away from doing what I wanted."

A different kind of relief filled Jesse.

This, he could understand. She wasn't as different from the other socialites he'd gotten to give him money. They were selfish, wanted things their way and when that didn't happen, they got angry or petulant. It sounded as if Erin fit into that mold, as well. Her father wouldn't let her attend whatever function she wanted to attend, so she'd run away.

On the heels of his relief came a rush of disappointment that settled in his gut like the heavy slab of bacon he'd just devoured. He'd wanted her to be different.

Pete returned at the same time the attendant was putting away the table, and Jesse visually checked him over for bulging pockets or any other sign he'd filched something that didn't belong to him but could see nothing.

The boy wrinkled his nose at the scrutiny, likely guessing what Jesse was doing. He ignored Jesse completely, turning to Erin and asking, "Are we going to read some more?"

Jesse had to admire him. The kid knew that between the two of them, Erin was more likely to be sympathetic to his lies and pretending than Jesse would.

"Certainly," she said with a wide smile, reaching for her satchel to bring out the book she'd been reading yesterday. Her Bible.

It had taken everything in Jesse not to get up and leave yesterday when she'd been reading to Pete. He'd heard the story before. Multiple times. Jim had read it aloud in their prison cell.

Jesse had been questioning his former cell mate's preaching. Wondering if he could believe in a God that had let Daniel die. He'd still had so many unanswered questions when Jim had died and figured maybe Jim's death was the end of it.

And he'd been shocked when Erin hadn't preached at Pete or himself yesterday, only read part of the story and then put the book up. As if she wanted to let them make up their own minds. Her manner was nothing like the way Jim had been.

Now she began to pull out the worn, leather-bound book and another volume fell to the carpeted floor, flipping open.

Jesse bent to retrieve it, admiring the sketch on the open page, several pencil drawings of a bird. One of it sitting on a bare branch, two of it winging in flight, wings spread.

"Oh, that's not— Here, let me—" Erin snatched the book from his fingers, closing it with a *thwack.*

"It's a nice drawing," he said. And it had been. The detail had made the pictures seem to be alive on the page. "Was it your work?"

"Are you an artist, Miss Erin?" Pete slipped the book from Erin's hands and had it open before she could protest.

Watching the boy touch the pristine pages with his grubby hands, Jesse expected Erin to rebuke him or at least take the book from his hands, but she simply watched him, a flush rising in her face.

"It's something I do for enjoyment… I dabble, really. They're not—"

"They're really good, Miss Erin," Pete gushed. Jesse couldn't tell by his manner if he was flattering her or if the boy honestly admired the pictures.

"Well, thank you, but I haven't had any formal training…"

Was her modesty a ruse? Most of the women he'd met before preened and fluffed up when they received compliments. But Erin seemed genuinely embarrassed by the praise.

"What's that kind?" Pete asked, not relinquishing the book but tilting it so Erin could see what he pointed at.

"This one is a common wren. A pair of them had a nest outside my bedroom window last spring. That one is a warbler." She pointed to something in the book and Pete pored over it curiously. "You can tell it's a male because of the coloring here..."

They continued flipping pages, Erin making some soft comments.

"Lookit that," Pete said, tipping the book in Jesse's direction. "Ain't she got talent?"

Even with the book extended toward him, Jesse had to lean forward to see.

He admired the bold pencil strokes; they made it easy to recognize the bird with its jaunty black hat and gray wings—it was the same kind that often flitted outside his cell window. He could imitate its whistle, he'd heard it so many times. And with very few things available to capture his attention in the compound, the little bird had been memorable.

"What is it?" Jesse asked. "I've seen one like it before."

Erin leaned forward in her seat, bringing their heads close together as they bent over the book Pete still held. Jesse could feel the warmth from her skin, could smell something flowery coming from her hair.

"A black-capped chickadee. Fairly common throughout the country. Most of the sketches in here are of ordinary birds."

Her breath fanned his cheek with little puffs of

warmth, making it hard for him to concentrate on the blurring image before him.

She seemed to realize how close they'd become and sat back abruptly. Her lashes fluttered against her cheeks as she glanced up at him and back down at the book. "I haven't had much of a chance to view the more unusual types." Was the flush on her cheeks getting bolder?

Jesse followed her example and sat back in his seat, allowing Pete to continue to pore over the sketches.

As he remembered the chipper little birds on the other side of the few square inches of freedom he'd been allowed, Jesse began to think Erin sort of reminded him of them. She was petite and had a cap of raven hair. And she chattered. She hadn't been quiet since he'd pulled her onto the train and sat down across from her.

"So you like to draw birds?" he asked.

"Well, I consider myself a bit of an amateur ornithologist..."

His face must've looked blank, because she went on, "A bird-watcher. It's sort of a hobby of mine."

"Hmm," he said. "Well, I'm not an orni—an..."

"Ornithologist," Erin repeated softly, as if she didn't want to embarrass him.

He nodded, running the word over again in his head. "But I've definitely seen some of those chickadees before. Sometimes with their chins all tucked up to their chests, riding a branch through the cold wind outside—" He broke off. He'd almost said "outside his prison cell." He needed to watch himself. How did talking with Erin discombobulate him so?

Erin's gaze rested on him. She tilted her head to one

side, assessing him. "You know, I can see you out on the range in frigid cold, riding your horse to watch over the cattle. You and the chickadees."

He hummed noncommittally. He could tell her he'd never ridden a horse—never even seen one up close, except for those attached to a cart or carriage on the Boston streets. But he wouldn't.

"Maybe your brother would like to hear some stories about life as a cowboy," she suggested.

Pete looked up at him, a look on his face as if asking, *Now what're you going to do?*

Jesse shook his head, forcing a smile. "Maybe later. I thought you two were gonna read."

He felt bad deceiving her. Something he'd never felt about one of his targets before. He counted on spinning stories for survival, but for a moment there, he'd wanted Erin to know the *real* Jesse Baker.

He could imagine the horror filling those expressive eyes if she knew who he really was, the things he'd done.

No, he could never tell her the truth about himself.

Not that they had that much time left together. By tonight, he'd been in Chicago, and she'd be on her way to Wyoming.

Erin accepted her sketchbook from Pete and opened her Bible to begin where they'd left off yesterday afternoon.

But even as she began to read, part of her wondered at the distance Jesse had enforced between them.

It was as if he didn't like talking about himself. While most of what they'd shared in conversation over the past day had been general things fellow travelers would talk about, she'd shared part of herself with him. And now she realized he hadn't opened up to her at all, hadn't reciprocated.

It was strange, because she *felt* as if they'd shared much.

She forced herself to concentrate on the words in front of her, not the man in the seat across.

"'And there were in the same country shepherds abiding in the field, keeping watch over their flock by night.'"

She broke off to tell Pete, "Perhaps sometime your brother can tell you what it is like to be out in the fields at night, with all the stars overhead…" Something she wanted to experience in Wyoming and hoped to talk her brother into helping her achieve. She'd never been anywhere as wild as the West and wanted to experience things her father had kept her "safe" from.

She glanced at Jesse briefly. He gave her a tight smile, nodded for her to go on. At least he was listening. Perhaps he needed the story, too.

"'And, lo, the angel of the Lord came upon them, and the glory of the Lord shone round about them: and they were sore afraid.'"

"I'd be scared, too, if some angels appeared out of nowhere," Pete muttered quietly from beside her. She kept going.

"'And the angel said unto them, Fear not: for, behold, I bring you good tidings of great joy, which shall be to all people.

"'For unto you is born this day in the city of David a Saviour, which is Christ the Lord.'"

Jesse tried to tune out Erin's words, but her gentle voice wouldn't be ignored.

"'Glory to God in the highest, and on earth peace, good will toward men.'"

He just had a hard time believing God meant for Jesse to have peace or good will.

He'd spent years trying to improve his life, and what did he have to show for it? He'd lost everything, been in prison. Had to start all over.

If there was a God up there, He didn't care one whit about Jesse.

Unbidden, Jesse's last few moments spent with a dying Jim flashed to his mind. Why had Jim given his life for Jesse?

"'Greater love hath no man than this, that a man lay down his life for his friends.'"

The words came to Jesse's mind, a quote his cell mate had said before. But Jim and Jesse hadn't really been friends.

Jesse couldn't fathom why his cell mate had done it, but he was determined to erase the burden of guilt he felt by bringing Jim's brother back to his mother and sister.

But what could he do about the heavier burden—the guilt of Daniel's death—that he'd carried for so long? He hadn't spoken to his mother in a decade, doubted she would allow any action on Jesse's part to redeem himself. How could he rid himself of *that* guilty burden?

Surely Jim hadn't meant he could be free from it, as well?

Chapter Six

Jesse had been quiet and contemplative all afternoon, not reaching out to his brother as Erin had hoped. Pete seemed agitated and uncomfortable.

By the time the evening meal had been completed and shadows lengthened in the train car, both men were antsy and tense. Their time together waning, they were probably ready to get on with their new lives in Chicago.

It seemed Erin was the only one regretting their time together was nearing its end. She wanted to have time to encourage Pete's curiosity about the Bible stories she'd been reading. She wanted to make Jesse's eyes light up with laughter again, the way he'd laughed this afternoon when she'd told a story about watching two birds attack a woman's feathered hat in the park.

She didn't want their time together to end. How had she allowed them to sneak into her heart so easily? They were like the children in the hospital ward; she couldn't help caring about them. But she also didn't want them to see her distress. The brothers needed to get off to a good start together.

Lip wobbling, Erin excused herself to the ladies' lavatory, determined to compose herself before the Chicago stop.

In the mirror, her face was pale compared to the roses she'd seen only yesterday.

Once she had shored up her smile, felt she could face them again and say goodbye, she slipped back out the door to return to her seat.

When she tried to make her way back up the aisle, a man blocked her way.

"Excuse me," she said politely.

He turned to face her and something lit in his eyes. His facial stubble and wrinkled clothing made him look disreputable, but then Erin considered that she probably looked just as wrinkled.

"Hullo, there," he said.

"Hello." Again she tried to angle her way past him, but the aisle was too narrow and he filled too much of it.

"Where ya traveling to, darlin'?"

She didn't appreciate the endearment, but decided returning to her seat was more important than correcting his impropriety.

"Out West," she said as kindly—and as dismissively—as she was able. There was something about the man that made her not want to be more specific. He certainly wasn't trustworthy, not like Jesse Baker. "Excuse me," she repeated.

He raised his brows, almost leering at her. She eyed the small space between him and the wall. What had she gotten herself into now? And more important, how could she get out of it?

Someone had followed Erin back to her seat.

The someone was a man who had a similar look to

the one who'd tripped her in the Boston terminal, slick and predatory.

Jesse bristled; Pete shifted beside him.

"These are my friends, Jesse and Pete Baker," Erin said with a look at Jesse almost as if pleading for help.

"Hullo," the newcomer greeted them. His smile was a little too wide, his gaze leering at Erin. Jesse noticed he also didn't give his name.

How had Erin attracted someone else's unsavory attention? She hadn't been gone that long.

"Nice to meet ya," Jesse said, sitting forward in his seat and extending his hand. When the man met his grasp, Jesse gripped his hand firmly, met his stare unwaveringly, warning the man without words that Erin was off-limits.

Except that the Chicago stop neared with every turn of the train's wheels. What if this character didn't intend to get off there? Would Erin be subjected to his advances? She was a young woman, traveling alone. Vulnerable.

A characteristic Jesse had thought he might exploit, and his time was running out.

But when she sent him another of those pleading glances, he couldn't ignore the protective instincts firing within him.

"Weren't you going to show Pete some more of your sketches this evening?" Jesse asked Erin. He shot the boy—who was starting to look a little green—a look, slanting his eyes back in Erin's direction.

"Why don't you switch places with the boy?" he asked the newcomer, making it sound more like a command.

The other man started to protest, but Pete was of the

same mind as Jesse and quickly jumped up. "That's right, Miss Erin, you promised you'd show me."

Thankfully, she caught on, and the other man had no choice but to move to Pete's vacated seat. Erin pulled her sketchbook out, even though the outside light was starting to fade as the sky darkened.

With Pete leaning over the book in her lap, she brushed against him, then paused and put a hand to his forehead.

"Jesse, he's burning up," she said softly, concern filling her eyes.

And at that moment, Pete tossed the contents of his stomach at their feet for the second time.

"Aw, kid," Jesse groaned.

The newcomer scrambled up, attempting to lift his feet away from the mess as Pete continued to heave; Jesse saw his ribs expanding and contracting against the thin material of his shirt. Erin ushered the boy into the aisle hastily.

"I'll take him to the washroom," she said.

Jesse saw her open satchel, where she'd dug out her sketchbook, at the same time he saw the other man eyeing it. Her purse was visible right on top.

The other man made a slight movement and Jesse stayed his reaching hand with a grip on the man's wrist. "You'll want to think twice about taking something that doesn't belong to you."

The other man gaped at him wide-eyed for a long moment; he must've seen Jesse's determination that he wouldn't get Erin's purse because his eyes narrowed but he brushed past Jesse and down the aisle, where he disappeared.

Leaving Jesse alone with Erin's cash.

The attendant bustled up. Some other passenger must have notified him. Jesse moved his feet as the man began wiping up the mess.

He couldn't seem to take his eyes off the purse. Right there was his fresh start. All he had to do was take it.

The conductor passed through the car, yelling that Chicago was the next stop. Erin and Pete might not even be back by the time the train pulled in and out of the station.

Jesse could get away with it, scot-free. Erin likely wouldn't even know he'd taken her cash—he'd be long gone, lost in the crowd before she realized he'd got off with it.

He was sure her father had plenty more where that had come from.

But something held him fast in his seat until Erin returned with a white-faced Pete.

"He's not doing well," she informed Jesse. "I think some others might be sick, as well. There were a few people clutching their stomachs and another man waiting for the lavatory when we exited."

The train's momentum began to slow. Outside the windows lights from different buildings made weird patterns against the dark sky.

What was Jesse supposed to do with a sick kid in a city he didn't know?

He really wished he'd never allowed the kid to sit with them in the first place. But the kid did look miserable, clutching his stomach.

"It's probably same thing as yesterday," Jesse said,

although he was beginning to have doubts of that. "He hadn't eaten in a while, and now..."

Erin shook her head, concern radiating from her. "It's more than that, I think. He's burning up with fever, and he can't even sit up straight."

She was right. The boy was folded over nearly double in pain. She asked the attendant for a blanket, but the man shook his head and hurried away.

"Well, what do you want me to do?" Jesse asked. The kid wasn't really his responsibility, but he couldn't just leave him in awful pain when they got off the train. "I've never been to Chicago before. Don't even have a place to stay the night."

Pete moaned.

"He may need a doctor," Erin insisted. She began gathering her belongings, hefting her valise in one hand and gathering her packages.

"Chicago!" the conductor shouted from the end of the rail car. The wheels began to squeal against the tracks.

"What are you doing?" Jesse stood, bracing himself against the change in momentum, and donned his leather duster.

"I'm getting off with you. I want to make sure Pete is taken care of."

"He's not your responsibility." He wasn't Jesse's, either, but Jesse wasn't going to abandon the kid, no matter if he had been a pain the last day and a half.

"My ticket will still be good to get me to Wyoming tomorrow. I'll help you two get settled somewhere and make sure he's going to be okay."

As the train screeched to a halt, Pete vomited again, this time hitting Jesse's boots.

"Aw, kid!"

"Jesse." The worried tone of Erin's voice drew his gaze to where she pointed, and he saw the blood amid the boy's mess. That was not a good sign.

"Don' feel so good," Pete slurred, slumping onto the seat Jesse had just vacated.

People began streaming inside the train car, bringing a flurry of snowflakes and cold air.

With a grunt, Jesse lifted the boy into his arms, cradling him against his chest as if he were a much younger child. That's what he felt like anyway, so light and skinny.

"Let's go," Jesse said to Erin, nodding her to precede him. He figured once she got the idea into her head they weren't getting off the train without her.

She moved quickly, elbowing her way past the new passengers. "Excuse us. Can you move, please? We've a sick child here."

And to his amazement, they all moved aside to let the trio pass.

Then he realized it probably wasn't her words that were moving the people. It was the stench. Pete had messed all over his clothing—which meant Jesse's only duds were now covered in vomit, as well.

Stepping onto the platform, a burst of cold air hit Jesse in the face. The chill wind was bracing to him with his coat on—what did it feel like to the boy with his tattered clothing? Jesse held him a little closer to his chest, even though he could barely stand the smell.

Pete moaned again. This close, Jesse could see the sweat beading his forehead. Pete began to shiver.

"Hang on, kid. We're gonna get you someplace warm."

He kept Erin's dark head in sight as he followed her through the pressing crowd. Someone jostled him and for a moment he was back in the prison yard, trying to back away from a fight. He whipped around, prepared to blast the other prisoner who'd pushed him, but a man in a dark coat hurried away into the swirling snow. Jesse blinked, and was back in the Chicago depot.

Four days out of the Boston prison, and he'd thought for a moment he was back there.

He wheeled around and barely caught sight of Erin at the edge the crowd. She spoke to someone from the depot, and Jesse joined her. With the wind whistling in his ears, he couldn't hear her words clearly, something about her luggage. When she set off again to the street outside the station, he followed.

On the street, the situation seemed even worse than the jostling crowd inside. A line of hackney cabs waited, but a flock of other passengers had gotten there ahead of them.

Jesse watched as Erin approached one of the cabs, waving a wad of money above her head. Coincidentally, a path opened between the other patrons and the cabdriver motioned Jesse ahead with Pete even as he helped Erin inside.

It was difficult getting inside while holding Pete, but Jesse didn't want to dump the boy inside and possibly jostle his tender stomach.

Inside, Erin alighted on the seat across from Jesse and Pete. The biting chill of the wind had gone, but the kid still shivered in Jesse's arms as if he were still out in the elements.

Pete groaned and tensed and Jesse closed his eyes; he was sure the boy was about to throw up all over him again.

But nothing happened.

Jesse peeked open his eyes to see Erin sitting forward, almost off her seat, one hand across the boy's face. Comforting him.

Jesse found a hard knot in the back of his throat; he couldn't speak.

The moment of consideration for someone so much less than she was caught Jesse off guard. He didn't doubt Pete had had a hard childhood, similar to Jesse's. But this merciful woman seemed to want to take care of the boy.

Jesse wished there had been an Erin for Daniel all those years ago. He was glad for her presence now and not just for her money.

Jesse wanted that kind of tender compassion for himself. But she would never offer it to him if she knew the real Jesse Baker. He had no doubt of that.

And he couldn't figure out why Erin would bother. She had no responsibility for the kid. She thought he was Jesse's responsibility, but even then she'd got herself off the train, derailing her own travel plans, to make sure the two of them got taken care of.

Why would she do something like that?

Chapter Seven

Erin noticed Jesse's discomfort by the stiffening of his posture the moment they stepped out of the hackney cab, but she was too worried about Pete to take the time to reassure him she would foot the bill. He stood looking up at the austere awning of the Grand Atlantic Hotel, mouth half-open.

"Erin—"

She interrupted whatever argument he would give by shoving him gently toward where the doorman held the large portal open, light spilling out into the freezing dark.

"Let's get Pete inside."

Jesse stepped foot over the threshold, but wouldn't go farther. "Erin, Pete and I can't stay here—"

She ignored him, relieved to be inside out of the bitter cold, and approached the massive front desk with its opulent ornamentation that matched the decor in the rest of the lobby area. She greeted the concierge and was quickly able to get two rooms next to each other, all the while Jesse sputtered in the background.

She thought it was better to override his wishes in

this case, else they'd never be settled for the night, and she was becoming more afraid as Pete got quieter and quieter. The boy had no extra flesh on him at all, and if he continued getting violently sick like he was, she worried he might not survive.

She made arrangements for the hotel staff to take delivery of her luggage when it arrived from the train station, and for a doctor to be sent up to their rooms as soon as one could be fetched.

Then she allowed a porter to attend her and her companions to elevator. It took several good tugs on Jesse's elbow to get him moving. On the elevator, he was silent, only inhaling a soft gasp when the conveyance began lifting them toward their rooms.

As they exited the elevator and followed behind the porter, Jesse hissed out the corner of his mouth. "I can't afford this place. Not even for an hour, much less a whole night."

She shrugged. "We'll worry about it in the morning. Right now, Pete needs help."

His jaw clenched and a muscle ticked in his cheek, but he didn't argue further, just allowed her to precede him down the hallway.

Inside the first of the rooms, she directed him to lay Pete out on the bed. Jesse took one look at the pristine bedcovers and turned back to her—she knew he intended to protest—but at her firm nod, he finally deposited the boy there.

She dismissed the porter and requested some hot water be brought up. When she turned back to the room, Jesse was removing Pete's worn sweater.

"He's still burning up," he said grimly. "But at least he's not vomiting anymore."

She wasn't sure that was a good thing. The quieter the boy got, the more she worried.

"I'll send his clothes down to be laundered if you want to undress him. He should be warm enough under the blankets. And what about your clothes, as well?"

Jesse looked down at himself, back up at her with a flush spreading up his neck. "To be honest, all I've got are the clothes on my back."

She opened her mouth, but no easy solution presented itself.

The flush spread farther up his neck and into his cheeks. "Don't need to worry about me, anyway. My coat got the worst of it. Maybe you could send that down."

She nodded and gathered his coat from the floor where he'd shed it before while he undressed Pete and got the boy under the blankets. With an armful of soiled fabric, she met a maid at the door, carrying a pitcher of hot water and accompanied by the doctor.

"Oh, thank goodness you've come." Erin traded her armful of dirty clothing for the hot water; the maid disappeared down the hall.

The doctor didn't look happy to have been called out from his home or office at this hour. But as he spent several minutes examining the boy, his face grew grave. He palpated Pete's stomach, causing the boy to moan and thrash on the bed.

Finally, the doctor drew Jesse and Erin toward the door, where Pete wouldn't be able to overhear them.

"It's most likely a bad case of food poisoning. Has

he eaten anything spoiled lately? Maybe something left out too long?"

Erin and Jesse exchanged glances. And then she remembered the older couple on the train who'd clutched their stomachs as she'd passed them in the aisle with Pete. And another mother with a young girl who'd been the same color green as Pete had.

"We've just arrived on the train from Boston. I think there were several others who had stomachaches, but I'm not sure if any of them got off the train."

"He had pork loin for dinner," Jesse said.

"It doesn't matter much now what he ate," the doctor said. "His body will try to expel whatever it was that upset his stomach."

The doctor paused, and Erin knew he wasn't finished yet.

"The problem is that he appears to be malnourished."

The doctor glared at both of them for a moment until Erin said, "Jesse is his older brother. He has recently taken Pete out of an untenable family situation." She wouldn't go into detail; it likely didn't matter to the doctor at this point. "He's only had Pete with him for a couple of days."

The doctor's gaze turned considering.

Jesse remained silent at her shoulder. Was it worry for his brother that kept him quiet?

"I'm afraid that the boy's body is weak, because he hasn't had the proper nutrition. The fever is trying to fight the food poisoning but he's just…not very strong in body. If he makes it through the night, it will be something but if he does then he'll likely be all right."

* * *

Jesse stared at the floor as Erin closed the door behind the doctor and then leaned back against it, her palms flush against her sides.

In the soft lamplight, she looked worn and a bit bedraggled from their rush off the train and to get to the hotel. Nothing like that first vision of her after she'd changed from the drab housedress into her fancy traveling gown.

But she still seemed to fit into her surroundings. The gilt lamps on the walls…the fancy bedspread…the wallpaper. Erin belonged here. He didn't.

She looked as hopeless as he felt. The doctor's visit hadn't been a comfort and the man hadn't been able to help Pete at all.

Jesse felt as helpless as he had when he'd watched Daniel's sniffle turn into a racking cough then into a rattle in his chest that had grown worse and worse…and Daniel's frail body had been much the same as Pete's. They had scrounged for food, but never had enough. Living on the streets with no one to turn to for help, there was no way Jesse could have afforded a doctor.

Was Jesse bound to watch another boy die? Unable to help, unable to do anything other than sit there?

Fury flashed through him like lightning. He hadn't asked to become involved with this boy. Pete had insinuated himself in Jesse's life, but Jesse had no real duty toward the boy. Why should he care if Pete lived or died? What Jesse should do was walk out that door and get on with his life. Find Jim's brother, release his burden of guilt. Live his own life.

Problem was, he did care. The little rascal had

wormed his way past Jesse's defenses. Oh, he didn't think of Pete like a little brother—more like a pain, an ache in his tooth that wouldn't go away—but he didn't want the boy to *die*.

The fury in Jesse's veins changed direction. If the God Jim and Erin talked about really did care about people, why would He let kids like Daniel and Pete die? Why couldn't He do something for them?

Erin pushed off the door, looking up and finally meeting Jesse's gaze. The look in her eye nearly made him take a step back. She was full of fire, too.

But instead of snapping her arm back to hit something—him—as his stepfather might've done, she threw herself into an embrace, twining her arms around Jesse's waist and burying her face in his chest. Jesse's arms hung lax at his sides; he wasn't sure if he should embrace her back.

She let him go as quickly as she'd embraced him, wiping her face with the heels of her hands. Was she crying? Jesse felt discombobulated and tried to keep up with her swinging moods.

She bustled into the small attached washroom and Jesse heard the splash of water from a pitcher into a bowl. When she returned, carrying a damp washcloth, face full of determination, Jesse's chest expanded. He was starting to care about her. Too much.

"We're not giving up," she said firmly. "Pete's proven his strength by surviving long enough for you to come find him in Boston. He'll get through this."

She moved to the bed and sat down next to the kid, arranging her skirts around her. "I rented two rooms. Why don't you take a few hours and rest in the room next door. I'll watch over Pete, try to get his fever down. Then you can spell me after you've had some time to rest."

"You're not worried about propriety?" he asked, because surely there was something inappropriate about them taking turns sharing a room.

"I'm worried about Pete," she said simply, looking up into his face with those guileless eyes.

Jesse did as she said.

And as Jesse drifted off in the bed softer than anything he'd ever experienced before, he realized maybe God had done something for Pete. He'd put Erin here to fight for the boy.

Erin dabbed Pete's face and neck with a damp cloth, hoping to cool the boy's fever. She prayed in a constant stream, words often escaping her, but she knew the Father understood the very groanings of her soul. Still, the shadows and darkness threatened to overcome her.

She was nearly as worried for the man sleeping in the room next door. He'd barely said a word since they'd got off the train. She imagined he was worried for Pete. Something deep inside told her he couldn't take another loss. He'd already lost his parents, so she refused to let go of Pete, for Jesse's sake. He couldn't lose his little brother, too.

Pete moaned and moved restlessly on the bed. She reached down for the basin she'd moved close and within minutes, he'd filled it.

He lay back on the bed, eyes glassy and fevered. "Ma?" he asked in a raspy voice.

Erin smoothed his sweaty hair back on his forehead. "Pete? It's me, Erin. Can you hear me?"

"Ma?" he asked again, and this time it sounded like a child's cry.

"Try to drink some of this water," Erin whispered, holding a cup to his lips. Against her hand, his skin was hot and clammy at the same time.

She was afraid the water would come right back up, but he needed the fluid to replace what he'd lost already. He dutifully sipped it and afterward, his head seemed to clear a bit.

"I miss my ma," he rasped as his head fell back on the pillow. "And Jenny. My little sister."

"It's all right, Pete." Erin tried to comfort the boy by taking his hand in hers. Still hot, too hot.

Why hadn't he mentioned his mother or sister before? She was afraid to ask, afraid of the answer. "Your brother is sleeping right next door."

"Ain't got no brother."

The boy must be delirious with fever. Erin dipped her washcloth in a basin of cool, clean water, wrung it out and began to dab it on Pete's face again.

"Sure you do. Remember Jesse? He came and got you in Boston and now you're going to live with him in Chicago."

"Ain't got no brother," Pete insisted stubbornly, though his voice was just a murmur. "Just me and Ma and Jenny."

Suddenly, he ratcheted up again and Erin grappled for the basin, moving it just in time for him to empty the contents of his stomach again. He heaved mercilessly; there wasn't much left inside him.

When his body could bear it no longer, she pushed him back in the bed and pulled the covers up to his neck. He shivered violently.

"I—I want my ma," he cried out.

"I know. Shh. I know. I'm not your ma, but I'm here." She clasped the boy's hand again and he finally fell into a fitful slumber.

Erin resumed her prayers, so exhausted she couldn't think about Pete's statement that he had no brother. All she could do was lift up the boy to the Lord.

Several hours later, Jesse awoke with a start, unable to determine where he was. The bed was far too soft and sweet smelling to be his prison cot.

Then, remembrance of the last few days since his release burst on him and he sat up in the bed. Rubbing one hand over his face, he tried to wake up, knowing he needed to go relieve Erin of Pete's care.

When he'd splashed his face with cold water from the pitcher and straightened his clothing as best he could, he crept out of one finely furnished room and into another, steeling himself for the worst.

He found the lamps turned down, the room almost in total darkness. Erin slept facedown on the bed, still half seated in a chair she'd pulled close to the bed, one hand outstretched and touching Pete's wrist. A basin at the side of the bed told the story that Pete had been sick at least once more, but when Jesse touched his face, his skin felt cool and dry, no longer feverish. Pete breathed easy.

Relief sliced through Jesse hard and clean.

He shook Erin's shoulder. She mumbled into the

blanket and turned her face away. He leaned down farther, loath to wake the boy, and shook her again, whispering, "Erin. Wake up."

She came to with a start, nearly upending herself out of the chair. He held back a smile at her hair that was half falling out of its pins and her cheek was pink where it had been pressed to the blanket.

His heart contracted at the picture she made, eyes soft from sleep and open to him.

He wanted…

She took his arm and tugged him with her toward the door, staggering a little as she adjusted to being upright.

"His fever broke a bit ago. I was only going to close my eyes for a moment, but I must've…" Her voice trailed off on a yawn and Jesse fought the urge to enfold her in his arms. A memory flashed of her in his arms from late last night. He was a knucklehead. He hadn't even gotten his arms around her that time.

"I must've fallen asleep. I think he's going to be all right."

Seeing the deep joy in her eyes, Jesse couldn't resist reaching out. He brushed a hank of loose hair off her cheek, slowly running the pad of his finger across the softness of her cheek.

Her eyes deepened with awareness and she leaned minutely toward him. Jesse reached for her waist with his other hand, determined to capture the kiss he'd nearly gotten on the train—had it only been last night?—but Erin raised both hands and rubbed them down her face.

"I'm sorry. I'm so tired I'm wobbly. And…I must be a sight." She stepped away from him, reached out and touched the door with her fingertips. She swayed. "I'll just sleep for a bit. If he gets worse, or you need me, just knock...."

She closed the door behind her quick escape. Leaving Jesse wondering if he'd dreamed the encounter, or her movement toward him. Had he imagined it? Even when he'd thought he might target her, he'd been immeasurably attracted to her. Were his feelings toward her influencing the situation with what he'd wanted to happen?

He sat in the chair Erin had pulled up to the bed and began to watch over the boy. He wasn't sorry that the kid had survived the night. He didn't deserve to die, just like Daniel hadn't deserved death.

But...part of Jesse wondered why one boy should be chosen over another. He didn't know. Just as he didn't know why Jim had sacrificed himself for Jesse.

Too tired and bleary to give the line of thought proper consideration, Jesse wondered if Erin would have an answer.

He slunk down in the chair, hoping to catch a bit more rest before the morning.

Trying not to think about the financial burden staying overnight was going to place on him. How could he pay for the rooms when he hadn't a cent to his name?

Chapter Eight

A soft knock roused Jesse from where he'd drowsed in the chair next to Pete's bed. Light filtered in around the expensive curtains draping the window.

Erin stuck her head and shoulders inside the door and motioned him toward her. Jesse's stiff muscles protested as he dutifully stood up. Pete's even breathing reassured him and Jesse stopped to splash his face with water from the basin before sneaking out into the hall.

By the time he had joined Erin, she was speaking to a matronly woman while a uniformed maid hurried off down the hall.

The woman moved past Jesse into the hotel room. He looked to Erin with raised eyebrows.

"I had the concierge send for a nurse. I know you've got things to do this morning trying to get settled. I thought we could leave Pete to rest as long as he had adequate supervision. Is that all right? Oh, and the maid just brought this up." She handed him his jacket, which smelled much better than it had last night.

"And we've a new errand to run." Erin smiled wryly as she headed toward the stairs, leaving Jesse to follow.

"I'm afraid Pete's clothes did not survive the washing. The maid said they simply fell apart…."

Jesse could believe it. They'd been threadbare to start with.

"We'll have to pick him up some new things."

Down the elevator and into the opulent lobby, Jesse studied the fine furnishings and wainscoting. He'd been too concerned for Pete last night to really take it all in; then he'd fallen into the spare bed and been out immediately. Sitting with Pete through the night, the darkness had hidden the well-apportioned features of the room and he'd nearly forgotten where they were. He'd never actually stayed in such a nice place, although he'd been inside a few times to run one of his schemes.

He followed Erin slowly, considering that this might be his chance to take his leave. Once they stepped foot out of the hotel it wouldn't be too hard to sneak away. Then he wouldn't be responsible for a hotel bill he couldn't possibly pay for. She glanced over her shoulder and their eyes connected and he knew he wouldn't.

Something had changed last night as they'd labored together to save Pete. Their struggle and victory had united them.

He had no funds, but he had his pride. He didn't want Erin to think he wasn't capable of taking care of himself. Didn't want her handouts, not when he was beginning to really care about her.

And there was the rub. Now that he'd let her believe him a cowboy, let her believe that Pete was his brother, he could either continue the charade or tell the truth and likely alienate her.

"Would you like to get a cup of coffee or some breakfast before we go out?"

Had she appointed herself his task-master, as well? It seemed that since she'd decided to get off the train, she'd been ordering him about. He didn't dislike it...not at all.

He stopped as they stepped off the elevator, guiding her by the elbow to one side, pulling her close. He spoke in a low voice. "Look, Erin... I tried to tell you last night, but I can't afford this place. I doubt I can even afford a cup of coffee here. And I don't have money to buy Pete any new clothes."

Her mouth softened. "We'll work something out."

He began to protest, because he didn't want to be beholden to her, but she crooked her arm through his and pulled him toward the heavy outer doors. They passed several wealthy patrons, and Jesse wondered if perhaps that was his solution. With a hotel full of wealthy people—none of whom knew him, nor his reputation like in Boston—he could easily spin a story and find someone to give him enough funds to pay for a night in the hotel. Maybe two.

Maybe enough to get him started here.

If he tried things the honest way, he'd be working for weeks to pay off the hotel bill, never mind funding a place to live or food.

But he didn't have to decide right now.

As they stepped outside into the brisk Chicago morning, Erin exchanged a sideways smile with him. She thought he was a good guy. It was obvious in the way she treated him, with respect and even...admiration. So different from the way he'd been treated the years while he was in prison, and if he admitted it to himself, even before that.

It made him want to be worthy of the way she looked at him. But he didn't know if he could.

"We'll go visit your friend first, then stop at a couple of shops on the way back," she said, leading him toward the already-bustling street with its shoppers and workers hurrying about their business.

His brows creased as he thought about Jared Kenner and the errand he had in mind. "It might be better if we went our separate ways." Better for Jesse that she not know his business. If she found out about his time in prison, she'd be disgusted with him. "I'll see my… friend and you can do your shopping."

"Nonsense. We're both alone in an unfamiliar city. It would be better to remain together, don't you think?"

Her words inspired thoughts of the man who'd followed her back to her seat from the lavatory on the train. The man had had no good intentions, Jesse was sure of it. And if Erin ran into something similar here, her naiveté would be a problem for her. Jesse was used to taking care of himself. Pete was, too. But Erin was not. After all, she'd helped the boy—Jesse owed it to her to get her safely back on the train first thing tomorrow and on her way to Wyoming.

She tugged him to a waiting hackney cab and looked to him with her eyebrows raised. Submitting with what grace he could muster, he gave the address that the Boston Kenners had given him. He didn't know whether it was a business or a home, but he helped Erin into the carriage and they set off.

Inside the coach it was a little warmer, and quieter,

though other carts and horses could be heard rumbling past.

"So what is the purpose of your visit this morning? Will your friend help you find a job or a place to stay?"

He hesitated. "No. I'm seeing him as a favor to a… an acquaintance back in Boston. Sort of a…last wish."

She gazed solemnly at him. "He died?"

Saving Jesse's sorry hide. He swallowed hard. "Yeah. I promised I'd try to send his brother back home to take care of his ma and his sister."

"That's quite noble of you."

It hadn't been, not really. Jim had been the one making the sacrifice—his life for Jesse's. And Jesse still couldn't understand why.

She turned those admiring eyes on him again and again he was hard-pressed not to lean over and kiss her. He focused on the traffic and pedestrians outside the cab window.

Their destination turned out to be a lumberyard in an industrial part of the city, and before Jesse could ask Erin to stay in the hackney cab, she'd descended along with him and was moving toward the door of the lone brick building on the yard, leaving him no choice but to follow.

Inside, the smell of freshly hewn wood was prevalent and sawdust gathered in the corners though it was obvious someone tried to keep the floors clean. Jesse inquired for Jared Kenner and a man in work clothes approached him. Thankfully, Erin hung back.

"I'm Jesse Baker." He stuck out his hand and the other man shook it politely.

"Jared Kenner. What can I help you with?" The man

cast a curious look over Jesse's shoulder, eyes flickering over Erin.

"I'm here because…well, this is sorta difficult." Jesse took a deep breath. "I was an…acquaintance of your brother Jim back in Boston."

The man's face instantly closed. "I haven't spoken to my brother in years."

"I know. But he…well, that is, your ma…" This was hard. Harder than Jesse had thought.

"What about her?" the other man asked warily. His words gave Jesse at least a little hope that maybe he could fulfill the vow he'd made to a dying Jim.

"Jim was…killed." A glance over his shoulder at Erin; he hoped she couldn't hear him. "And he asked me to see to your ma and your sister."

The man crossed his arms. "Yeah? How'd you know Jim anyway?"

Jesse clamped his jaw. The man's suspicions were well-founded, obviously, since Jim had been in prison and that's where Jesse had known him, but he wasn't making this easy for Jesse.

"That's not important," Jesse insisted. "But I went to see your ma in Boston and she isn't doing well."

The other man didn't respond, just studied Jesse with narrowed eyes.

"Your ma didn't come out and say it in so many words, but I know she'd like to see you before she… passes."

Still the other man didn't say anything.

"And if she passes, your sister would need someone to take care of her."

Now the other man shook his head. "I moved away

when I was sixteen to get away from my family and their problems. I can't go back there."

That sounded familiar. Jesse had run away to get away from his stepfather and the man's temper. He'd promised never to go back, not for anything. And then after Daniel's death, he'd figured his ma would never want to see him again.

His stomach clamped tight like a vise. If a similar break had happened between Jim and his brother, Jesse might never convince him to go back to Boston. Then who would take care of Jim's mother and sister? If they didn't have anyone to take care of them, how would they survive?

The burden of guilt pressed heavily on Jesse's chest. Would he never be free of the debt he hadn't wanted in the first place? Jim had had no right to place Jesse in this position.

"Plus, I've been saving money to rent a bigger place." Kenner flushed slightly. "Thinking about asking a gal to marry me, ya know? If I spend that money on a train ticket to Boston…and my job…" But something in the man's tone told Jesse he was wavering. Jesse just needed to convince him.

"You want your sister to be thrown out on the streets?"

The man's eyes narrowed suspiciously. "What you got to do with my sister?"

Jesse raised his hands in front of himself defensively. "Nothing. I only met her the once. The truth is, I didn't know Jim well. We didn't have a lot in common. But he saved my life, and I owe him."

"If he's dead, you don't owe him anything."

Jesse didn't argue, but he *felt* like he owed Jim. The burden pressed heavily on him.

"I can't just up and leave my job." Kenner shifted his feet as if impatient to be done with this conversation.

"I'm sorry to interrupt, gentlemen." Erin joined them and placed a hand gently on Jesse's forearm. He started, unused to the gentle touch and lost in thoughts of Jim. He'd nearly forgotten she was there. She squeezed his arm as if in reassurance.

Kenner's narrowed eyes followed the exchange, then flicked to Jesse's face.

"I'm sure Mr.…" She trailed off, and Jim's brother was quick to say,

"Jared Kenner."

"Mr. Kenner needs to return to work. Why don't you join us for supper tonight and we can discuss this further?"

The man opened his mouth and Jesse knew he was going to refuse. Erin rushed on.

"We can eat at the restaurant in the hotel—the Grand Atlantic—"

Kenner's eyes went wide. But Erin wasn't done yet.

"You should bring your… I thought I heard you say you had a girl that was particularly special to you…? Say seven o'clock?"

The man nodded silently, looking a bit like Jesse had felt last night as Erin had ordered him about from the train station to the hotel—railroaded.

"Perfect. All right, Jesse. We should finish our errands and return to check on Pete."

She started for the door but Jesse's feet remained

rooted to the floor. Erin looked over her shoulder at him, beckoning him to follow.

Kenner spoke in a low voice. “She know about your connection to Jim, whatever it is? Bet she wouldn’t look at you like that if she did.”

He was right. Jesse walked out of the office, torn—part of him wanted to go back in and demand Kenner do the right thing and get back to Boston to take care of his family, but Jesse followed Erin helplessly.

Erin looked up at him with an apologetic smile as he took her elbow. “At least he didn’t say a final no. Perhaps we—you—can still persuade him.”

Jesse shook his head, boosting her into the cab and then settling next to her, acutely aware of her warmth as they were pressed together in the seat. “He seemed determined, set in his ways.” And Jesse couldn’t blame the man, being estranged from his own mother.

“You’re an intelligent man, and I’ve got some ideas, as well. Between the both of us, surely we can come up with some way to get him back to Boston.”

How much had she heard? Was she suspicious about his connections to Jim’s family? Jesse couldn’t tell from the corner of his eye, but she wasn’t treating him any differently than before.

Erin was more convinced than ever that there was much she didn’t know about Jesse. Neither her dear friend Pat nor her father were men who liked to chatter, but Jesse seemed to keep even more about himself private.

After Pete’s statement last night that he had no brother, she’d begun to reflect on the small discrepancies she'd sensed between the two brothers. Was it possible they weren't actually related? They didn't seem close, but neither was she close to her older brother, Chas, even though she had embarked on this Christmas visit.

She sensed there were things the two Bakers weren't telling her, but what? She'd already decided to ask some pointed questions when they returned to the hotel, but she really wanted to talk to both brothers together. She'd bide her time.

"I asked the driver to take us to some shops." The carriage slowed and stopped even as she spoke. "And here we are."

She followed Jesse out of the conveyance, allowing the driver to assist her before she slipped him a coin for the ride.

It was still quite early, as she hadn't known how long Jesse's errand would take. They had plenty of time before she'd told the nurse they would return.

People moved quickly along the sidewalks, some carrying Christmas packages, most with heads ducked into their collars against the biting wind. At least it wasn't snowing. When someone accidentally shouldered into Jesse, he half turned with a shout of "Hey—" before he bit off the word as if coming to his senses. The person who'd bumped him didn't even notice, kept right on going.

She thought she'd seen him do something similar at the train station last night as they'd fought their way through the crowds trying to help Pete.

"Are you all right?"

He nodded, face drawn and with that muscle ticking away in his cheek.

The storefronts were decorated for the holiday, some with posted signs declaring discounts. A boy hawked papers on the corner, shouting loudly above the din of voices and carriages. There must be a bakery down the street because yeasty, doughy smells wafted on the brisk breeze to tickle her nose.

The Christmas spirit seemed to abound, except in the man standing next to her. "Erin, I already told you I can't afford to buy anything."

"Well, Pete can't very well go around without clothing, can he? Especially not in this weather." She meant the words as a tease, but his expression didn't waver from its seriousness.

A muscle jumped in his jaw. "I don't like taking charity." There was something behind the words he bit out, some deeper emotion she could see behind his eyes but that she couldn't decipher.

"Consider it a Christmas gift from a new friend," she said softly, imploring him with a hand against his arm. "There's nothing wrong with accepting help when it is needed."

She thought he groaned, but she couldn't be sure because a horse and buggy clattered its way down the street just at that moment.

"All right. As soon as I get a job, I'll pay you back, though. Where do you want to go?"

She pulled him into a clothing store on the ground floor of a multistoried building. "We should be able to find something in here."

He seemed lost in thought as he absently followed her

through the rows of hanging clothing toward the children's section. A sales clerk directed them toward the boys' clothing, and Erin began browsing, though she noted how the other woman's gaze lingered on Jesse.

Erin bypassed the fancy suits and fine woven shirts for the sturdier wool pants, noting that shirts to match were nearby. She'd love to gift the boy with both a Sunday suit and play clothes—it wasn't as if she couldn't afford it with the allowance she'd put aside for months—but she doubted Jesse would agree to such a large gift.

"Do you think Pete would prefer brown or gray?" Either color would keep too much dirt from showing.

"Hmm?" Jesse looked up from several feet away and their gazes clashed.

She lifted a pair of brown trousers for his perusal, but he shrugged helplessly. "I suppose they're fine."

He seemed distracted and tense. She put the pants back and moved toward him. "If you really don't want me to purchase these for Pete—"

He shook his head. "It's not that. I was just thinking...about some other things."

"What other things? Perhaps another opinion could be of help."

He smiled, but it was stiff. "I doubt you could understand. It's not something someone like you could—I mean—"

She stiffened. Someone like her? A woman?

Now he sounded like her father, who often claimed that Erin was too naive or uneducated to be able to understand. Did Jesse think of her the same way?

Blinking against a sudden sting of tears, she turned away, blindly reaching for something nearby. A shirt crumpled to the floor, slipping from her numb fingers. She knelt to pick it up, grateful for a moment to keep her face down, so he wouldn't see the embarrassing emotion she knew he would be able to see there.

She'd thought they were friends. Equals.

"Erin?" he asked.

And then he was there, kneeling before her, reaching for the shirt as well, enfolding her hand between both of his.

She pulled away, wiping at a stray tear that slipped down her cheek. "I'm all right. Just overtired and anxious over Pete, I suppose." It was partly true, but she desperately didn't want this man that she was coming to admire to pity her. She rose and turned her back, pretending to look at a rack of light blue shirts.

But Jesse followed her relentlessly, his large palm covering her outstretched hand with its warmth.

"Did I offend you?" His voice came low in her ear.

She shook her head, unable to force words past the lump in her throat.

"What did I say? That you wouldn't understand?"

She stilled, and knew that her actions had given her away.

"I only meant that you're…obviously very well-off. We're from very different circumstances."

She turned to face him, aware that her eyes probably sparkled with unshed tears. "You mean you didn't say that because I was a woman?"

His brows drew together comically. "No!" he blurted. "Of course not. It's just… The last time I'd been in a store like this was with my ma…a long time ago."

She let out a deep breath, bringing her emotions back

under control. She *must* be overtired from the trip and Pete's long night. Usually, her emotions weren't so close to the surface.

"You and Pete don't speak of your family often," she said, watching his face. Perhaps this topic was skirting what she hoped to talk about when they returned to the hotel, but she couldn't pass up the opportunity to learn more about him.

"Hmm." He half turned away, fingering one of the shirts on another rack. For a moment she didn't think he would elaborate, but then he went on, voice low. "I can't speak for the kid, but for me most of the memories are…painful."

"Do you miss her—your mother—very much? I imagine you must."

He stared at the rack of suit jackets before him, not seeming to see it at all. "I miss the way things were when I was a kid. Younger than Pete."

What a curious statement. "What changed?"

"My father died and my ma remarried. And my stepfather was… He wasn't a kind man."

"Was he why you left?"

His face darkened, turning stormy. He nodded tightly and turned toward the clothing, "We'd probably better get back. Let's find some things for the kid," he said, changing the subject.

She allowed it, because he'd finally opened up and told her something personal. But she couldn't resist laying her hand on his arm and saying, "But you've turned into a fine man in spite of it. You came back for Pete, after all."

He stilled and looked down at her, almost as if he

couldn't believe what she'd said. She squeezed his arm and held up the pants she'd been considering earlier. "Brown or gray?"

He squinted at them, then cut his eyes to her. "You want both, don't you?"

She nodded, not daring to smile. He shook his head, but his lips quirked and she knew he would agree.

"You're a good man, Jesse Baker," she murmured, pivoting to find the shirts.

"Do you think the nurse will be all right for a bit longer? I'd like to walk through the park." Erin nodded toward a swath of trees across the busy street. She juggled the wrapped packages in her arms and Jesse belatedly moved to take them from her.

"Thank you," she murmured, her gratefulness shining up at him in her eyes. "The sales clerk said our hotel is only a few blocks over, past the park. I'd love to stretch my legs a bit more before we retire to the hotel, but only if you think Pete will be all right…."

"I'm sure he's still asleep." He was already following her, as she'd set off before she even finished speaking.

"With all the sitting on the train, I felt quite restless when I woke this morning. And two more days to go."

He let her chatter flow over him. He liked that she hadn't pressed him for more details while they'd shopped for Pete's things. He liked that she admired him, even if she shouldn't.

Inside the store, he'd been caught in remembrances of what it had been like when he'd been a successful con man, with full pockets. He'd had several fine suits and two pairs of nice shoes.

And now he had to start all over. Even the clothes on his back weren't his own. He didn't kid himself that it would be easy finding honest work, but when he'd gotten out of prison he'd been determined to try.

He should ask Jared Kenner about getting work tonight when he saw the other man. Perhaps the man might know of something.

Thoughts of how easy it would be to spin a story for one of the patrons at the hotel plagued Jesse. If he got some quick cash, he could set himself up and be that much ahead.

But something inside him balked at the idea. He had a niggling idea it might be Erin's influence.

The internal debate whirling through his brain had distracted him as Erin had started shopping and then she'd gotten upset and he'd blurted the first thing that had come to mind to keep her from crying.

Then he'd got his head on straight and they'd enjoyed selecting several items for Pete. Jesse hoped the boy would be pleased at Erin's thoughtfulness when they returned.

Stepping into the park was like stepping into another world. The brick-paved walkways had been shoveled clear by someone, but snow drifts buried the rest of the landscape in white, only broken by the dark skeletons of bare trees. The bright morning sun glinted off nearly every surface, making Jesse squint.

Beside him, Erin took it all in with wide-eyed wonder, her expressive face open.

They walked in silence among the snow, soaking up the late-morning sunshine, when a pair of birds swooped down before them, chattering and fluttering for all they were worth. They swooped up into a nearby tree and settled, still chirping at each other. They sounded like two little neighbor ladies upset about something.

"Oh!" Erin exclaimed in a hushed whisper, tugging on his arm. "Can we stop? Just for a moment?"

She began to rifle through the satchel she'd carried with her all morning, finally coming up with her drawing book.

"Ah, the ever-present sketchbook," he teased.

She thwapped him on the upper arm as she dug in her satchel, at last holding up a pencil with a triumphant but soft "Aha!" Then she edged toward the birds in their tree, moving slowly and with only the soft shushing of her hem against the snow on the ground disturbing the peaceful morning.

He advanced slowly, watching the quick movements of her hand over the paper, watching her eyes dart to the birds and then back to her page. She flipped to a new page in the book and began again.

She was much more interesting than any birds or scenery.

Her eyes jumped to him briefly, as if to assess his level of impatience. "Just another moment..."

He started to say, "I'm not in any hurry—" but a bright red projectile hurled toward his head.

Chapter Nine

His first instinct was to duck or flinch, but Erin's cry of "Oh, don't move!" froze him in place quicker than any command from a prison guard had done in five years.

Something tapped on the brim of his Stetson, then a soft flutter made him aware that a bird—a red one—must've landed right on the brim of his brown hat.

And Erin was furiously attempting to capture it on paper.

He remained still, more from the joyful light in her eyes than her command. He watched her eyes flick from a point above his head to her sketchbook as her pencil skimmed over the page. Her concentration was marked in the small purse of her lips. Drawing his attention there.

And then her focus changed. It was subtle, but for someone who made details his business, he noticed. Now her eyes traveled his face, and the hint of a smile played at the corner of her lips.

"You're not drawing the bird any longer," he accused softly, moving toward her.

The bird flew off with a sharp flutter of its wings.

Erin stepped backward, still feverishly filling the page with her sketch.

"I don't know what you're talking about," she said. But the small smile trembling on the edges of her lips belied her words.

"You're drawing me. Let me see."

"No!" She snapped the book closed, now with a full-fledged smile aimed at him. "And why shouldn't I use you as a subject? It's a fine, strong face you have."

Heat flooded his face, and triumph expanded his chest at her flirting admission. Something was growing between them, and he didn't know what to do about it. But he knew what he wanted to do about it. He advanced on her, dropping Pete's wrapped packages in the snow. She allowed him to catch her much too easily, and he captured both her elbows in his palms, holding her close enough to count her eyelashes, close enough that his breath riffled the fine hairs at her temple.

She looked up at him with those luminous blue eyes, and his gut tightened. He couldn't resist her. Jesse leaned close and brushed his lips over hers in a kiss.

It had been more than five years since he'd kissed a woman, but even if it had been five days, Erin's kiss would have erased all memories of kisses before it. She was fire in his arms for the brief moment their lips met, and then she pulled away, or he did.

He didn't—couldn't—release her arms and they stood close in the bright morning stillness, his chin brushing her forehead as their breaths misted in front of them.

He was shaking.

When she pulled away, he squatted to gather the packages he'd so heedlessly dropped, trying to hide his rioting emotions.

She seemed to know the kiss had thrown him, because she simply threaded her arm around his elbow and set off toward the hotel.

He wanted it—whatever was between them—to be real. He knew she was far above his station, knew that if she discovered his past, she would shun his company. But it didn't stop his heart from nearly beating out of his chest at having her close by his side. It didn't stop him from *wanting* what couldn't be.

He felt fifteen again, wanting something just out of reach. Would he never get it?

By the time they had walked the few blocks to the hotel, Erin was able to compose herself. Or maybe the shock of warmth inside compared to the blustery wind outdoors roused her.

Somehow, she ordered refreshment to be sent up to their rooms while Jesse waited near the elevator, watching her with hooded eyes.

He seemed as discomfited by the kiss they'd shared as she was. But surely he was more experienced than she—it had been her first kiss. She never could have imagined the swirling emotions that the warmth of his lips would evoke. It had frightened her. And she had liked it.

She glanced around at the other hotel guests in the lobby. Could they tell just by looking at her that her life would never be the same?

Her father never would have permitted the intimacy,

but she was no longer in her father's safe little world. She thought perhaps Jesse would have said something about the kiss by now, but he hadn't.

She joined him at the elevator and when she took his arm, the awareness still simmered between them. She could see it in his gaze, as if he didn't quite know what to make of her.

She didn't know what to make of him, either. She'd never been attracted to one of the men her father had paraded before her, not like the way she felt now with Jesse.

Heat climbed into her cheeks as they rode the elevator up, but he *still* didn't say anything, and she began to wonder if he regretted the impulsive action. Had she done it incorrectly? She couldn't be sure, not if he didn't say anything.

She usually wasn't one to avoid an issue—her angry flight from her father's home had been an aberration more than anything—so she shored up her courage to just ask Jesse outright, but then they arrived at Pete's room and before she could open her mouth to question him, Jesse pushed open the door.

Inside, the curtains had been drawn back, flooding the room with light.

Pete was just waking up, groggy and grumbling about being hungry, but with beautiful color filling his cheeks and rumpled hair indicating he'd had a good rest. The nurse said he should be fine to eat, and then she left.

She must've cleaned the room while they'd been gone, because it certainly smelled better than when they'd left.

Pete's eyes turned on Erin with surprise. "What're you doin' here?"

He started to get out of the bed and then seemed to realize he was missing some clothes, because he burrowed back under the blankets, splotches of red climbing in his neck and cheeks.

"It's a little late for modesty," Jesse told the boy. Erin couldn't see his face as he approached the bed, but she thought his voice sounded teasing. "Miss Erin spent half the night sponging you with cool water to keep your fever down. Do you remember much of last night? Miss Erin got off the train with us and brought us here and fetched you a doctor. And then she stayed up with you to make sure you were going to be all right."

Erin left her satchel on the sideboard and brought the packages to the bed, while Pete self-consciously held the blanket before his bare chest. His skinny arms almost brought tears to her eyes. Focusing on him was a welcome diversion, since she wasn't going to mention the kiss in front of him.

"And Jesse spent the other half the night doing the same." Her fingers tangled with the twine securing one of the packages as she tried to open it. She kept her eyes down, fearing that if she looked at Jesse, her confusion and uncertainty would be plain on her face.

"You—you did? Why?" The poignant note in Pete's voice brought her eyes up. When she met his gaze, his eyes seemed to hold a deeper question, but then he blinked and the moment was gone. "And—where's my clothes?"

She finally untangled the knot and began folding back the paper. "Your old clothes were very soiled, and when I sent them down to be washed…well, they didn't survive."

"Miss Erin picked you out some new clothes. Store-bought ones," Jesse said.

She didn't look at him when he spoke, still afraid of showing emotions that were too close to the surface.

Now Pete began to look decidedly suspicious of her. "Why'd you do that?"

She'd expected him to be a bit more thankful, not question her motives. She kept a smile on her face. "Because you needed them. Consider it a Christmas gift from a new friend."

His brows wrinkled and he looked as if he might protest, but Jesse's wide hand came down on his shoulder. "It's polite to say thank you," the older brother said, tone brooking no-nonsense.

Pete shrugged his hand off quickly, looking from Jesse to Erin, eyes suspicious of both of them now.

Erin didn't need thanks, didn't want to be a source of contention between the two. And as she wasn't as composed about the kiss in the park as she'd thought she was, she needed a moment alone to gather her thoughts.

She laid the pants and shirt out on the bed, smoothing a wrinkle before backing toward the door. "Someone will bring up a meal soon. I'll freshen up a bit and give you both a chance to do the same, and then I'll join you again. How does that sound?"

She turned to leave but then remembered what she wanted to ask about, so she turned back. "Oh, and Pete, I'd like to know more about what you said last night. Some things about your family…?"

For a moment, she imagined she saw a flash of panic

enter Pete's features, but then he turned his face down, away from her gaze. She determined to get to the bottom of things over lunch. With that, she excused herself.

The door had barely latched behind Erin when the kid vaulted out of the bed and began pulling the new clothes on, paper crackling as he snatched the pants off the bed.

"What happened between the two of you?" Pete asked, hopping on one foot when he got tangled in the pants.

"What do you mean?" asked Jesse, though he was pretty sure the kid had read the tension between Erin and him after that kiss. He was too smart for his britches.

"You kiss her or something? She was acting about as skittish as a wife whose husband is about to come home from the fact'ry when the chores ain't done."

Paper crackled. Pete struggled into the shirt, shaky fingers fumbling with the buttons. His stomach rumbled, loud in the quiet room. Jesse could relate. He was mighty hungry after all their running around last night and this morning.

The kid glanced up at Jesse, pausing in his frantic movements. "You *did* kiss her."

Jesse didn't want to talk about that. Not with Pete right now. Not with anybody. It was a memory he was going to hold with him for as long as he lived.

"What's your rush?" Jesse asked, thinking the kid sure was in a hurry to get dressed. "She's not going to barge back in here, if that's what you're worried about. At least, not without knocking." And if she did as he expected, she was going to hide out in her room for a while.

The kid shook his head, opening his mouth to say something, but then he went still as he knocked away the paper from the last package, a new pair of leather shoes. He went perfectly still, all the nervous energy in him seeming to freeze.

"Shoes, too?" The question was barely a breath, so low Jesse almost didn't hear it. Pete touched the boot, just ran one finger across its shiny, new surface.

And Jesse knew that he was feeling the same thing Jesse had felt when she'd wanted to spend the morning helping him—first with locating Jared Kenner and then with purchasing Pete's clothing.

Why had *someone like her* chosen to give *someone like him* such a gift? Like Pete, he got the feeling that something was off here, but Erin's pull on Jesse was too strong for him to think about walking away. If she pushed him away after that kiss, he'd go. But if she allowed it, he wanted to spend the rest of the day with her, as she most likely was going to hop on the first train headed West tomorrow morning.

Pete snatched up a pair of thick woolen socks from amongst his spoils and began tugging them on, leaning against the bed. "I've got to get outta here."

And Jesse realized he'd been in a hurry to get dressed because he was trying to *leave.* Jesse intercepted him before he got to the door, still in his sock feet. "Wait a minute—"

Pete jerked away from the hand Jesse clamped on his shoulder, but he spun toward the room, not the door, where Jesse planted himself with arms crossed.

"I'd think you'd want to split, too," Pete said. "Erin find out you've been in prison yet?"

Jesse froze and knew he'd given himself away. "Good guess. How'd you figure it out?"

"You sure ain't a cowboy." Pete began ticking things off his fingers. "I ain't never seen anybody turn up their nose at potatoes so much—what'd they do, serve them three times a day?"

Jesse stayed silent, the kid's words hitting close to home. He *was* tired of potatoes.

"And you're plumb particular about your space. Anybody brushes up against you and you tense up."

That much was true, too. Jesse hadn't got used to being among the regular population just yet.

"You let me go now and Erin never finds out," Pete cajoled.

"I can't do that." Jesse sighed, knowing this was a mess. But he had no intention of walking away from Erin before he had to. She was special and he wanted to experience being with her even if it could only be for hours, only for today. "I want the rest of the day with her."

The boy stuck his chin up in the air in an expression Jesse was coming to recognize.

"It's gonna cost ya."

Jesse tensed as the little blackmailer threw the words out there. "You got out of Boston. We both did. Can't you give me the rest of the day?"

The kid shot Jesse a look that said clear as day, *You've got to be joshing.*

"You know I don't have any money," Jesse protested.

"Don't mean ya can't get some—what were ya in for?"

It was Jesse's turn to be stubborn. The kid might've guessed he'd been in prison but he wasn't volunteering information that could be used against him.

Pete shrugged. "Whatever you get for yourself before we part company, I get half."

Still conflicted, Jesse didn't even know if he planned to run a swindle in the next twenty-four hours, so the agreement might not be so bad.

"Fine, but no pickpocketing."

"What?" the kid howled. "Nuh-uh. Let's just cut our losses. Look, I ain't even gonna take the shoes, all right? She can take 'em to the store and get her money back."

Jesse should his head. "It's not about the shoes. Erin *got off* the train and helped you because you were real sick. She's bringing lunch up now—"

The kid shook his head, eyeing the door again. Jesse couldn't understand what he was so afraid of.

"Look, I—"

"Knock, knock!" Erin's sunny voice rang out and the door opened behind Jesse, nudging him farther into the room. "Lunch delivery."

Erin could feel the almost palpable tension between the brothers when she stepped back in the room.

Pete was dressed and in his sock feet, standing in the middle of the room. Jesse looked much the same as when she'd left, but he'd been standing near the door. What had they been doing in the short time since she'd left?

She allowed the attendant rolling a white-clothed

cart to follow her into the room. He began unloading silver-covered dishes onto the table, filling the room with decadent smells that had Erin's mouth watering.

The table in the room only had two chairs and Jesse pulled it over next to the bed, allowing Pete to sit cross-legged while Jesse and Erin took the chairs.

Pete began stuffing his face, much as he had on the train, until he realized both Erin and Jesse watched him a bit incredulously and he slowed to a more polite speed. Occasionally, he glanced toward the door, and he kept shooting speaking glances at his older brother.

The manners her mother had drilled into her demanded Erin wait until after the meal to discuss an unpalatable topic, so she ate mostly in silence. After Pete leaned away from the table, patting his stomach in satisfaction, and Jesse had laid his fork on the table, she took a deep breath.

"There's something I've been curious about since last night," she said, pushing her chair back away from the table a bit. "I think you were probably delirious, Pete, but you called out for your ma and your sister."

He fidgeted in place and began to rub one palm against the new fabric on his knee. He wouldn't look directly at her.

"I only want to make sure there isn't someone back in Boston that needs care," she went on in her most reassuring voice. "If your sister is still under the care of the same aunt and uncle that allowed you to...well, to get in this condition, then I want to... I could send a telegram to my father and ensure someone removes her from the situation."

Pete still wouldn't look at her, and when she glanced

at Jesse, that familiar muscle in his cheek was jumping, though he held himself as if he was entirely relaxed in his chair. One leg crossed over the other.

"You also told me that you didn't have a brother," she reminded Pete softly.

And watched the transformation as both man and boy froze. Nothing in particular changed in their expressions, but it was the very act of becoming so still and emotionless that confirmed what she had begun to suspect in the wee hours.

"You aren't really brothers," she stated clearly. Growing agitation made her stand up and pace toward the door.

"Erin, wait—" Jesse was already out of his chair, one arm outstretched toward her, when she whirled back toward the room.

"I wasn't leaving," she said, crossing her arms over her middle. "I want to know what exactly is going on." Her stomach flipped at the thought that they had lied to her all this time—or at least if they hadn't outright lied, they had let her believe that they were brothers when they really weren't. She felt slightly sick.

Pete and Jesse exchanged guilty glances and then both began to talk.

"We first met on that train out of Boston."

"I didn't think the conductor would let a kid like me travel on my own—"

"The kid seemed harmless enough, and I was heading out of town anyway—" As he spoke, Jessed rubbed the back of his neck as if the muscles there pained him.

"My ma passed about a year ago and my sister and

I got taken to an orphanage—" Pete fidgeted with the cuff of his new shirt.

"It just seemed easier to let people—you—think we were related."

"She got adopted by this real nice family, but I ran away."

"And once we'd started the story, it was harder and harder to tell you the truth…."

"And then I didn't want to be in Boston no more so I got on a train." The young man's story finally petered out just after Jesse's explanation. Both seemed resigned, waiting for her reaction.

She kept an even stare directed at them, the man standing with shoulders slumped, and the boy with chin nearly meeting his chest. The sunlight streaming in the windows behind them seemed incongruous to the tension inside the room.

"That's not all of it, is it?" she asked.

She remained silent, waiting. During this prolonged pause, they didn't look at each other, both stared resolutely downward. She wondered if they knew just how much alike they were.

Finally, Jesse took a deep breath and seemed to be steeling himself to speak again, but it was Pete who blurted out, "It's all my fault, Miss Erin. I'm the one who sat down next to Jesse and…er—" he squirmed a bit in his seat "—*convinced* him to take me along on the train. It wasn't his idea at all. I'm the one who said he was my brother."

Jesse stood tall. "Yeah, but I didn't have to agree to it. Some of the blame for this misunderstanding falls to me."

Misunderstanding. She almost giggled aloud at the overexaggeration but was afraid they'd think she was in hysterics. Which she nearly was.

Her mind whirling, she suddenly remembered the cryptic conversation between Jesse and Pete that first night on the train, after the conductor had brought Pete back from wherever he'd escaped to.

"You're a thief," she said faintly. "A pickpocket."

Pete's face turned white, almost as white as it had been last night when he'd been weak from food poisoning.

"And you knew about it," she accused Jesse, spinning to face him. She pressed a hand against her now-roiling stomach. She'd hardly eaten, but what she had now lodged inside her uncomfortably, making her feel distinctly sick.

Jesse's face had hardened into a mask she couldn't recognize. "I guess a boy will do just about anything to survive," he said simply. "To eat."

Just as quickly, the memory came of Pete loading his face that first morning, until his cheeks pouched out like a chipmunk's. She could still feel the bones of his spine beneath her hand as she'd helped him to the washroom when he'd gotten sick. He *had* been starving.

But that still didn't make it right. And it didn't erase her lost trust, now that she found out they'd been pretending to be something they weren't the whole time she'd known them.

"Are ya real mad?" Pete asked, voice small.

She shook her head, then shrugged. "I don't know what I am." She lowered herself into the chair again when her legs went weak. Mostly, she felt numb, but also betrayed and hurt.

And then she remembered that she only had to face this situation for another few hours—in the morning she would board a train to Wyoming to see her brother for Christmas.

Surely, she could stuff away her hurt feelings until then.

"So what do you plan to do now?" she asked. "A young man such as yourself can't do enough factory work to support himself. Hawking papers or something like that won't pay much either, not enough to support you." She faced Jesse again. "I don't suppose you've thought much past today, either?"

Jesse shook his head, expression downcast. "I don't have any plans past talking to Jared Kenner, trying to get him to go back to Boston for his mother."

She'd completely forgotten about the dinner she'd insisted on at the lumberyard earlier.

Pete's chin had come up again. "I ain't going to no orphanage," he said tightly.

"We'll figure something out," she said, and was surprised to hear Jesse's words echo her own, a half step behind her statement.

Her eyes lifted to his in surprise and she was further shocked to see the determination in his expression. He and Pete shared another of their wordless exchanges.

Her head began to pound.

"Then I'm going to go lie down for a bit." She put a hand to her forehead. "I'm still tired from sitting up last night. I'll be dressed and ready for supper at seven. Knock on my door and we can go down together."

At the door she turned back. “Is there anything else you’d like to tell me?” she asked, encompassing both of them in her gaze.

Jesse sucked in a breath like he had something to say, but when their eyes met once again, he shook his head, mouth tight.

She left without looking back.

Chapter Ten

Jesse stuck a finger in the tight collar of the starched white shirt. Something else borrowed, a suit that didn't fit quite right. Jesse hoped the concierge hadn't steered him wrong when he'd loaned him the suit. The suit was too tight, and the black jacket he wore bore down on his shoulders like a wooden stock.

Or maybe it was the weight of what he hadn't confessed to Erin earlier that afternoon, when he'd had the chance. He'd started to say it all, but had chickened out. She'd already been upset, and Jesse hadn't wanted to add to her hurt feelings.

But the real truth was he'd been scared of how she would look at him if she knew the truth. He'd seen disappointment in many different eyes—his stepfather's, his mother's; disdain in others, like Catherine's, but he desperately didn't want Erin to look at him in either of those two ways.

"How do I look?" he asked Pete as they were about ready to join her for the evening meal.

"All right, I guess." The boy shrugged.

Jesse scrutinized him with his new clothes and hair

slicked into place with water and a comb. "You're not having second thoughts about our deal, are you?" The last thing he wanted was the boy tattling on him now.

Jesse tried to take a breath, but felt as if he were suffocating.

"I'm hungry," Pete complained, moving to the door.

Jesse stopped him with a hand on his shoulder, a hand that the boy quickly shrugged off.

"Erin's been nothing but kind to you—to both of us," he amended, "and as disappointed as she was earlier, she'd probably be even more disappointed if you pulled something like trying to steal a wallet out of someone's pocket. And I don't want her disappointed tonight, all right?"

The boy looked as if he wanted to make an angry retort, but finally just nodded.

Jesse knocked softly on the door next to their room and Erin opened it.

He gulped, sure as he'd ever been about anything that he was about to make a big fool of himself.

In the soft lamplight from the hall, her fancy gown was an ivory that deepened her eyes even more than they already were, and the shape of it accented her tiny waist. When she turned to close the door, he noticed her hair swept up in a fancy style, with curly dark tendrils clinging to her slender neck.

He pulled at the neck of his shirt again because he couldn't seem to breathe properly. When she turned around again, her straight, white teeth flashed in a smile. Probably at how dumbfounded he appeared.

"You look real nice," came Pete's voice as if from very far away.

All he could do was nod his agreement, but that seemed to be okay, because she took his arm and they were moving toward the elevator and she still wore that smile on her pink, pink lips.

He didn't remember the elevator ride, unable to concentrate on anything other than the beauty at his side. Until they arrived in the lobby, where Jesse came to earth when he saw the masses of people in dolled-up dresses and dark suits and waiting to be seated at the fancy dining room.

He could dress up in a suit like them, but he didn't belong here. Pete hesitated slightly beside him.

"That kid's got a dog," Pete muttered.

Jesse looked up and decided maybe Pete had paused for a different reason than Jesse had.

Across the lobby, near the wide check-in desk, a rather stout lady in a wrinkled traveling suit raised her voice at the harried-looking clerk. A boy chased a small, fluffy, yapping white dog the likes of which Jesse had never seen before around the lobby until the woman turned and sniped at him, too, and both dog and boy moved to stand next to her with downcast faces.

"I don't see your friend yet," Erin said, still hanging on to Jesse's arm.

He was proud just to have her near him. He tried his best not to stare directly at her, but he didn't have to be looking at her to know she outshone all the other women in the room. Probably all the women in the entire hotel and Chicago, too.

And for tonight, she was on his arm.

He knew he'd hurt and confused her earlier, and he still didn't have the courage to tell her the truth about himself, but he resolved to make tonight a good night for her.

The lobby doors opened, sending a rush of cold air in their direction, and Jared walked in with a pretty brunette on his arm. He wore a dark suit, probably his Sunday best, but it looked more like something Jesse would have owned back before his incarceration—not quite in the same class as these rich folks. Folks like Erin.

And yet, she'd taken in Pete and befriended the both of them without any preconceptions about them. She was something he'd never experienced before.

"I'm really sorry about everything this afternoon," he murmured so only she could hear him.

Her smile slipped. She glanced at his face and he saw the hurt lingering in the depths of her eyes; she hadn't forgotten what had happened, no matter that she was putting on a cheerful face.

"It was certainly an unexpected afternoon," she said and he sensed she was going to leave it at that until she suddenly turned her head and their eyes connected. "I have to ask—you're not even a real cowboy, are you?"

He held her gaze, but didn't say anything and she knew the truth, he saw it in her gaze. Something flickered inside her eyes and he closed his other hand over the fingers she clasped on his forearm, wanting to hold on to the moment, on to her regard. She lowered her eyes, hiding her emotions from him behind her sooty lashes.

"If I could go back and change things, I would," he murmured again, conscious of Jared and his gal approaching them. And he *would;* he'd tell her from the start that he wasn't a cowboy and that Pete wasn't really his responsibility. He'd have found another way to stay on the train to Chicago, to be near Erin…

But he'd started out with the deception and now there was no turning back. He was a con man, after all.

It was silly to be disappointed. Erin knew it, but it didn't stop the stinging hurt that lanced her insides and prickled behind her eyes.

Before they'd met two days ago, Jesse had been a complete stranger to her. He didn't owe her honesty, he didn't owe her anything.

But she'd thought there had been something between them. Especially after their morning together and the kiss in the park, she'd hoped…

But that was foolish. She was leaving to continue on to Wyoming first thing in the morning. And he was staying here to start his new life as he'd said before. It wasn't her business what he did or how he did it.

Although she did worry about Pete. Without a real big brother, without a mother or any relative to take care of him, what would happen to the boy?

She knew Jesse probably thought there was a distinction between not telling her the truth—his omissions—and outright lying; she'd thought the same as he and Pete had scrambled through their explanations earlier that afternoon. But even his omissions smacked of lying and all of the deception reminded her entirely too much of what had happened with her father before she'd left Boston.

She'd told herself that afternoon after she'd escaped to her room that it didn't matter, that she would be able to go on her way to Wyoming without further thought of the man beside her and his unlikely young companion, but perhaps she was even getting good at lying to herself. She wanted to make excuses for him, wanted to think perhaps he hadn't meant to deceive her, but he certainly hadn't been forthcoming about any of it.

She took a deep breath to steady herself as his friend approached, and was able to greet them with a smile.

"Evening, Mr. Baker," the newcomer said, looking a little uncomfortable and glancing at all the couples surrounding them. "I didn't get a proper introduction earlier..." He allowed his voice to trail off but indicated Erin with his eyes.

"This is Miss Erin O'Grady of Boston," Jesse said, and then placing a hand on Pete's shoulder, which the boy promptly shrugged off. "And a...friend we met on the train, Pete. Erin, this is Jared Kenner."

"And my best gal, Amelia Minor." Jared completed the introductions with a proud glance at the young woman on his arm, who glanced around with starry eyes.

"It's lovely to meet you, both of you," Erin said, disengaging her hand from Jesse's arm to shake hands. Pete followed her example, mumbling a hello.

"Shall we see if our table is ready?" Erin tucked her hand back into the crook of Jesse's elbow.

Pete kept pace with Jesse and the other couple followed behind as Erin and Jesse approached the maître d' to see if they could be seated.

"I've never even been inside anywhere this fancy before. Are you sure you can afford a dinner here?"

Erin glanced at Jesse to see if he'd heard Amelia's whisper from just behind them. Judging by the tightness around his mouth, she knew he'd overheard the whisper, as well.

"Baker invited me," came Jared's soft answer. "I'll work it out with him."

She knew Jesse was concerned about money, but even if she paid for both hotel rooms and the dinner tonight, it wouldn't put a dent in her pocketbook. She'd been saving up her weekly pin money for a while, in hopes that her father would allow her a trip on her own, or possibly to do something worthwhile with the hospital. Certainly she'd been blessed and didn't mind sharing those blessings with others.

But she sensed that Jesse's pride might make it difficult for him to accept it if she paid for everything.

They were seated at a lovely white cloth-covered table, and Erin immediately saw Jared and Amelia and Pete all glance warily at the table settings in front of them. Jesse seemed frustrated, glancing with hooded eyes at the man across the table. Erin knew it would be up to her to smooth things over, start the conversation.

Certainly it wasn't a bad thing that her mother had insisted on extensive training on matters of etiquette. She smiled warmly around the table, first nudging Pete's elbow in the seat next to her.

"I don't know about you, but I'm starving. I heard someone say they have an excellent chocolate cake here."

The boy's eyes lit. "I can have cake?"

"Certainly. As long as you don't eat so much you make yourself sick," she teased gently.

He wrinkled his nose at her, but his shoulders lowered from up around his ears.

"How long have you two known each other?" She directed the question to Amelia, hoping to draw the other woman into conversation. "Jared mentioned earlier that you were fairly serious."

Amelia blushed, becoming pink roses blooming in her cheeks. She glanced affectionately at the man next to her. "We met about a year ago. He asked me to accompany him to a reading at a local university and we came to realize how much we liked to spend time together."

She and Jared shared a smile. Erin envied that they seemed to be able to converse without words.

"How do you know Jared?" Amelia asked Jesse, seeming to warm to the conversation.

"I don't. I knew his brother, Jim, back in...Boston."

The hesitation in his answer and the quick cut of his eyes to her made Erin wonder just what he wasn't saying about this Jim.

A waiter arrived and filled their glasses and explained the evening's menu. Pete grinned when the man mentioned the chocolate cake Erin had heard about earlier in the day.

"I'm trying to convince him to go back to Boston to visit his sick ma," Jesse continued with a winsome smile.

The other woman suddenly drooped and sent a pointed look at her companion. "Your mother is sick?"

Jared glowered at Jesse. "I haven't heard from my ma herself. Don't even know if it's serious."

"His sister says it's plenty serious. The doctor isn't sure his ma will make it."

Jared shot Jesse another glare and Erin thought that

perhaps this wasn't the correct conversational route if Jesse intended to convince the other man to return to Boston. Jared certainly seemed to bristle at the very mention of his mother, which caused Erin to wonder about his character.

"Perhaps you could send a telegram to check on your mother and sister," Erin suggested.

"That's a grand idea," Jared agreed quickly with a relieved glance at Erin. "I could find out without having to leave here."

"If your ma is sick, you should go to her," Amelia insisted quietly to Jared.

"She didn't protest when I left home and I doubt she really cares if I'm there now," he said, voice low so that it almost didn't reach Erin above the gentle hum of other diners' conversations. "She's probably worried about my sister."

"Well, she may have reason to be worried," came Amelia's answer. "If she's really sick, she probably wants to get everything in order, and taking care of your sister must be important to her."

"I'm not *leaving,*" he answered firmly. He seemed to realize that the rest of the table was attempting not to overhear their private conversation, and said a gruff, "Sorry."

"Excuse me," said Amelia. "I've got to visit the powder room." She scooted away from the table and disappeared.

It was clear she was upset and the glare Jared turned on Jesse was fierce. "I'd appreciate it if you'd change the subject."

When Jared looked away, Erin was able to see something beneath the raw anger—genuine concern.

"Amelia's ma has been sick for a good while and Amelia has the responsibility for taking care of the both of them." It was obvious by his tone he respected her, loved her. Erin realized that by bringing up Jared's mother's situation it was putting Jared in an awkward place. Amelia would feel that he should go, while it was obvious he was torn between staying and supporting the woman he loved or returning to help his mother.

"It should be the obvious choice to go help your ma—"

Erin touched Jesse's arm gently, breaking off his sentence.

"Come into the lobby with me," she murmured, then turned to the table. "Excuse us a minute."

He looked as if he wanted to protest, to stay and press his case, but when she stood, he reluctantly joined her.

Pete barely looked up from his plate when they left.

Jesse followed close behind her, looking back toward the table. "Erin, I want to get back and talk to him while his girl is away from the table—"

"Jesse."

He stopped when she said his name and allowed her to tug him into an alcove half hidden in shadow. They could speak with more privacy here, where the other noises of the restaurant were muted.

Jesse looked at her, waiting for her to speak, and she realized how far off her assumption from earlier at the clothing store had been. He valued her opinion.

"I know this is important to you, getting Jared to go back to his mother in Boston. It's an admirable task that you've taken upon yourself. But perhaps it might be time to start thinking that you've done as much as you can. You came and told Jared that his mother is in bad health and needs him. You've completed the task you set yourself."

He stood silent, gazing over her shoulder, with that familiar muscle ticking in his jaw.

"It's not for any admirable reason you might be thinking," he finally said. "Jared's brother Jim? He saved my life. Someone…came after me with a knife and Jim stepped in front of it. I owe him."

Again, she had that sense that he wasn't telling her everything, was possibly sparing her some of the details of such a violent event.

"I watched him die." Jesse stared away, eyes focused on events of the past. "For me. I promised I'd take care of his family."

Erin reached out and touched him. Not a touch on his arm, through the material of his jacket as she'd done before. She slipped her hand into his, palm to palm, and laced their fingers together. It was all she dared in such a public place—if they had been alone together she would have thrown her arms around his neck.

His hand closed around hers and he blinked, seeming to come back to the present. The open emotion still on his face struck to her core. She squeezed his hand tightly, unable to help her reaction even though—especially after the events of the afternoon—she knew she should keep her distance from him. Even with her brain telling her to be wary, her heart was drawn to him….

"You know I'm not one to preach at you, but whatever guilt or burden Jim's actions have set on you, you can find relief by giving your burdens to God."

The instant the words left her mouth, his face closed. Part of her wanted to take the statement back, but she couldn't. She truly believed it. And part of her really wanted Jesse to come to believe it, as well. But she wouldn't nag him about his beliefs.

She squeezed his hand again, hoping to give further comfort with her presence, their connection.

"If he won't go back to Boston, I'll have to," Jesse said quietly, looking down at their joined hands.

She admired his conviction. She knew he hoped to find a fresh start in Chicago, but to be willing to return to Boston to see to the care of an old woman and her daughter showed true character.

"You've brought the situation to Jared's attention. Now let him deal with it," she said. "I'm going to see if I can fetch Amelia from the powder room."

She felt his eyes on her back as she moved away. She found the other woman in the small vestibule, eyes red-rimmed as if she'd been crying.

"Did Jared send you after me? Oh, I'm so sorry to have ruined a nice meal together like this. I don't get to dine out often." Amelia sniffed and Erin was afraid she would become upset again.

"It's all right," Erin comforted her, pressing her own lace handkerchief into the other woman's hand. "Jared didn't send me, but I wanted to come check on you. Are you all right?"

"Yes, I'm fine." She sniffled again and Erin knew the other woman's tears were still close to the surface.

Erin guided Amelia to a small sofa just inside the vestibule and they both perched on the edge of it.

"Jared mentioned a bit about your mother's health concerns. I know it must be trying to be responsible for someone else's care at all times. Are you the only one who cares for her?"

Amelia fiddled with the handkerchief, looking down. "My older sister tries to help, but she's got her own family to worry about."

"What about you? Your plans for starting a family? Jared seems a fine man."

Amelia looked up, eyes bright with emotion. "He is, to be sure. We've spoken of marriage a couple of times in passing, but I couldn't ask a man to take on the burden of supporting both my mother and I."

"Do you honestly think Jared is the kind of man who would let that matter?"

"No." Amelia sniffled again, and pressed the handkerchief beneath her nose. "That's why I know he'll choose the right thing and go to his mother in Boston."

It was clear Amelia thought the world of Jared, and expected him to do right by his mother. And leave her behind to do so.

While Erin saw his devotion to Amelia when he'd said at the table, "I'm not leaving," and meant he wasn't leaving *her*.

Clearly the two were in love and only needed a little push—and possibly a little help—to make things right for them both.

"Let me ask you a question," Erin said, an idea forming. "What would you be willing to do for Jared...?"

* * *

Jesse couldn't help wondering what was taking so long when the women didn't immediately return to the table.

Not that he was in a big hurry to see Erin again. He had the thought that he'd disappointed her with his reaction to her faith statement, but his initial reaction had been to distrust what she said. Her words had brought back everything Jim had tried to pound into him with his preaching. But as Jesse had walked back to the dining room alone, he'd realized that she'd actually been trying to help him. Not that he thought God or anyone wanted Jesse's burdens, but it was kind of her to try.

Jared glared at him across the table, seeming to think the same thing about the women. Only Pete didn't seem to notice anything amiss, as he continued to clean his plate.

Jesse was disheartened. The remainder of the juicy steak on his plate held no interest for him; he'd lost his appetite.

If Jared refused to return to Boston, Jesse himself would have to do it. He'd promised Jim as the other man had died that Jesse would care for his family. And when Jared's mother had asked him to bring back her second son, Jesse thought it would be the easiest way to get absolution. He never thought Jared wouldn't want to return.

Thinking about returning to Boston made Jesse feel green, like Pete had been on the train.

He'd desperately wanted a chance to start fresh, to make a new life for himself away from Boston. Honest work, not being a confidence man any longer, or at least not after he'd made a few bucks to set himself up.

He was starting to want to be the kind of man Erin would be proud to be with.

"Where are they?" Jared demanded, finally plunking his fork down on the table.

"Probably gabbing in the powder room." Jesse wasn't too worried, not yet. "Erin likes to chat and she's only had me and the boy—" he hiked his finger at Pete "—to talk to for the last couple days. She's probably talking Amelia's ear off."

Jared's expression softened. "Amelia, too. She's cooped up a lot with only her mother for company, and sometimes she just needs to talk to another woman. Someone her own age."

It was clear the other man adored his sweetheart. Jesse's mind began to work as he tried to figure out a way to work that to his advantage. Could he somehow play Jared's love for Amelia to make the other man want to return to Boston?

"Maybe this dinner was a good idea after all," Jared said with a reluctant smile.

It had been Erin's suggestion in the first place. She continued to help Jesse, offering him comfort in the lobby just now, even when she'd been disappointed by his and Pete's deception earlier that afternoon.

"Amelia certainly seems like a nice gal," Jesse said casually.

Jared nodded, digging back into his food, and Jesse attempted to follow suit, even though he wasn't hungry.

"She's the best thing to ever happen to me," Jared said between bites.

"Seems like you would want to get a ring on her finger then."

The other man choked on his bite, face turning red as he reached for and gulped water to try to dislodge it.

"I'd love to," he finally spluttered, "but a man's got to be able to support his woman, and I'm just now getting set up, with the new raise at the lumberyard. I won't ask her until I've got some funds in the bank."

Something Jesse could understand. And again, it came down to money. If he had the funds, he could offer to help with Jared's expenses and free the man up to go to Boston. Without money, how could he get Jared to agree to go?

"I don't suppose they're hiring?" Jesse asked.

He wasn't sure he could make it in honest work, but he wanted to try.

"I see Pete's nearly cleaned his plate." Erin's cheery voice turned his head and Jesse was struck anew by her beauty as she approached the table. Her face shone, and Jesse realized what set her apart from all the other women, even high-society women, he'd known. It was that peace she carried with her.

"Yes'm," Pete said. "Seems a shame to waste food this good."

"You're entirely correct." Amelia settled into her seat next to Jared. Amelia was smiling, too, with a shared glance at Erin that suddenly made Jesse feel they'd hatched some plan and perhaps he and Jared had better watch out. "Forgive us for our absence. I see it hasn't stopped you men from enjoying your meals," she said with an affectionate nudge of her man.

Jared studied her face closely and seemed to be relieved at what he saw there. Jesse watched as he reached over and swiped a stray bit of hair that had caught on her cheek. "You all right?" Jesse had to read his lips to catch the words; they were spoken too low to hear over the other diners.

Amelia nodded and bent to say something to him but Jesse's attention was diverted when Erin leaned close enough that her breath warmed his ear when she whispered, "It will take care of itself."

He wanted to question her further and find out just what she'd done, but she leaned away and engaged Pete in conversation.

By the time everyone had emptied their plates, the waiter returned with the dessert cart.

"We should get a slice of that cake Erin mentioned earlier," Amelia said to Jared. "To celebrate."

"Celebrate what?" he asked absently, eyes on the sweets presented before them. He didn't notice her trembling smile, but Jesse did.

"Our engagement."

Jared went wide-eyed. "What?" He half laughed.

Amelia's chin went up slightly. Her eyes didn't waver from Jared. "Would you refuse me?" she asked softly.

Jared considered her in silence for a long moment. "Of course not." Slowly, a smile stretched across his face. "You'll really marry me?"

Jesse looked down when he found that Erin's hand had again slipped into his. For someone who hadn't experienced kind touches in years, her softness was a balm to his soul and he found he was getting quite used to it.

A glance at her face that mirrored the joy shared by the couple across from them now sharing a hushed conversation, and he knew she'd had something to do with Amelia's agreeing to marry Jared. Had she offered a monetary gift? The thought made Jesse's stomach roil again as he thought of the growing amount he owed to either the hotel or Erin herself.

After congratulations had been exchanged and thick slices of cake consumed, Jared and Amelia took their leave and Pete, Jesse and Erin made the trek back upstairs to their rooms.

After riding the elevator up, Pete's jaw cranked open in a wide yawn and Jesse imagined he was still exhausted after surviving his bout of food poisoning just the night before. The boy excused himself to go to bed, but Jesse lingered in the hallway outside the door to Erin's room. Without the excuse of a sick boy to care for, he knew it wouldn't be proper to be in the same room with her at this time of night.

"Did you offer money to Amelia to get her to propose to Jared?" he asked bluntly.

"No!" she said with a surprised laugh. "They are so in love…offering a bribe like that would've diminished what they felt for each other." She shook her head, eyes scrutinizing his face. "All I did was talk to Amelia and help her see she was putting obstacles between them that didn't have to be there."

She continued studying him and Jesse wondered what she was looking for in his features.

"I'm happy things worked out for them," Erin said softly. She seemed in no hurry to go inside her room.

Jesse nodded, but his mind still whirled with his dilemma. "I'm glad for them, too, but I don't see how getting married is going to get them to Boston to take care of his ma." He leaned his shoulder against the wall, standing close but not too close to Erin as to be considered inappropriate.

"Amelia and I talked things over a bit. She wants to marry soon and she's determined to talk him into a honeymoon trip to Boston. When they get there, they can decide what to do about Jared's mother. If she isn't too bad off, she thinks they could bring her and his sister here and combine both households. If Jared's sister agrees, it might actually relieve some of the burden on Amelia, if the two of them can work out a way to share the duties of caring for two older women."

"I thought Amelia had to care for her ailing mother? How can she take a trip?"

"Amelia has a sister who can care for their mother if they aren't gone too long."

His little fixer had everything all figured out, but Jesse still felt the heavy weight of his responsibility. He needed to be sure Jared would return to Boston for his mother. Sending money wasn't enough. Jim's death had to mean something.

The weight of it felt impossible to lift.

Jesse thought of the other thing that was bugging him.

"I'll find a way to pay for the meal," he said, aware that she'd had the entire sum charged to their rooms. He had no intention of allowing Erin to foot the bill, not when she'd staged the entire thing for his benefit in the first place.

"That's not necessary," she replied, shaking her head. He noticed the back of her intricate style was beginning to fall out, curls raining down on her slender neck and shoulders. His hand ached to bury in them and pull her close for a kiss, but he knew that was impossible. He pushed both hands behind his back, pressed them to the wall.

He made his voice firm. "It's what I want. I'll figure out a way."

"Fine," she said brusquely, staring down at her hands where she'd clasped them in front of her. "I'll pay for the hotel in the morning and leave my address for you. When you've earned an appropriate sum, you can forward it to me."

He frowned, but imagined it was an acceptable solution to her, seeing as she didn't think he could have a way to pay for his part by the morning.

"Listen, I don't want to talk about money right now." She twisted her hands together, and then looked up at him with those incredible blue eyes. "In the morning, we'll be going in our separate directions and..."

She seemed to run out of words, an unusual thing for her. He was used to her chatter.

She watched his face again, but he worked to keep his expression neutral, even as she talked about her departure and he felt like his heart was being ripped from his chest. Breath left her lips in a soft exhalation, and she went on.

"Is there anything I can do to help you? I don't have any connections in Chicago, but perhaps I could wire my father to see if any of his business connections could help you."

He knew the admission cost her, because he remembered her saying she'd left Boston to get away from the man's manipulations, but Jesse didn't want to be beholden to her any more than he already was.

"That's very kind of you, but I'm sure I'll be able to find something."

"But what about lodgings? Where will you stay?"

"Erin." He said her name when really he wanted to silence her by placing a kiss on her warm, enticing lips. He fisted his hands behind him. "I've been taking care of myself since I was fifteen." Not that he'd always done such a good job. "I'll be all right."

Her concern made his resolve waver. His own mother had offered only a token protest when he'd left home at fifteen, but most of her worry had been for Daniel. As it should've been.

Who, other than Erin, had offered Jesse any concern? No one. And he was afraid he might be falling in love with her because of it. He imagined her concern was only an outpouring of the gentle, generous spirit she exhibited constantly. And he knew he didn't deserve it, not one bit.

"What about Pete?" she asked, looking down now. "I meant to do some checking on local orphanages this afternoon, or perhaps contact a nearby church, but with all the other goings-on, I lost track of time."

There wouldn't have been much time after she'd found out Pete wasn't his brother and before their dinner plans.

"He's not your responsibility," Jesse reminded her.

"That doesn't mean I can just leave him to fend for himself," she argued hotly, about as he expected her to. She liked to fight for the underdog, he knew that about her now. "He's only a little boy," she went on.

"Maybe I should stay another day and see him settled somewhere..."

"And maybe he won't even be in the room when we wake up in the morning."

Her eyes went wide, and Jesse held up his palm to forestall her disgruntled argument.

"The kid is streetwise. The only reason he's stuck around this long is he thinks he's found a cash cow to bleed dry." Right now Jesse wasn't sure if it was her or himself.

She bit her lip, but he still didn't stop. "He might've approached me first, but when he figured out that you've got about the most generous heart a body's ever seen, you'd better believe he latched onto you."

She raised her chin in a little imitation of Pete. "I don't care," she said defiantly. "If he needs help, and I can give it, why shouldn't I?"

"Because he'll take everything you've got," Jesse said. Aware that two days before, Jesse had seriously thought about it himself. "I was only a few years older than Pete when I left home. If I had met someone like you back then—" or before he'd gotten to know her "—I would've had your purse in the work of a few moments and been on my merry way."

She stared at him as if she didn't know him at all, as if he'd accosted her in the hall instead of spent the better part of two days together and become almost...friends.

Her distaste stung, and even worse was the thought that pickpocketing was the *least* of things he'd done to survive on the streets, or done to get ahead a few bucks. He shoved off the wall where he'd been leaning, half turning away from her because he couldn't bear that look.

But she didn't allow him to escape. She reached out and tangled their hands together again, the way she'd done twice at dinner. The simple touch of her hand threatened to unman him.

"I would've given it to you," she said softly, looking up into his face with those guileless blue eyes, and he knew what she said was true. "I wish I would've known you then so I could've helped you."

"I don't understand you," he said, his own honesty surprising him as he just blurted it out. "I've never met anyone like you, and I don't understand how you can be so..." Generous, giving, unselfish, perfect, amazing. "I don't deserve your help, much less your friendship. You're too generous."

She shook her head. "There's no such thing."

"Sure there is. One of these days, you might get taken advantage of."

She shook her head again, laughter dancing in her eyes. "I can take care of myself."

She'd said it before but he still didn't believe it.

"How'd you get this way, anyway?" he asked, wanting nothing more than to keep her here next to him, holding his hand.

Something darkened behind her eyes and he wanted to take whatever pain that was away from her. Something in her past?

"When I was a young girl, I was very sick. Very sick, for a long time." Emotion flickered across her face and he squeezed her hand, encouraging her to go on. "I wasn't allowed to have any friends for fear they would make me sicker or that I would tire myself out and be unable to recover. It was a very lonely existence for me."

"I can only imagine," he teased her gently, chucking under her chin with his bent finger. "A young Erin O'Grady chattering endlessly to a bed full of dolls, all lined up." He could identify with the loneliness she must have experienced; he'd felt desperate for someone to talk to immediately after Daniel's death when he'd been alone on the streets. For someone like Erin, someone who enjoyed the company of others, it must have been unbearable not to have any friends.

"That's when I first developed my love of birds," she said smartly, knocking his hand away from her chin, her fire returning. "There was a large window right across from my bed and a family of sparrows nested there year after year. And sometimes there was a mockingbird that would roost in the tree outside..." She cut herself off with a shake of her head.

"That's beside the point. I had a nurse who stayed with me nearly all of the time."

"What of your parents?" he interrupted.

"My father's businesses engage much of his time, and always have. And my mother, while graceful in social etiquette, didn't quite know what to do with a sickly daughter. So my nurse, Miss Kettleblum, stayed with me."

The affectionate note in her voice showed exactly what she thought of this woman. She looked straight at Jesse. "You might not like this part of the story, but it's my story, so I'll tell it anyway.

"Miss Kettleblum taught me about Jesus and how much he loved a lonely little girl like me. She taught me about God's mercy and how He sacrificed the Son He loved so much for me. And she taught me how important it was to share that mercy, not hoard it. She showed it in her life, providing care for a lonely little girl.

"So that's what I try to do. Pass it on," she finished quietly, not quite meeting his eyes.

The words were simple but Jesse knew Erin's actions weren't.

"Good night." She leaned up and bussed his cheek, slipping into her room before he could protest or embrace her.

Leaving him empty and aching for the mercy he expected wouldn't come. Not for him.

Chapter Eleven

Jesse slipped out of the hotel and into a softly falling snow. He'd changed out of the rented suit and back into his cowboy clothes, and now he pulled the lapels of the leather coat up around his ears as best he could.

It was the middle of the night—no one else was around, and even the breeze whistling around the corner of the building sounded lonely.

He'd been too restless to sleep. Pete had been snoring softly—who knew boys could snore like that?—in the wide bed, and Jesse had left him there, sneaking out of the hotel room and now out into the night.

Erin's description of her childhood played over and over in his mind.

She was such a wonderful person. He couldn't understand how her parents could just lock a sick child away, with only a hired nurse to care for her. What if the nurse they'd hired hadn't been the loving person she'd turned out to be? What if it had been someone more like Jesse's stepfather, who didn't care about anyone other than themselves?

And why wasn't she bitter about it? He had trouble

moving on from the pains in his past but she seemed to just accept what had happened to her and move on.

Jesse stomped through the snow, passing into the deserted park where he and Erin had walked earlier. Now it was shadowed and dark and the tree branches clacked together and creaked eerily, covered with ice as they were.

Beneath thoughts of Erin's childhood and how her story affected him—much more than any of Jim's sermons!—were worries about how he could repay Erin for the hotel and their extravagant meal. Even the train ticket and Pete's clothing should be his responsibility, but Jesse didn't have any idea how to get the funds.

He'd seen several hotel patrons still awake as he'd passed through the lobby on his way out. It wouldn't take much to concoct a story and relieve someone of the contents of their purse. The people staying in that fancy hotel could surely afford it, and Jesse couldn't even afford his breakfast.

But he didn't want to.

He didn't want to think he'd changed that much since just knowing Erin, but her generous spirit and gentleness with Pete, even the way she'd seemed to forgive them for their deception—at least the one she knew about—had made him want to be a better person.

The fact was, he couldn't stomach taking someone else's money. Not when Jim had given him the slightest hope that Jesse could change. Knowing Erin had rekindled the desire to live straight.

And he didn't want to prove his stepfather right when the man had said, *"You'll never be more than a petty thief."*

Jesse didn't want to be that anymore. But he didn't know another way to get the money he needed.

He wanted Erin to see him as capable, someone who could take care of himself, not someone else who mooched off her. Even if she didn't mind giving her money to him.

Apparently, he had some pride left after prison, small though it might be.

Even if he got a job tomorrow, it would be a long while until he could repay anything to Erin, because he'd have to find a place to stay, buy food, and he'd eventually need some new clothes.

He just couldn't see a way to do it.

A small yipping broke into Jesse's thoughts and he turned on his heel, looking for the source of the sound. Was some small animal out in this cold? He peered through the snowy drifts, looking for the source of the slight noise. A whine…there!

Jesse squatted and spotted a shivering, small dog beneath a bush just off the footpath. Muddy and gray over a white coat, it almost faded into the landscape.

"Here, boy," he called, but the dog barely moved. How long had it been out in these elements?

Jesse approached slowly, thinking the animal might be hurt and lash out at him. But a friendly, though slow wag of the animal's tail expressed things might be looking up.

"You all right, boy?" Jesse crept closer, watching the animal for any sign it might attack. It didn't look big enough to do him damage but a person couldn't be sure. Then he spotted the fine quality ribbon attached both to the animal and wrapped tightly about the base of the bush and realized it might've been stuck here for quite a while.

And after he'd untangled the shivering, sluggish creature, he lifted it into his arms, wrinkling his nose at the wet dog smell. The animal looked familiar. Was this the same dog that had been running and yapping around the hotel lobby, the one Pete had noticed when they'd gone down to dinner?

He didn't feel ready to end his walk, hadn't solved any of the problems plaguing him, not even his whirling thoughts, but the animal burrowed close, seeking Jesse's warmth. Its owner was probably worried about it.

He trudged back to the hotel, the small white ball of fluff shivering against his chest as he cradled it close, hoping to share some of his warmth with it.

Maybe Erin *had* turned him into a do-gooder if he was going out of his way to take a mutt like this back to its owner.

The clerk at the hotel desk looked at him askance when he first walked up to the desk but when a manager came over as Jesse was explaining where he'd found the dog, the man's face lit up.

"Oh, you've found Mrs. Smith's little Georgie. Bless you, sir. Her son lost the animal earlier and we've had several of our employees out scouring the streets for it. If you knew her, she's been quite upset, thinking the little dog might've been crushed beneath a carriage wheel on our busy streets or stolen… I'm going to send someone up to her room to fetch her—"

Jesse tried to turn over the dog to the man behind the desk, but the fellow would have none of it and insisted Jesse stay to return the dog to its owner.

Moments later, a woman in an obviously hastily donned dress with hair in a gray braid down her back dragged a small pajama-clad boy cross the lobby from the elevators.

"Oh, Georgie!" she cried. "Oh, is this the man who rescued you?"

The dog tried to jump out of his arms, and Jesse thought to himself he'd like to run the other way if that was his keeper, as well. Jesse managed to keep hold of the dog and turned it over to the woman, who snatched it to her ample bosom.

"Where did you find him?"

Jesse explained how he'd found the dog shivering in the park, and by the time he was done, the woman was sniffling and had tears in her eyes. Save him from crying females.

"I just don't know how I can thank you for saving my baby. He was the last gift from my late husband. I don't know what I would have done if he'd been lost forever—I know! I'd like to give you a reward."

"That's not necessary," he protested. "It was a complete accident that I stumbled on him in the park."

"Things like this are never accidents, young man," she said in all seriousness. "God put you in that park to find my Georgie, and I'll reward you as I see fit."

She shoved a bill into his hand. He glanced at it and then looked again. It was a crisp hundred-dollar bill. Something he'd only held once in his entire life and certainly more than the dog itself was worth.

"Ma'am, I can't take this." He tried to push it back into her hand, but she was holding the poor dog up to her face and allowing it to lick her chin. He wrinkled his nose. "I didn't really do anything. I was just in the right place at the right time—"

"Young man, don't argue with me. I thank you for finding my Georgie and now I've got to return to bed. Come along, Franklin."

The boy obediently followed her, drooping from tiredness.

Leaving Jesse staring after her, more money than he'd seen in quite a while in his palm.

Just before he'd found the little animal, he'd been desperate to find a way to make money—any way. And now he held more than enough cash to cover the hotel, supper and pay Erin back for the ticket to Chicago.

It couldn't be a blessing for him—could it?

And suddenly he knew what he wanted to do with his life…or at least the next forty-eight hours of it.

Jesse shook Pete awake early the next morning.

"Wha—" Pete thrashed beneath Jesse's hand, finally throwing back the covers.

Jesse threw open the curtains, flooding the room with early-morning sunshine. "Get dressed. We're taking Erin to the train station."

He hadn't slept much the night before, but his sleeplessness had been from excitement. He was still thrilled about the cash he'd received last night for what he'd thought was a silly task, returning a dog to its owner.

Erin might've said God orchestrated the event, knowing Jesse was in need of cash. He didn't know if he believed that, but he sure wasn't going to give back the money.

"What's yer rush?" Pete moved sluggishly to the edge of the bed.

Jesse tossed several bills on the cover, half of what had been left after paying the hotel rooms and for their supper. And he'd sent an amount for an engagement gift to Jared Kenner at his workplace.

Pete's eyes went wide.

"That's half." Jesse snatched it back when the kid reached for it. "You'll get it when we get to Wyoming."

Pete pulled on his new pants, shirt and shoes, with new urgency. "I want my half now."

Jesse paced toward the door, anxious to get moving. He couldn't wait to see Erin's reaction this morning. "No. Then I'd have no guarantee you'd keep your mouth shut until we get there."

The boy wrinkled his nose at Jesse but Jesse wouldn't back down. Pete stuffed the extra pairs of socks Erin had bought him into the center of the shirt and rolled it all up into a bundle that he tucked beneath his arm.

"Can we get breakfast?" Pete asked on the way down the elevator. "I'm hungry."

"You're always hungry," Jesse murmured.

Stepping off the elevator, they saw Erin at the desk. She appeared to be arguing with a flustered clerk.

"How can the rooms be paid when I've just got down here?"

"Because I paid for them," Jesse said.

Erin whirled to face him. "You? What— How?"

"I had a busy night," he explained.

Pete looked sideways at him, a skeptical smirk on his lips.

"It was all on the up-and-up." Jesse held up his palms

outward to show he was being honest. "It involved a walk in the park, a lost dog and a reward. C'mon, we've got to get to the station."

Erin allowed him to take her valise and the porter wheeled a trunk out to the street for her and hailed a hackney cab. "You're seeing me off?"

Jesse squinted against the morning sunlight, his hat not providing adequate shade for his eyes due to the angle of the sun. "Something like that."

He assisted her into the carriage and gave Pete a boost, too.

"No breakfast?" the kid whined, looking longingly over his shoulder at the hotel.

"No time," said Jesse. "We'll see about getting you something later."

"So what happened?" asked Erin, and Jesse explained the events of the evening after he'd left his room last night.

"Amazing," she murmured, her face shining with real joy for him.

Pete continued to consider him skeptically but Jesse didn't have anything to hide. Not this time.

"So, I started thinking about you traveling to Wyoming all on your own, and remembering that man who approached you just before we got to Chicago—Pete, do you remember that guy?"

"Pete was pretty nauseous by then," Erin protested.

"Nope, I remember him. He was sleazy." Pete leaned back in his seat, still clutching the rolled-up shirt, and grinning.

"I'm a little concerned about Miss Erin traveling the rest of the way by herself," Jesse went on. "And…

it's only four days until Christmas. Her family might be upset if she didn't make it out to see them by the holiday."

She nudged his booted foot with the tip of her prim little shoe, huffing, but he knew she was aware he was teasing.

"She does get in an awful lot of trouble," Pete put in.

"Huh!" she exclaimed. "Only with you two around!"

"So I was thinking maybe Pete and I better go with you the rest of the way."

She leaned her head to one side, assessing him for so long that Jesse wondered if she didn't *want* him to accompany her.

"It's two more days of travel. It's really not necessary," she said. "I thought you were going to make your new start here, in Chicago. Now you've got the funds to do it."

She had the right of it. But lately he had been thinking he could find a fresh start in Wyoming as well as anywhere. With the amount remaining of his hundred-dollar reward, he could come back to Chicago if that was what he decided. He still didn't know what he wanted to do, what he could do.

But he knew he wanted to stay close to Erin for as long as possible. If it was only two more days, then he'd take those two days.

"You've been plenty kind to Pete and me," he said, low and serious. "I'd like to make sure you get where you're going without any trouble. And I thought it might give us a chance to solve the dilemma of what to do with..." He let his voice trail off and cut his eyes to Pete.

Okay, so he wasn't above using a little manipulation. He knew she was worried about what would happen to the kid.

"But if you don't want us to go with you…"

"No, no," she was quick to interject. "I'd love to have the both of you travel to Wyoming with me. At least to Cheyenne, where I'll have to change trains to travel up to Calvin, the town where they live."

"All right, then we're riding along with you."

Chapter Twelve

As the noon meal neared, Erin reflected that this leg of the journey had been particularly uneventful. It hadn't been quite as pleasant as traveling on the sleeper car. With no sleeping berths available out of Chicago going westbound, they'd been crowded onto a passenger car with a lot of other people. Erin imagined the volume of passengers was due to people traveling for Christmas to see their families.

The seats in this car were narrower than they had been in the sleeper car, and whomever was seated closest to the window couldn't completely stretch their legs. So far, Erin had remained on the inside, and Jesse and Pete had traded turns next to her, where they could stick their legs out into the aisle and get a little relief.

She was thankful she'd repacked her trunk at the Chicago hotel and put the parcels she'd brought for gifts for Chas and his family inside. Even keeping up with her valise was more difficult in this tightly packed railcar.

The conversations were closer, louder, and the smell of unwashed bodies at times threatened to overpower Erin.

And they had to endure another day and a half of it. Including somehow catching some sleep on the train tonight.

Thankfully, she had no complaints about the company. Jesse and Pete had kept her entertained all morning, making up stories for the various passengers in their car. The man two rows up with the funny hat was traveling to see his estranged daughter in Arizona. The woman with the loud, yapping voice near the front of the car was going all the way to California to meet her grandson for the very first time.

At last they were nearing the next stop—a place where they could get off and stretch their legs while they ate the noon meal. They'd have an allotted time to eat and then get back on the train. Erin hadn't paid much attention to the disembarking and reloading of passengers on the trip from Boston to Chicago, but now that her stomach was rumbling for some sustenance, she was ready to pull into the station.

When the call finally came from the conductor, who passed quickly through the car, she already had her coat and scarf on.

"Take your satchel," Jesse cautioned her, half turned toward the aisle and glancing over his shoulder at her. "And keep a good hold on it. You don't want it to fall—or someone to grab it—in the hurry to get off."

The train pulled up to the platform with a hiss of brakes, and Jesse grabbed her arm and hauled her into the aisle in time for the other passengers to get out of their seats as well, pressing in on her from all sides. The crowd surged forward and Erin received an elbow in her back as she tried to maintain her balance.

"Jesse!" she cried out when she lost her footing.

"I've got you." He kept her upright with his hand beneath her arm, and when he could manage it, passed her beneath his arm, so she was in front of him. He changed his grip so his left hand rested beneath her left elbow and his right arm snaked behind her back, steadying her further.

"Watch it, bud," he called over his shoulder as he was jostled. "Better?" he asked, right in her ear.

She nodded, unable to find air in the press of bodies to answer him verbally.

They passed down the steps to the platform and she breathed a little easier as the fresh, cold air hit her face and the dispersing crowd gave her a little more room to move.

"Next time, I might wait until the crowd passes," she panted as Jesse moved in front again and pulled her in the same direction the crowd was going. She realized she had no idea if Pete had made it off the train with them.

"Pete? Pete!"

"Right behind ya, Miss Erin. Ya know I'm not going to miss the noon meal."

She didn't have time to turn her head, but she could hear the grin in his voice.

"If you wait until after the crowd gets off the train, you're likely not to get a seat," said Jesse as he ushered her into a ramshackle building full of long tables, already filling up with other passengers. "Hurry up and find a place."

Erin climbed onto the bench seat in the first location where there were three seats together, and before she'd even settled herself, a steaming plate appeared in front of her, along with a sweating mason jar of iced tea and a mug of coffee. She turned to ask for a glass of water instead of the tea, but the girl who'd plunked down her plate was already gone, bustling down the line of patrons.

"Best eat fast, miss," said a snaggle-toothed man across from her. "Be gettin' back on the train afore you know it."

Erin glanced over to see Pete shoveling food into his mouth—the sharp lines of his face had already begun to soften after only a couple of days of eating well—and Jesse, too, was digging in. She followed suit. Apparently, they weren't going to share any scintillating conversation over this meal, but that was all right.

The chaos of other diners talking, clanking silverware and people shouting for the server had Erin on edge but she attempted to ignore it all and just eat.

Her stomach appreciated the food more than her tastebuds. The meat was flavorless and hard and smothered with some unidentifiable gravy. And she didn't particularly like tea; the coffee was much too strong. She ate anyway, conscious that they wouldn't get another chance until the evening meal.

She noticed Jesse pushed all his potatoes to one side of his plate. He had ordered steamed carrots last night at the restaurant and she'd meant to ask him about his aversion to potatoes but gotten distracted from her aim.

She opened her mouth to ask him now but looked up and saw a frazzled-looking mother with several children huddled around her like a mother hen with chicks. The little group stood just away from the edge of the tables, with the mother craning her head as if looking for a place they could all sit together. None of the other passengers seemed to pay her any mind, but Erin couldn't ignore the hungry gazes of the young children.

She pushed away from the table, nearly toppling Jesse as she used his shoulder as leverage to disentangle herself from the wooden bench and table.

"What're you doing?" he asked, reaching out one hand to steady her even as he took a drink from his mason jar.

"There's a mother, just there—" Erin pointed "—looking for a seat. She looks worn out and she has small children. I count…one, two, three, five of them. I'm going to send her over to sit here."

"What about you— Erin!"

She shrugged as she passed Pete, and called back over her shoulder, "I can certainly eat standing up."

She made her way back through the tables, excusing herself when she couldn't avoid bumping into other patrons, some of whom shot her disgruntled looks. Some even cursed her, but she wouldn't be deterred.

Erin reached the young mother and pointed out her now-empty seat, and Jesse, who stood half out of his seat now. He was waving down the server who'd brought their food and was now at the other end of the long tables.

The mother slanted a suspicious look at Erin before she guided her children down the way Erin had just come, and again the passengers they couldn't get around complained.

"Excuse me," Erin called out to a man who'd said a foul word right in front of the children. "But the children need to eat, too. Would you like to give up your seat for one of them?" she asked sweetly. He went back to his food in silence, shooting a glare at her.

Jesse joined her a moment later, juggling two tin plates. He thrust hers into her hands with a mock scowl. "You couldn't just stay in your seat, could you? Can't let anyone fend for themselves…."

"You gave yours up, too."

He smiled crookedly. "Only because I thought I'd better keep you from causing more trouble."

She nudged his elbow with hers as they both stood with backs to the walls and ate. There really wasn't much room between the edge of the tables and the wall, but there was enough.

"Feels good to stretch my legs," she said at one point and Jesse only raised his eyebrows at her. She shrugged. It also felt good to provide a kindness for someone, and as Erin watched the young mother try to corral her five children to eat and behave at the crowded table, she was glad she'd done it. Although the woman hadn't exactly been grateful.

Eating so quickly while standing up caused the food to settled like a lump of lead just behind Erin's sternum, but there wasn't time to ask for a seltzer water as shouts from the conductor from outside indicated they needed to hightail it back onto the train.

As the passengers started moving and standing up, Jesse waved Pete to hurry up. The boy stuffed one more roll between his teeth and stood up, jostling the little girl who'd been squished in next to him. She started to wail, but the sound was lost in the noise of passengers leaving.

"We should help them get back on the train," Erin said, having to shout a second time for Jesse to hear her.

He rolled his eyes, but didn't argue. He pushed back through the crowd, Erin following close behind, and stopped Pete with a hand on the boy's arm, then approached the young mother and her brood and Jesse leaned down to speak with her.

Erin couldn't hear what was said over the hum of passengers, but the woman looked over his shoulder at Erin with narrowed eyes. She didn't protest as he loaded Pete's arms with two small children, then scooped up another two and moved toward Erin, ushering the young mother with him.

The conductor called out from the platform again and Jesse ushered them all toward the train, rushing now. Erin took one of the small children from Pete—a girl of about two—and led the way back to the train. They were some of the last ones on, and had to take the last two and a half rows, those closest to the door, where they'd get a draft at each stop.

Jesse shot her a wry smile, but she was starting to see that beneath his bluster was a kind heart. Whether he wanted to admit it or not. He never would have helped Pete—deception or no—if he hadn't seen that the boy was in trouble.

"I'm Erin. This is Jesse and Pete," she introduced as the young mother and her brood began getting seated. The children shed their coats and scarves like an instant molt of feathers.

"I'm Andrew!"

"I'm Matt! And we're twins!" chorused the two boys.

"Oh, my," Erin murmured with an amazed look at their mother.

"I'm Nora," the woman said with a frown, juggling baby and bag on her lap as she struggled to loosen her own coat. "And these are Emma and Rachel and baby Roy. Boys, sit in your seat."

The two younger girls, probably two and three, pressed their faces shyly into their mother's arm, while the baby gave a gurgle and a toothless grin.

"You got a lot of kids," Pete said bluntly.

"Pete!" Erin exclaimed, while Jesse only chuckled. When Erin scowled at him, he only shrugged.

"What? Five is a good number of kids."

"Humph," Nora said, blowing air through her lips to move her bangs off her face. "At home, they aren't such a handful."

Erin could only imagine.

As if to illustrate her statement, one of the twins pinched the other, who slugged him in the arm and they tumbled to the floor, wrestling and writhing, knocking into passengers across the way.

"Boys!" Nora cried out, but with the baby in her lap, she only had one hand to reach out and try to grab them, but nearly unseated herself trying to do it anyway.

"Here!" Erin scrabbled in her purse to find her sketchbook and two pencils.

Jesse cleared his throat from beside her and she turned a glance on him that revealed a crooked smile. She knew he was thinking about lunch and giving up their seats. She shrugged. He could think she was silly or interfering if he wanted, but what could she have done differently?

She tore several blank pages from the back of the book. “Here—”

“C’mere, you two.” Jesse pulled the fighting boys apart. “Miss Erin is going to show you something fun to do to pass the time.”

They goggled at her as Erin handed them both a sheet of paper and a pencil.

“You’re old enough to know your letters, aren’t you?”

“Most of ’em,” one of the boys answered, wiping beneath his nose with his sleeve.

“Well, why don’t we practice them? And then when that side of the paper is full, you can draw a picture on the other side.”

Erin helped settle the boys on the floor between the two facing seats. When she righted herself in her own seat, Nora grimaced at her, suspicious again.

“Well, thank you, I guess.” She didn’t sound very thankful. “Most of the other passengers would’ve just ignored us.”

Jesse read the tension between Nora and Erin, but the kindhearted girl beside him seemed oblivious. He’d seen Nora’s suspicious look when he’d approached in the restaurant with an offer to help them get on the train. It seemed her suspicions about Erin’s motives remained.

It was some comfort to him that someone else thought Erin’s kind actions were unusual.

Unaware of the vibes, Erin asked, “Where are you traveling to?”

“Oregon.”

“We’re meeting our auntie,” one of the boys said, looking up from the floor.

"Just in time for Christmas, hmm?" asked Erin. "I'm visiting relatives, too. My brother and his family."

One of the smaller girls came hesitantly across the space between the two benches, shyly holding up her ragdoll for Erin's inspection.

"Emma, leave the fancy lady alone."

"Oh, I don't mind," Erin told Nora. "May I see your doll? Thank you."

As she leaned forward to engage the little girl, Jesse caught sight of Pete's face where the boy was catty-corner, sitting across from Erin in the other. The boy's face was confused, as if trying to understand Erin's interactions with the other children.

After the confessions they'd made to Erin yesterday, Jesse knew a bit more about the boy's past, that he'd lost his mother and been separated from his sister. Was he feeling a bit of jealousy to see Erin sharing her kindness with these other passengers? Or was it something else?

Self-preservation urged Jesse to put some distance between himself and Erin. But with her generous outlook, she made him want to be better than he was. She thought he was noble, and good, and he wanted to be those things. But he knew he wasn't.

The conductor came through the car, calling out the next stop.

Pete stretched his arms above his head and stood. "I'm going to visit the washroom."

There was only one washroom on this car and it was at the opposite end from where they sat. Pete looked back from halfway down the aisle and a gut feeling had Jesse out of his seat and following the kid before he realized he was up.

There were a few folks standing near the outer door—probably anticipating a quick jump off at the stop. Pete seemed to have disappeared until Jesse noticed him wedged between a portly man and the wall, in a narrow corner. Jesse edged close and the kid's face changed color when it was clear he'd been spotted.

"I'm not gonna stop you from getting off, if that's what you want," Jesse said, keeping his voice low so the other passengers wouldn't pay them any attention. "Erin wouldn't, either, if you would've told her you wanted to go."

"She's too busy with her next charity case to even notice."

Jesse spotted the insecure boy behind the words just as he'd spotted Pete trying to hide. "She doesn't think you're a charity case. In case you haven't noticed, she's special."

Much too special for the likes of him.

One of the disembarking passengers stared unabashedly, obviously listening to their conversation. Jesse resisted the urge to tell him off. He only had a few minutes to convince the boy to stay.

Pete kept his eyes trained on the wall, chin raised in that familiar defiant posture.

"For some reason, she seems to genuinely like us both, even after we let her think we were brothers."

Pete's eyes flickered once to the opposite side of the car, where Erin remained, but he made no other sign he was listening.

"I think we owe it to her to go to Wyoming with her—"

"You just want me around to look good to her," the kid spat.

"Maybe so." Although the kid *was* starting to grow on him. "But our deal was you had to come to Wyoming to get your half of the cash."

The kid raised his chin, staring at the wall.

Jesse wasn't getting through to him. The train started to slow, and Jesse knew he was running out of time for talking. Why did it matter to him anyway? This was just another kid. Who reminded him of Daniel.

"I wish I'd had someone like Erin to try to help me when I was fifteen—just a couple years older than you. I was living on the streets with my younger brother, Daniel. I was in charge of us both."

Saying the words aloud seemed to release something in Jesse—he'd never talked about it before. "We were doing all right, finding enough food, mostly warm places to stay. There were times we went hungry, but I thought we were making it…and then Daniel got sick. I couldn't help him and he just kept getting sicker and sicker…"

Jesse had to swallow hard before he could go on. "And then he died."

Pete's eyes were on Jesse now, but he remained silent.

"If I would've had someone like Erin to help me, maybe Daniel could've got the help he needed. Maybe he would've lived.

"She's already saved your hide once," Jesse said with a pass of his hand over his mouth to still his rising emotions.

The train stopped and Jesse knew the kid was going to get off. He reached in his pocket and pulled out the reward money. Peeling back a couple of bills, he shoved them into the kid's hand. "Here."

Then he turned to go back to his seat. He'd done all he could to convince the kid to stay.

When he slid into his seat, Erin looked up at him curiously, a child perched happily on her lap, although Nora looked a little disgruntled. "Where's Pete?"

He hesitated. He wanted to spare her knowing Pete had snuck off the train, but he didn't want any more secrets to come between them—not with what he was already keeping back about his past.

"He…"

"Had to wait for the washroom," came the kid's voice and then he appeared in the aisle and went back to his seat. He met Jesse's eyes and nodded slightly. Jesse's words *had* penetrated, had made some difference to the boy. Or maybe he just wanted the rest of the money Jesse had promised him.

Jesse returned Pete's nod, settling back into his seat. He caught an enigmatic glance from Erin, but she didn't ask him about the exchange between him and Pete.

"We're just about to read some more of the story I've been reading to you and Pete," Erin said. Jesse noticed what he hadn't before, that she had her Bible open on her lap, juggling both it and the sleepy toddler.

Jesse tuned out, not wanting to hear a sermon, until she read, "'And when they were departed, behold, the angel of the Lord appeareth to Joseph in a dream, saying, "Arise, and take the young child and his mother, and flee into Egypt, and be thou there until I bring thee word: for Herod will seek the young child to destroy him." When he arose, he took the young child and his mother by night, and departed into Egypt—'"

"You mean, the king wanted to kill the baby Jesus?"

The shock in one of the young twins' voices brought Jesse out of his doze.

Jesse listened as she explained the hatred that had led a king to try to kill the Christ child.

She had the kids completely engaged; Jesse was, too.

She was so different from Jim. Where he'd preached things like living right, and God's love, Erin lived those things. Without apology, she lived her beliefs in every moment.

It made someone like Jesse believe when he never had before.

But he couldn't forget the things he'd done, the guilt he carried. How could God?

Chapter Thirteen

"That one's trouble," Nora cautioned as Erin watched Jesse and Pete head to the washroom for evening ablutions.

In the melee of getting off the train for dinner and back on, somehow their larger group—Erin, Jesse and Pete, along with Nora's troop—had gotten seats in the center of the train car. Although farther from the boiler, this area of the car retained more heat because the drafts from outer doors opening was diminished.

Nora's little ones had finally worn themselves out and were sprawled across each other, coats and scarves on but askew. Erin held the baby against her midsection, where he'd dozed off.

"Which one?" asked Erin with a grin. "They're both a little troublesome."

She'd meant the words as a joke but Nora didn't share her smile. Erin had been attempting to get to know the prickly woman all afternoon without much success.

"I meant Jesse. I see the way you look at him, and you need to watch out."

"How do I look at him?" Erin asked with a half

laugh, determined not to be offended at Nora's abrupt manner.

"Like a woman falling in love," Nora said bluntly, and it was clear she thought this was a bad thing.

Erin started to deny it but the words stuck in her throat. She couldn't be falling for Jesse, not after the way he'd misled her. Could she?

"We're planning to go our separate ways once we get to Wyoming," she said at last, because that much was true.

Nora scrutinized her with narrowed eyes. "He's trouble, I'm telling you. What do you know about him anyway?"

"Well..." She was going to say he'd proven himself trustworthy on the trip so far, but it wasn't entirely true, was it?

"He reminds me of my husband—slick, too slick." Nora's mouth firmed into a white line. "Six years together, and he left two weeks before Christmas. Said he wasn't coming back."

And suddenly Erin understood why the other woman seemed so tightly strung.

"Is there anything I can do to help?" she asked softly.

The other woman's look of vulnerability was quickly replaced by a glower. "I didn't tell you so you'd feel sorry for me. I'm trying to warn you off that Jesse—he's no good—"

Nora cut herself off as a shadow fell over them. Jesse and Pete returned to their seats.

"Ladies," came Jesse's greeting, though his voice was subdued.

Nora gave Erin a knowing look as the two males

retook their seats. Erin smiled tightly. She could certainly understand the woman's disappointed dreams and dashed hopes for her life, but it didn't mean she should look down on Jesse.

Besides, Erin wasn't falling for Jesse.

Their group remained in awkward silence as it grew colder and darker until finally Nora drowsed off, leaving Erin and a tense Jesse awake. Pete had finally succumbed to sleep as well, his head leaning against the corner where the seat and edge of the wall met. Erin still held the baby snugged against her chest, his thumb held loosely between his gums.

She was afraid Jesse had overheard Nora, but when he spoke, it was with a teasing inflection in his voice.

"I thought they'd never go to sleep," he groaned softly, just above a whisper. He rested his head against the back of the seat, exaggerating a yawn.

"They weren't that bad." Erin nudged his elbow, careful not to jostle him. She hadn't taken off her coat after they'd got back on board the train after the last stop, but even with the baby cuddled against her creating heat, a chill slipped down the back of her neck. "They're pretty good kids," she went on. "The boys might be rambunctious, but the girls are darlings."

"They reminded me a bit of my brother and I when we were young."

Erin barely dared breathe. Jesse was revealing something of his past to her. "You were darlings?" she teased lightly, pretending to misunderstand.

"No," he said, more seriously than she would've thought. "We were into everything. Drove our mother crazy. Constantly harassing our sister. Getting into scrapes with other neighborhood boys. Playing pranks on our teachers until we were old enough to work in the factories."

"You were close?"

He nodded. "He always followed me, from the time he could crawl."

He ran a hand over his mouth, watching the darkened window with vacant eyes. "He followed me when my stepfather kicked me out. And that loyalty cost him his life."

"What happened?"

"My stepfather and I constantly fought. He was nothing like my father. He had a mean streak and was often cruel. I hated him. When I was fifteen, my mother's birthday arrived… Daniel and I both worked in the factories to help support our family, but our stepfather wouldn't let us have any money to get our mother a birthday gift. So I…I stole a trinket from one of the shops close to where we lived. When my stepfather found out, he was livid. We got into a screaming match and he…kicked me out."

She sensed there was more than that. Why hadn't the mother intervened?

"And Daniel sided with me. Followed me. We lived on the streets—like Pete, doing whatever we had to do to survive."

"Why didn't you continue working at the factory?"

"My stepfather talked to the boss at our factory, all of the foremen at all of the factories within walking distance. He turned them against us. Spread lies about us to ensure we wouldn't be able to get jobs. I didn't have any skills to apprentice on—we didn't have any options."

"I suppose you were too old for an orphanage, but what about a church?"

He looked at her, really looked at her face for a long moment. "Not every churchgoer is like you, Erin."

She brushed off his words with a wan smile and a small shake of her head before she laid her cheek against the baby's head. Jesse was starting to think she didn't see herself in the same way he did—she was amazing, selfless. Erin O'Grady was something else.

She hadn't judged him for what he'd just told her about his rebellious youth.

But his stomach was in knots at what he was about to say, and this wasn't even all of it. Thinking about his stepfather and the vitriol the man had spewed at him that last night—*You'll never be more than a petty thief!*—still wasn't as bad as thoughts of his beloved brother and what had happened only a few months later.

The car had grown quiet as they'd talked, most passengers nodding off to sleep. Erin's gentle, steady gaze, gave him the courage to say it, even if only in a whisper.

"In the winter, we were always cold. It was hard to get warm. If we stepped into a shop, the shopkeeper would chase us out, afraid we would steal something."

He grinned ruefully. "They were probably right. We were so hungry, all the time..."

He swallowed hard, trying to find the strength to tell her.

And she reached over and laced her fingers through his, so that their hands were tangled together on top of his knee. The comforting contact made his heart pulse powerfully. He was afraid he was falling in love with her…

"When we were kids, Daniel was—" He forced the words out to block thoughts of Erin. "He was this cheerful little person. Always had a smile—sometimes causing mischief—but always happy."

He drew a deep, shaky breath. "Those last few weeks, he was like a shadow. It was as if he just faded away, and there was nothing I could do to bring him back…

"One day he started coughing. A dry, raspy cough at first, then deeper, like it had settled in his chest. He started burning up with fever, and I didn't have any medicine, no money to take him to a doctor. I even thought about taking him back home—I would've begged my stepfather to help him. I would've done anything."

Jesse's voice broke. He bowed his head, had to forced out the last words, had to tell her all of it.

"There wasn't time to get him back home, because he died a few hours later."

Jesse squeezed his eyes shut against the pain of saying the words aloud. He still felt as if his heart had been flayed open and left bleeding. He would never forget holding Daniel's hand as those last few rattling, ragged breaths took his brother from him.

But then a new sensation overtook the pain radiating out from his heart. Warmth.

Jesse lifted his head to acknowledge that Erin had leaned her head and shoulder against him. She still clasped his hand tightly, still held the sleeping babe tucked against her.

Jesse couldn't resist, couldn't stop himself from half turning in his seat and taking her—the both of them—in his arms. She fit there so perfectly, just as he'd guessed she would. She leaned into him with the same abandon the child had shown her—as if she trusted him implicitly. Her face pressed into the juncture of his neck and shoulder, her breath warming his collarbone through his shirt.

And he realized the neck of his shirt was becoming suspiciously damp. He pushed back enough to see her face, his arms still around her.

"Are you crying? For me?" His own voice choked up as he stared down at the silver tears on her cheeks.

"It wasn't your fault," she whispered. "You were barely older than a child yourself."

No one had ever shown him such empathy, such mercy.

Overwhelmed with emotion, Jesse did what he'd told himself he wouldn't do again, and kissed her. His hand slid against her damp cheek into her upswept hair, the curls already coming loose from a day manhandled by children and other travelers. He was careful not to jostle the little bundle in her arms—

She met him fiercely, melding her lips to his as if she could erase his pain by her kiss…and maybe she did, because when they drew apart moments later, ragged breaths mingling, he couldn't remember pain, could only hear his own heartbeats thundering in his ears, could only see the vibrant blue of her eyes, the teardrops spiking her lashes, the pink of her cheeks.

She reached up with one hand, the other still holding tightly to the sleeping babe, and put her palm to his jaw. When he thought she would simply gaze at him, she surprised him by tugging him down to meet her kiss, this one sweet and searching and…hopeful.

He pressed her close to his chest again, holding her as his emotions calmed until one panicked thought crystallized in his thoughts.

He wasn't falling in love with Erin O'Grady. He was already *in love with* Erin O'Grady.

But he knew he didn't deserve her—there was no way he could. So the noble thing to do would be to walk away.

But he didn't know if he had the strength.

Erin had never felt closer to another human being than she did right now, ensconced in Jesse's arms, the memory of his kisses lingering on her lips.

Her mother would be ashamed of Erin's actions, kissing the man like that in public—or at all, given that they weren't anything more than friends—but she couldn't find it in herself to regret it.

She should probably be worried about opening her heart to a stranger. Part of her sensed there were still things Jesse wasn't telling her about his past. But she couldn't help what she felt, and what she felt was drawn to Jesse. Even with his initial deception, even with whatever it was he wasn't telling her, she couldn't make herself wish they'd never met. She wanted to find a way to be with him.

Perhaps if she could convince him to return to Boston, he might find work there and they'd be able to continue in a courtship.

Or perhaps they could write, if he wanted to stay in

Chicago or elsewhere. She'd known of relationships, marriages, built on less.

But she was getting ahead of herself. Right now she needed to concentrate on getting to her brother's place in Wyoming and perhaps convincing the man beside her to stay for the holiday.

Cold air seeped down the back of her neck and she shifted slightly closer to Jesse and his warmth.

"Will you tell me about your father?" Jesse's voice rumbled against her ear. "Why you decided to come out and see your brother?"

She stiffened but forced herself to relax back against his side. She didn't want to talk about something that would intrude on this place of happiness, but she would because he asked and because he'd shared something obviously very painful to him with her.

"My father has always been protective of me. You know about my childhood. As a teen, I often rebelled against the strictures my father placed on me."

"You rebelled?" he teased gently.

She turned her face briefly into his shirt, a hot flush rising in her cheeks. "No matter what you think of me, I certainly wasn't a perfect daughter. I threw tantrums, refused to see my father…"

"Hmm," he said, and she tickled his side with her one free hand. He clasped it quickly in his and held it. "Go on."

"Recently, my mother became a benefactor for a hospital that helps many underprivileged families. Children whose families can't afford care otherwise."

His chest froze on an inhale, and she imagined he was thinking of Daniel.

"I visited with my mother and felt… Well, I suppose the truth is, I identified with those children, many of whom were too sick to even sit up in bed. I can remember the loneliness of times like that…."

He squeezed her shoulders, and she relished the comfort he offered.

"When my father found I was volunteering my time, he asked me to stop going to the hospital. I think he probably worries I will contract some disease and waste away." She snorted at that. "I tried to explain to him how much this hospital and the children there mean to me, but he didn't—wouldn't understand. He believes the doctors and nurses that we support with our funding should be enough for the children."

She bit her lip, ashamed of what she was about to say. "I kept visiting anyway, against his wishes."

Again, Jesse squeezed her shoulders. "I wouldn't expect anything less. You have a heart for helping others, I've come to discover."

She preened at his praise. "Thank you. I believe you do, too. If I understand the undercurrents that passed between you and Pete earlier, may I assume he attempted to get off the train but you talked him out of it?"

"Don't change the subject," Jesse said. "You were telling me about your father."

She lifted one eyebrow at him, so he would know she wasn't just going to forget about what he'd deftly sidestepped. But she went on.

"My father began arranging functions for me to attend. It was so subtle, I didn't notice it at first. My mother would suggest a ladies' tea she wanted me to accompany her to. Papa would encourage me to attend parties nearly every night of the week, I suppose hoping to make me too tired to attend the hospital the next morning. And a young man began calling."

It was Jesse's turn to stiffen beside her. "You have a beau?"

"No."

The tension in him eased. She explained.

"I found out that my father had paid him to come courting, to keep me too busy to go to the hospital."

Just thinking about it fueled her ire. "My father lied to me—got others involved in his lies. He manipulated me to get what he wanted without regard for my feelings. Or for the poor, unfortunate children I want to help."

Jesse was silent, thoughtful beside her.

"I suppose…running away was a selfish thing to do." She looked down at the little one sleeping in her arms. "Certainly, it didn't help the children. I had thought… if I could make the trip on my own successfully, then father might see me as an adult, able to make my own choices. It was a rash thing to do…"

He touched a finger beneath her chin, drawing her face up to meet his frank gaze. "I don't think you're selfish. How could I?"

"Perhaps not, but I am strong-willed—"

"Independent," he corrected.

"Prone to tantrums—"

"Passionate."

She raised her brows at his second interruption and he quirked a smile and amended, "Irish."

She elbowed him in the ribs.

"I want my own way in things."

He grinned. "Now there's one I can agree with. You are stubborn."

She started to elbow him again but he caught her elbow in the cup of his hand.

"I suppose I've only proved myself as immature as my father thinks I am," she said, sharing the fear she hadn't dared put into words until now. She couldn't bear it if Jesse saw her that way, too.

"C'mon, Erin. You haven't done too badly on your own." He gave her an encouraging smile. "Even if you have fallen in with a couple of reprobates." He waggled his eyebrows at her. "Another day, and you'll be in Wyoming with your brother and his family."

She shook her head at his teasing. "I meant I should've sat down with my father and talked things out instead of running away like a spoiled child. But I was afraid he would twist my actions and words around on me. He can be very persuasive."

Jesse shrugged. "Who am I to say you shouldn't have come out to visit your brother? I've made my share of mistakes. Sure, it was impulsive, but I don't know that it was bad."

Well, at least he didn't seem to think less of her for her rash actions.

Would he think differently if he knew her next impulsive action was falling in love with him?

The baby fussed, and Jesse watched Erin soothe it back to sleep. Nora peeked her eyes open, but when she saw Erin was taking care of the baby, she went right back to sleep. For someone so surly, she was sure quick to let Erin help.

His ears still felt hot from overhearing her say he was good for nothing. He'd half expected Erin to agree, but her actions indicated she thought the opposite of him. He still couldn't figure it.

Erin shivered, and he gathered her close under his arm again. It *was* getting colder in here. He couldn't see out the darkened windows, but earlier the conductor had mentioned it looked like snow.

She didn't say anything more, only leaned her head against Jesse's shoulder. She was probably exhausted from a long day of travel; Jesse would let her go to sleep if that's what she wanted.

He kept replaying her words from moments ago. *My father lied to me. He manipulated me.*

She'd been so quick to dismiss any fault he might've had in Daniel's death. But he imagined she might not think so kindly on the part of his past he still held back from her—the lies and trickery that had led him to five years in prison. He'd thought being a con man would build a life for himself, but instead he'd lost five years behind bars. And now, if Erin found out about it, he would likely lose her, too.

Honesty was important to her; he could see how badly her father had hurt her with his tricks and deceptions.

Jesse had thought for a good part of this journey that he might trick Erin's wallet away from her.

Even if he'd changed his mind about that, it didn't change what he'd already done, who he was.

He couldn't see any way that she would accept him if she knew.

And now that he knew he loved her—and he could

only surmise she had strong feelings for him as well, or she would never have kissed him—how could he hurt her by telling her?

"What happened with Pete earlier?" she asked sleepily, interrupting his frantic thoughts.

With her head tucked between his jaw and his shoulder, he couldn't see her face. He'd thought she might be asleep, but apparently she still wanted to talk.

"Just what you thought. He was down at the end of the car, half-hidden behind a few people. Planning to get off at the next stop."

"How did you get him to stay?"

He didn't want her to know about their agreement. "I told him about Daniel. He was the first person I'd ever told. And now you."

She hummed sleepily, obviously pleased.

"I told him that if I'd had someone like you in my life back when I was fifteen, Daniel might not have died. If I'd been that lucky, I never would have turned away from someone like you."

She lifted her head and her eyes weren't clouded with sleep, as he'd supposed. "Jesse, I'm more than happy to help Pete get settled into a new, better life, but you're missing the whole point. He stayed because of *you*."

Yeah, but not for the reasons she thought. Because Jesse had paid him.

"Me? What are you talking about?"

She began to get that impassioned look. "He came to you in the first place. He understands you—you're both of a similar background."

Jesse shook his head. "You're not suggesting I take him on, are you? I can't take care of a kid right now—I can barely take care of myself. I don't have a job, a place to stay—" And Pete didn't really *want* to stay with Jesse anyway.

"Jesse, you have to admit there's a reason the two of you—the three of us—met on the train that first day. I believe God put you in Pete's path for a reason. I can facilitate some things, but Pete needs *you*."

He shook his head again, as what she said began to make sense. He could take Pete if he had a job. But the thought didn't bring comfort. It brought panic. "Didn't you hear what I said about Daniel? He died because of me."

"But you were just a teenager—now you're a grown man—"

"That doesn't mean I know how to take care of somebody else, especially somebody as needy as the kid is! I thought *you* could help the lad."

"His name is Pete."

"I know what his name is."

The conflicting emotions inside Jesse made his tone sharper than he wanted it to be, but he couldn't even consider what she was suggesting—he couldn't be responsible for another boy. Not someone like Pete, who needed love, and Jesse didn't have it in him to give.

"I can't," he said.

"All right." She didn't sound happy about it, but at least she'd stopped arguing. "We'll figure something out. My brother is a deputy in this little town in Wyoming. I'm sure he'll know what to do with Pete, what the best thing to do to help will be."

She settled back down, snuggling against him again. "It's gotten colder."

Before he could say anything else, the train began to slow. Passengers shifted in their seats, some mumbling questions. Jesse didn't know what the next stop was supposed to be, but it didn't seem that long since they'd had one.

And then the conductor came in, announcing, "We're in the middle of a blizzard, folks. The tracks are blocked up ahead and with the snow swirling the way it is and the temperatures below freezing, it's too dangerous to try to send men out to clear it. We're going to go back to the nearest town."

As he spoke, the train began to reverse, but before it got any momentum, stopped with a reverberating clanking noise.

"Just sit tight, folks. I'll be back with any further news."

Most of the passengers had woken by now and were getting louder as they tried to understand what was happening. A groggy Pete peered around, blinking blearily. Nora's children slept, except the baby, who peeped, and Nora took her from Erin. Erin crossed her arms over her middle.

"A blizzard. Do you think we're stuck out here?" she asked.

"He said we're going back to the last stop," Jesse reminded her.

"We ain't moving," Pete put in.

Just then, the conductor bustled back in. "Folks, it's snowing so fast that the tracks are covered going back toward the nearest town, and it's drifting pretty bad. I'm afraid we're going to have to sit here until the storm clears."

The passengers began to murmur, and the conductor whistled to get their attention again.

"We've got plenty of coal to keep the cars warm. Most likely the storm will blow over by morning and we'll get the tracks cleared and be on our way. Best thing for you to do is stay calm and get some shut-eye."

And with that, he left, leaving a mass of grumbling, alert passengers in his wake.

Pete stood and brushed past both of them into the aisle. "Goin' to stretch my legs."

"Don't go too far," Erin cautioned. "If the passengers get upset about being stuck here, they might start causing trouble."

Jesse touched the kid's arm, expecting it when Pete shifted away from his touch. "And don't take anything that doesn't belong to you."

Pete grunted without meeting Jesse's eye and wandered off.

Erin settled back into her seat, sliding close to Jesse's side. She leaned her head onto his shoulder, relaxed and apparently ready to doze off.

Sure, she could go to sleep without anything weighing on her mind. How could she expect him to take on Pete? The kid wasn't Jesse's real brother, and after what had happened with Daniel, Jesse didn't want the responsibility for taking care of another person. He couldn't risk getting close to someone.

Yet, Erin's obvious disappointment rankled, as well.

"Get some sleep," she whispered. "We'll worry about things when we get to Wyoming."

He settled his head against the back of the seat, but

doubted he would get comfortable enough—in mind or body—to actually sleep.

But the car had grown noticeably colder when he was shaken awake, and he realized he had dozed off.

"Wha—"

"Jesse. Wake up." The urgency in Erin's voice had him instantly alert, trying to rub some feeling into his face.

Glancing around the dimly lit car with its sleeping passengers, he couldn't guess what had disturbed her.

"What's wrong?" He reached out one hand to her, and she grabbed onto him, squeezing tightly.

"Pete's gone. I don't think he ever came back from stretching his legs."

"You sure?"

"No! I fell asleep, and just woke up but his seat is empty and it doesn't look like he's come back at all."

"Try not to panic." He didn't know whether to reassure her or just go find the kid to wring his neck. "He probably just got caught with his hand in someone's pocket and the conductor has him. I'll go look."

She started to stand up, but he glared her back into her seat. "You stay here. I don't want you coming up missing, too."

But he wasn't with the conductor when Jesse finally tracked the man down. He wasn't in any of the other rail cars, not sleeping in any of the berths in the nicer—and full—sleeper car, nor in any of the washrooms. Jesse checked them all, disturbing the other passengers.

When he made his way back to Erin, she was more frantic than before.

"You don't think he would try to get off the train, do you?" she asked, plainly worried.

It had occurred to him, but… "It would be a foolish thing to do. We all heard the conductor say that it's below freezing and still snowing."

His words didn't calm her. "Then where is he?"

"I don't know. But we'll find him."

She wrung her hands. "I just keep thinking…what if he overheard our argument earlier? About what to do with him. He seemed like he was sleeping but he could've woken up, and if he thought we didn't *want* him—"

She broke off with a loud sniff.

Jesse realized what exactly the kid might've heard if he had been awake. That Jesse didn't want him around, and Erin was young, too young to want to take on a kid.

And if their careless argument had sent Pete out into the snow, he might die. Jesse could be responsible for the death of another kid who didn't deserve it.

"Let's check with any of the passengers and see if they saw him get off the train. Maybe he didn't wander off." Even as he said it, Jesse knew what a long shot it was. And if the kid had gotten off in the storm—who knows how long ago?—chances were he was already frozen.

If another boy died, it would be Jesse's fault. Again.

Chapter Fourteen

Two passengers seated near the door remembered seeing Pete exiting the car. They thought he was probably going into the next car over, because who would go out in a blizzard?

But none of the passengers in the next car over had seen a boy fitting Pete's description enter the car. Because it was late, most of the passengers hadn't been moving around much—a lot of them had been sleeping.

Erin's stomach cramped with her worry for Pete; panic seemed to claw at her throat. Why would the boy get off the train in the middle of a blizzard? Even if he'd overheard her argument with Jesse and decided to leave, why wouldn't he wait until they got to the next town? Why do this? He was probably freezing, and what if he'd gotten hurt? Or lost?

Jesse shrugged into a sweater one of the other passengers had loaned him. His coat was slung over the back of the next seat and Erin held a woolen scarf someone else had insisted he wear, ready to wrap it around his neck.

Several other men were adding warmer clothing

from their luggage or borrowed from other passengers; they'd volunteered to go search when they'd heard about a boy lost in the snow.

Jesse slid his arms into his coat; his face was drawn and sharp. Erin knew he blamed himself for Pete's departure, even though they'd both participated in the conversation. Movements jerky as he buttoned his coat, she knew she had to calm him down before he left and did something reckless.

She looped the scarf over his head and tucked one end inside the other, looking at his chest so he wouldn't see the sheer panic she felt and feel even worse. "Be careful."

"I will."

"Don't get lost."

"Try not to."

"I'm serious." She thumped his chest and her hand was shaking.

He clasped it in his and raised it to his lips, pressing a kiss against her knuckle.

Her eyes went to his face. "Come back." What she really wanted to say was *come back to me.*

He held her gaze with his serious brown eyes. "I'll bring him back."

And then he was gone, disappeared into the blowing white snow.

Jesse could barely see in the blinding white wind. Fear clutched his innards as he stumbled down the train's stairs and then took the long jump down to the ground from the last one. He landed in a knee-high drift.

The three other men brave enough to follow him off the train exclaimed in surprise when they hit the ground. Ensconced in the safety of the train cars, they hadn't expected it to be this bad.

"Follow the tracks," Jesse shouted. It was only a reminder, they'd already talked out a plan inside, but he didn't want them to forget and get lost, too. "Don't lose sight of the tracks!"

Two of the men set off in the opposite direction and Jesse and one other fellow followed the tracks along the body of the train.

Within minutes he realized how useless their plan was, because the tracks were completely covered in snow in many places. If they wandered away, there was a chance they wouldn't be able to make it back to the train.

The wind bit through all the layers Jesse wore, as if he'd come out in nothing at all. He'd borrowed a pair of gloves from a man on board the train, but even with gloves on and his limbs buried in his pockets, his hands were becoming numb. Feet, too, making it hard to clomp through the drifts of snow.

"Pete!" he yelled, but the wind stole his voice, snatched it away into the black darkness. "Kid, if you can hear me, come to my voice."

The other man stumbled, going to his knees in the snow. It felt like they'd been out for hours, but they hadn't gotten far at all.

"I gotta go back!" the other man called out.

Jesse waved him away. He couldn't turn back until he found Pete. He'd driven the boy out into this storm with his careless words. He would bring him back.

Or die trying.

* * *

Erin paced to the end of the train car again, peering through the windows as she went. Offering up constant prayers for Pete's protection and for Jesse's. From inside, she couldn't see anything. The darkness and snow obscured everything.

Most of the passengers had settled again, the conductor had turned down the lights and it was dim inside the car. No one else seemed to share the anxiety she felt.

As she paced back toward their seats, the empty seats that taunted her, Nora settled a hand on one of her sleeping children. "You should sit for a bit. If they find— When they find him, you'll be up trying to help everyone get warm."

Erin perched on the edge of the seat but quickly stood back up. "I'm too nervous to sit."

Nora looked at her for a long time. Frowned. "They've snuck into your heart, haven't they?"

Erin looked down, played with one of the folds of her skirt. "We started out as strangers, but somewhere along the way…" She'd been falling in love with him the whole time.

Nora patted her hand. "They'll find the boy."

Erin returned to her pacing and praying. What was taking so long? Surely Pete couldn't have got far, not with the blowing snow and drifts…

As she neared the end of the car, the door burst open. Her heart thundered in her ears as she rushed toward the white-covered shapes that stumbled inside.

"F-f-freezing out there," one man chattered. She helped pull them inside—three of them—and then turned back toward the door, but no one else entered.

"Where are the others?" she asked, because Jesse wasn't among the men. "Where's Jesse and Pete?"

"Fool man kept on going—there's no way you can see anything in that."

"He'll never find the kid in that mess. Prob'ly get himself frozen looking for 'im," another of the men said through chattering teeth.

She rushed out onto the platform, screaming, "Jesse!"

But the wind screamed back at her.

Someone pulled her back inside. Nora.

The other woman shoved her farther into the train car. "Erin. Stop. Don't panic."

But she couldn't stop shaking, and it wasn't from the cold. "I w-want them back. Both of them."

Nora kept nudging Erin forward. "They'll come back. And when they do, they'll need you."

Erin prayed she was right.

Jesse trudged through the drifts, head down against the wind.

"Pete!" he shouted, voice hoarse from breathing the cold air and shouting.

How long had he been out here? He'd lost all sense of time to the swirling white world that now encompassed him.

His hands, feet and face were numb. He couldn't feel any warmth whatsoever. Every now and again he had to wipe the ice clinging to his eyelashes so he could see.

Was there any way the kid could survive this? Even with the new coat Erin had bought, Pete would be sorely underdressed. Probably freezing.

"Pete!" The timber of Jesse's voice changed as his

despair took over. "Kid, please! Don't be dead!" *Don't be dead.*

God, don't let him be dead!

Then…a flash of color in the white landscape.

"Pete!"

Jesse changed direction and within a few feet, his boot nudged against something half buried in a drift.

"Kid!"

Kneeling in the snow, Jesse dug with hands that were about as effective as blocks of ice, but somehow managed to uncover Pete's face and shoulders.

Thank you.

The kid's eyes blinked open. They were hazy and unfocused. His face was blue-tinged.

"Stay awake, Pete."

Pete's eyes started to close again, but Jesse shook him by his shoulders. "Kid! Do you hear me? Don't you dare go to sleep!"

He knew if the kid succumbed to the cold, there was no saving him. Jesse hauled him to his feet, keeping both arms around him.

"Can you walk?"

It would be better if the kid could walk. It would get his sluggish blood flowing. Also, Jesse was already so exhausted he didn't know if he could make it back to the train. He was pretty sure he knew where the train was, but needed all his wits about him to find it again.

"C-c-can't f-feel m' feet," the kid mumbled. If Jesse hadn't been holding him close to his chest he never would have heard the words in the screaming wind.

"Let's try it, kid," Jesse said, but when Pete tried

to step forward, his legs folded underneath him. Jesse hauled him up.

"All right. We'll do it this way." Jesse used the last of his strength to lift the kid into his arms. If Jesse took a tumble he might not be able to get up again.

He wheeled to go back toward the train, hoping the wind and blowing snow hadn't altered his sense of direction. Feet numb, he could barely lift his legs to walk. Yet somehow he pushed on.

"Don't fall asleep, kid."

"How can I with you yappin' at me?"

"What'd you run away for anyway? Pretty stupid thing to do in snow like this."

"Didn't think it was this bad."

"Yeah? That all?"

There was a long pause and Jesse shook the kid's shoulders again. "Don't doze off."

"A'right."

"So?"

"You don't want me around. Thought I'd walk back to the next town."

"Pete…"

Jesse could barely see through snow-encrusted eyelashes, but he recognized the rebellious tilt of the kid's chin.

"It's not that I don't want you around," he said through half-frozen lips.

"Don't lie." Pete's vehemence was probably a good sign. "The only reason you kept me around was to impress Erin."

"Maybe in the beginning, but not now. It's just hard for me. I told you my history with my brother."

"I'm not your brother. I'm not gonna die."

"You might if you keep pulling stunts like this." And still might, if Jesse couldn't find the train. He'd thought they would've been close enough to bump into it by now. He started sweeping his feet in front of him, hoping to encounter the tracks beneath the mounds of white snow.

The kid didn't say anything again and Jesse thought he'd better keep him talking.

"Erin's gonna help you find a place. She's got the resources—"

"Erin's nice, but she helps everybody!" Pete burst out.

And that was the crux of the matter. It was true. Erin did help anyone she came into contact with—as evidenced by Jesse himself, as well as Nora and her brood, who didn't even want her help. But Jesse also knew she had a special place in her heart for kids.

And Jesse couldn't risk caring for someone else. He already cared too much about Erin—and was about to get his heart ripped out when she went on to her brother's place. If he cared about Pete and something happened to the kid, he'd be heartbroken, again.

Pete coughed, a jarring rattle of his chest that for a moment threw Jesse back in time to Daniel's death.

"I just want somebody to want *me,*" the kid said, another of those bone-jarring coughs shaking his entire frail body in Jesse's arms.

Jesse could relate. Since Daniel's death nobody had bothered to get close, not truly, not until Erin. He and the kid were so similar in so many ways… Jesse couldn't risk letting Pete into his life, but how could he refuse, knowing how much the kid needed someone? Needed him.

A hulking shadow ahead gave Jesse a beat of hope. The train. He stumbled forward, frozen head to toe. "We're almost there, Pete."

No answer. Jesse looked down at the face that had become dear to him in the last few days. Pete was pale, and lifeless, snow building on his now-closed eyes and in his hair.

"Don't die, kid!" Jesse shouted, shaking his shoulders again. "We made it. And…*I* want you around."

God, don't let him die.

Chapter Fifteen

The outer door burst open again and a snow-covered figure backed inside. Erin rushed forward.

When the man turned, she saw he carried a smaller person across his chest, also covered with snow.

Jesse and Pete.

Heart beating furiously, she ran to them.

"You found him!" she cried.

"Take him." Jesse pushed Pete awkwardly at her. Snow fell from him in a miniature avalanche.

Erin couldn't look away from Jesse's face, his eyelashes matted with snow, a blue tinge around his lips. "Are you okay?"

"Kid was talking to me," Jesse gasped. "Fell unconscious. Is there a doctor?" he shouted hoarsely, and a man rushed forward.

"Pete?" Erin asked, stumbling under the boy's weight when Jesse released him. Jesse collapsed against the wall near the door, sliding down. The snow pooled around him and began to melt into droplets of water.

"Can you help him?" Jesse demanded of the man in a bowler hat and nice suit who approached.

"Bring him over next to the boiler. Not too close!"

Erin looked over her shoulder but Jesse wasn't moving. "Jesse!"

He waved her off. The fact that he could still move and talk must mean he was better off than Pete. Erin would see to the boy and then go back to help Jesse.

"Looks like some frostbite. I'll need some warm water—not hot!" the doctor said as he bent over Pete. "Hypothermic, most likely, if he's been outside for any length of time. Are there any blankets? Let's get him out of these wet clothes."

One of the attendants, probably from the sleeper car, rushed in with some blankets and left them at Erin's elbow. She helped undress Pete down to his long underwear, her hands shaking. She couldn't think anything other than a desperate prayer for God to save Pete.

They wrapped him in a blanket and then the doctor showed her how to briskly rub Pete's skin, only taking one arm or leg out of the blanket at a time.

Suddenly, Nora bustled in and nudged Erin out of the way. "Jesse needs you. I'll help out here."

She shooed Erin away. Erin went, grateful even though the other woman hadn't been particularly kind before this.

Erin found Jesse slumped on the floor where she'd left him. He didn't appear to have moved since he'd delivered Pete into her arms. She knelt beside him.

"Jesse? Did you fall asleep?"

"'M not asleep," he slurred. "Can't go to sleep in a snowstorm 'r you'll freeze, ya know."

He started, opened his eyes. "Where's the kid?"

She sighed. "His name is Pete."

"Know his name. Where is he?"

"The doctor and Nora are taking care of him. There wasn't room for me, too. Can you get up?"

"Prob'ly."

She took his arm and tried to assist him in sitting up. He barely moved. She jerked away; his coat was covered with ice and freezing.

"Prob'ly not," he murmured.

She suddenly became afraid. She'd thought he would be all right once he'd gotten inside, but what if he had a case of hypothermia, too?

"Come on," she coaxed, tugging on his arm again. "Don't you want to go sit by the warm boiler and get heated up? I'll help you over there, but you have to stand up."

He didn't move and she began unraveling his scarf, tugging enough to jostle his shoulders when she found part of it frozen together. She moved to unbutton his coat, but his hand moved sluggishly to cover hers. His skin was like touching a block of ice.

"'Re you undressin' me? What about propriety?"

"Stop joking, Jesse." She found her voice was shaking. "You're frozen through, you big oaf. Stand up, or I'll get some of the men to get you up."

Their eyes met and held, his a little less hazy than she expected. He huffed a sigh, but began pushing himself up off the floor, using the wall for support.

"I'll be all right," he mumbled. "Quit worrying."

She moved beneath one of his arms and held him

around his waist, taking some of his weight. "Between you and Pete, I've got plenty to worry about."

They made their way down the aisle step by painful step. Each movement felt like needles sticking in the bottom of Jesse's feet. The rest of him still felt frozen through.

But he was more worried about Pete than himself.

When Erin guided him down onto a clear space of floor near the boiler, he craned his neck to see the kid. Nora and a man Jesse assumed must be the doctor bent over him.

"He awake?" Jesse rasped.

"No," the man said. "But he seems to be all right. Lucky for him, this frostbite isn't going to cost him any of his digits. His body is exhausted—and he appears rather undernourished—but I expect he'll come to in a couple of hours. Perhaps it's better for him to sleep anyway, it's probably rather painful coming out of the frostbite."

Yes, Jesse could understand what he was talking about. Closer to the boiler, his clothes steaming around him, prickles of uncomfortable sensation crawled all over his body. It wasn't pleasant.

His fingers fumbled the buttons of the sweater he'd worn beneath his leather coat, and Erin was there, kneeling before him, taking over.

He seemed to fade in and out, a strange buzzing in his ears.

"Soaking wet." There was Erin's voice, something to ground him as the pain beneath his skin intensified and he gritted his teeth to keep from crying out.

He felt the weight of his shirt come off, and a scratchy blanket come around his shoulders in its place.

"There are a few too many people around for the pants to come off," she said softly in his ear, hand on his shoulder. "But you're close enough to the heat, I think they'll dry out in a bit."

She moved to his feet, sliding off his boots with some difficulty, then replacing his wet socks with some warm, dry ones. The intimacy of the action was not lost on him, but Erin was businesslike and quick in her movements.

He couldn't stop shaking. He'd gone from shivers to full body tremors, nearly rocking with pain as his body flashed hot and cold.

"Body heat—"

And suddenly Erin was lifting the corner of his blanket. She slipped beneath it and she drew her arms around his neck, pressed her warm cheek to his jaw and ear.

"Wh-what're you doin'?"

He tried to move away, but the warmth she was generating felt too good and his limbs felt like jelly.

"I'm warming you up," she whispered directly into his ear. "We're both still dressed. It's all right."

"But—but—"

"There are ten people here in the five closest seats—most of them watching us. It's not improper."

Still, he pushed away from her. He didn't want to taint her in any way. But his hands tangled in the blanket and they didn't seem to work right.

"Stop," she ordered softly, right in his ear. Then she

sniffed, and he realized with a moment of clarity in the mush of his brain that she was still quite upset.

"'S all right," he slurred. "We made it."

She tucked her face into his neck, her skin hot like a brand. "I was so worried," she whispered. "Afraid for you."

He realized she was crying for him. Again, like she'd done earlier when she'd comforted him about Daniel, though that other moment seemed like aeons ago now.

"Nobody's cared about me since Daniel. Nobody 'cept you."

She moved her head, pressing the other side of her cheek against his jaw and neck, spreading her warmth there, as well. Her hair, falling out of its pins, tickled his shoulder and neck.

"I'm afraid it's a bit more serious than that," she whispered.

Her warmth began to seep into him, began to slowly penetrate the frozen tundra of his body. He groaned at the sensation. Still painful.

"When you were out looking for Pete..." Her voice seemed to waver in and out. "Thought you wouldn't make it, I..." He tried to focus on her words, to concentrate, but he felt like slipping into sleep. His eyes fell closed, the darkness deepening. "How much I've come to care for you."

She paused. "I think I'm falling in love with you."

"Can't," he said matter-of-factly, not sure whether he was dreaming or not. He seemed to be floating, half-asleep. "'M not good enough."

She half giggled, half sobbed. "Sure you are. You're a

decent man. Kind enough to help a lonely boy and brave enough to fight through a snowstorm to save his life."

He shook his head, the bristles on his chin catching in her loosened hair. Just the small movement depleted the last stores of his energy. "Ya don't really know me."

She reached up and smoothed away her hair, touched his jaw briefly. This entire situation was so bizarre he felt sure he was dreaming. So he told her, "Don't know about my past, where I been. Things I've done. 'M not a good person."

She clung to the back of his neck with both hands. "Your past doesn't define you, Jesse."

"Done some bad things. Real bad."

She stiffened. It was slight, but he still registered it in his half-asleep state.

"Maybe we should talk about that in the morning, when you're more aware."

He tried to shrug, but his jellified muscles wouldn't obey him.

"How did you find him?"

"I think I…prayed. Called out to God."

"That's…really good, Jesse."

"Hasn't ever listened to me b'fore. Took my dad. Took Daniel."

She was crying again, her tears hot against his warming skin. "He doesn't promise to answer with a yes every time. But tonight He did. Tonight He answered your prayers…and mine."

She sniffled again, was quiet but only for a moment. "Was Pete able to talk to you when you found him?"

"Yep. Kept him talkin' most the way back to th' train."

"Why did he run away? Because he'd heard us arguing?"

"Yep. But I told him… I told him I wanted him around."

She squeezed him tightly.

"Don't know what to do with a kid…."

He couldn't fight the darkness any longer, finally succumbed to sleep, but as he drifted off, he heard one last whisper.

"We'll figure it out. Together."

Chapter Sixteen

Jesse was overly conscious of the woman at his side, afternoon sunlight streaming in the window and burnishing her hair.

Not only because of what they'd shared last night—inadvertent though it might have been on his part—but because the clock was ticking down on their time together. The snowstorm had cleared, the tracks had been uncovered and they were rushing toward Cheyenne, slated to arrive by late afternoon.

I'm falling in love with you.

He still couldn't believe she'd said…what she'd said. He'd tried to shy away from it in his thoughts, but basically had awoken obsessing over it. The way he'd been out of it, he couldn't determine what had been real or if the entire episode had been a dream.

And he'd been terrified to ask her. Terrified that he'd imagined it. Terrified that she'd really said it.

He felt guilty because he was still holding back a load of secrets from her. That he was a con man, that he'd been in prison, that he'd let Pete blackmail him to keep his secrets. Jesse didn't think those were things that she could just overlook.

And his burgeoning feelings for her—feelings that apparently mirrored hers—made him loath to hurt her.

He was in a pickle.

If he told her, she might not want anything more to do with him. Even Catherine had only pretended she was okay with his life, who he was, and that had only been for the purpose of getting close to him so she could betray him.

Since his father, he'd been missing out on love. How could he expect Erin to really love him, when she was such a fine lady, not only in her status but as a person?

He needed to steel himself for when they went their separate ways. It seemed inevitable that they would part ways, possibly on bad terms.

"Are you all right?" she asked, settled back into her seat, one of Nora's rugrats on her lap, playing pat-a-cake with Erin's hands. "You've been awfully quiet this morning."

He was a bit angry with himself for sleeping away most of the morning. He'd roused briefly when Erin had helped him and Pete back to their seats, once they'd warmed and when the train had been ready to move again, then fallen into a deep, dreamless sleep. When he'd woken midmorning, he'd found Nora's crew, Erin and Pete all in animated conversation, playing games.

He'd been ravenous and Erin had procured a steaming breakfast for him, probably bribed from an attendant on the sleeper car. Her manner was very much the same as before the nighttime escapades, so he hadn't been able to tell if she'd really said what he'd thought she said.

"Not regretting what I told you last night?" she asked softly now.

He watched roses climb in her cheeks and knew suddenly that he hadn't imagined what had passed between them.

"You can't be serious," he said when she wouldn't quite meet his eyes.

The blush blooming in her cheeks grew darker. "I—I can't help my feelings."

"No, that's not what I meant," he said quickly. "I meant, you can't seriously think that...*what you said* would offend me in some way."

She finally met his eyes and the soft joy shining in the endless blue depths cut him in the gut.

He clenched his jaw to keep from blurting out the truth—that he returned her love.

"I'm honored," he said quietly, truthfully. "I can't understand it, but I..."

He swallowed back the words that wanted to come. How could he burden her with his feelings when he was keeping so much from her?

"We getting off for supper at the next stop?" Pete asked, leaning forward with elbows on his knees. It was a needed reminder that Jesse and Erin weren't alone.

"No," was Jesse's reply. "We'll get off in Cheyenne, with Erin."

"Aw, do you gotta go?" asked one of Nora's twins, sitting on the floor and leaning his chin on Erin's knee.

"Yes, and I'll be sorry to leave you lot," she said,

ruffling his hair with one hand that wasn't clutching the squirming toddler on her lap.

"Remember, Miss Erin is going to visit her brother for Christmas," Nora said. She still hadn't warmed up to Erin and it puzzled Jesse.

"I've got a new little niece that I've never met before," Erin reminded them.

Taking in Erin's excitement when she talked about the new addition to her brother's family and the way she was always touching the children, giving impromptu hugs or pats all around, Jesse could easily see her with a passel of her own children. She would make a good mother, was loving and kind, generous and sweet. And with her confession last night, Jesse longed to have what he couldn't have—Erin as *his* wife, the mother of *his* children.

"Supper?" Pete broke into Jesse's thoughts again.

"You must be as hungry as I've been today," Jesse said. "I could've eaten a bear earlier and now I'm hungry again."

Pete grinned. "Saw you even ate your potatoes, so you musta been starving."

The abrupt reminder of what Pete knew and Erin didn't sent an icy chill through Jesse and he shifted uncomfortably. He hadn't known his aversion to potatoes had been that obvious, but he didn't want Pete's teasing to lead to a question he really didn't want to answer in front of Erin.

"I was thinking we should wait until Cheyenne. It isn't much farther past the supper stop and the fare at a hotel would likely be better than what we'll get at the railroad stop. Erin?"

She raised her brows slightly. “You know I’ll be going on to Calvin from Cheyenne, right? It’s a small town, farther up the Belt Line.”

“But you don’t know when the connecting train will be, do you?” Jesse asked.

“Aren’t we going on with Miss Erin?” Pete asked, curious. “To keep her outta trouble?”

He felt Erin tense beside him.

“Seems like Miss Erin’s been mostly keeping you two outta trouble, or at least bailing you out of it when you get into it,” Nora commented with a frown in Jesse’s direction.

Jesse chuckled, but it was halfhearted and even he could hear it. “Well, now that I’ve got a little brother to watch out for, seems like I’d better be making arrangements for a job and a place to stay.”

Pete’s face lit up momentarily, then he glanced guiltily at Erin. “But…”

“You don’t have to travel on to Calvin with me,” Erin said quickly, false cheer ringing in her tone. “I’m certainly capable of getting there safely on my own.”

“Maybe there’ll be enough of a break in the train schedule for you to stop for supper with us,” said Jesse. “Then we can figure out what to do.”

Erin’s lips tried to tremble, but she forced them into a semblance of a smile.

They’d had no formal agreement, but Erin had thought he meant to come with her all the way to Calvin.

What had changed? She could guess… She’d bared her soul to Jesse last night, thankful and overjoyed that he was alive, that he'd survived the storm and found Pete, but now he was pulling away from her.

He'd said he was honored that she was falling in love with him—what did that mean? It certainly wasn't the return of her feelings that she'd hoped for.

Last night he'd been so open…and said he didn't think he was good enough for her. If that was what was stopping him from returning her feelings, perhaps they needed to sit down and have an honest conversation.

But if he was staying in Cheyenne and she was going on to Calvin, would there be time for that?

Then again, how could she fault him when he was taking on a new responsibility of caring for Pete? He'd clearly said he had no cash to speak of and was looking for a new start, now he had the responsibility of another mouth to feed, and she knew he'd been reluctant to take on Pete's care in the first place.

Just because they were parting ways a bit sooner than she'd thought, it didn't mean they couldn't write each other. And maybe in a few weeks when she was on her way back to Boston, she could stop back in Cheyenne and look them up, if they were still there, and catch up a bit. Maybe share a meal.

But it was small comfort, and she struggled to maintain a cheerful facade.

Until one of the twins bounced in his seat and cried, "Miss Erin, Miss Erin. You said you'd read some more of Jesus's story to us today. We've been real good!"

So they had. And if her time with Jesse was running out, what better way to spend it than trying to subtly share God's love with him?

Even if her heart was breaking as she did it.

* * *

Jesse watched Erin wave to Nora's crew as the train huffed and hooted its way out of the station.

Before they'd disembarked, she'd exchanged an awkward hug with Nora, the other woman thanking Erin stiffly for her help with the children on the train. Jesse had seen the nickels Erin had snuck each of the children to get their mother something nice for Christmas.

Now she adjusted her satchel on her arm, turning to face him and Pete where they stood a few paces away. "I'll be all right if you want to go along to see about a hotel. I've still got to find out when the next train to Calvin is and make arrangements for my luggage."

She moved toward the small ticket counter, and Jesse joined her, Pete trudging along a half step behind him. This station was smaller than the one in Chicago, but its new construction made it a handsome sight.

"We'll stick with you. We're not in any hurry, except for the boy's stomach," Jesse said, nudging Pete's shoulder. Surprisingly, the boy didn't move away from his touch.

They waited nearby as Erin spoke to the ticket agent. She turned back to them with a wry smile. "It looks like I'll be joining you for supper, after all. The next train to Calvin isn't until the morning."

Part of Jesse was relieved he wouldn't have to say goodbye yet. But part of him was reluctant to let Erin just walk out of his life.

"I'll take your bag, Miss Erin," Pete said, taking her satchel from her and walking out ahead of them, head swiveling curiously as they left the depot with its tall clocktower.

Jesse craned his neck, as well. Out here, the blue sky seemed to stretch on forever.

"What about your trunk?" Jesse asked.

"The ticket agent said he'd have someone store it overnight and I'll just need to make sure it gets on the train in the morning."

She wasn't really looking at him as they walked down the boardwalk—a far cry from Boston's sidewalks!—at least not the way she'd been looking at him last night.

He wanted to explain…

"I hope you don't think I'm breaking my word to take you to Calvin, but I believe I should get a start on my new life, now I've got Pete to look after."

The words, the lie, slipped out so quickly and effortlessly. In Chicago, he'd wanted to be a new man for Erin, a worthy man, but her confession from the night before, that she was falling for him—it had frightened him, and his past behaviors took over.

Another sign that he could never be right for Erin.

"Of course, I understand," she said. "It's admirable that you're going to take him on. I can see you've already made a difference with him."

He didn't want her to think less of him for his past, wanted her to have good memories. There was no chance they could end up together, so it was better to part ways now, wasn't it? If he pretended that anything could be between them, it would only result in hurt for them both. Erin would be hurt when she realized he hadn't been completely truthful with her, and when he lost her regard, his heart would be ripped apart.

He wouldn't see her again after supper. They would

say their goodbyes and she would go on her way to Calvin, and then he'd figure out something to do with Pete.

But as he and Erin followed Pete down the dusty street, he felt hollowed-out and broken.

Chapter Seventeen

Erin watched Pete lick the spoon after taking his last bite of the pudding he'd ordered for dessert, then lean his chin on hand on the elegant white-covered table. In the background, other conversations and tinkling silverware swirled around them.

Jesse had surrendered soon after she had, laying his napkin next to his plate and sitting back with hands steepled over his belly, watching Pete enjoy the food with relish, a small smile playing on his lips.

The byplay between the two males had changed greatly since she'd first met them on the train out of Boston. Now, when Jesse made a dinner selection, Pete considered it gravely and chose the same thing. Jesse teased him about his bottomless stomach.

They were acting more like real brothers, and Erin was grateful and amazed to see the change and know Pete would have someone who cared about him from now on.

How could she be sad for herself, that Jesse was ready to move on?

She would say what she had to say and then retire to

her room. Rushing to fill the lengthening silence, afraid that if she thought too much she'd start to cry.

"I came down earlier, before we met for dinner, to stretch my legs a bit. I spoke to the hotel manager and he told me the livery stable down the street is looking for a stablehand. It probably wouldn't be much pay, and I wasn't sure if you even liked horses... And then as I was walking down the boardwalk, the milliner was closing up her shop for the day and we began talking, and she said her brother has a cattle ranch about ten miles out of town and needs cowboys, but I wasn't sure if Pete would be allowed to go with you. Then I thought of going to the telegraph office to wire my brother that I'll arrive tomorrow, but of course it was closed, but the clerk there mentioned the bank was looking for a bank teller. It could possibly be an option for you..."

Jesse knew Erin was disappointed. The connection between them had only strengthened since the moment they'd met and he knew that her smiles and conversation throughout dinner had been forced. Plus, he'd trained himself to be attuned to people's small gestures and she hadn't been as upbeat as their previous days together.

And now this. She'd spent the afternoon scouting for employment for him, when she might have been resting in her room.

His heart swelled with love for her.

But he was still afraid to tell her about his past.

If he told her the truth, she would walk away. He knew it. On the small chance that she didn't right away, what if she came to realize his true nature and changed her mind later?

"Thank you," he told her. "The milliner's brother wants cowboys and I might be a bank teller if I'd had more schooling."

"You'll find something," she said with a trembling smile. "I know you will."

"Maybe you could be a lawyer," Pete offered. "You're smart enough."

His face warmed.

"Gentlemen, I'm afraid I'd better retire. Only a short jaunt tomorrow, but I want to be fresh to see my brother."

They stood and accompanied Erin out of the hotel's dining room and into the lobby area. It wasn't as opulent as the Chicago hotel, but a far cry nicer than a lot of other places he'd slept. He was looking forward to a real bed after cricking his neck on the passenger car.

And he'd paid for his room himself.

Jesse saw the surprise on her face when Pete slung an arm around Erin's waist in an awkward hug. "'Night, Erin."

"Thank you both for getting me here in time for Christmas. Only two more days!" She half laughed and wiped beneath her nose as she embraced the kid. He faded up the stairs, giving them some privacy as Erin and Jesse followed more slowly.

The upstairs hallway was quiet and dimly lit, offering them a quiet place to talk.

"Would you walk me over to the rail station in the morning?" she asked, eyes on the stairs in front of her feet.

"I—don't know. I'll likely be busy hitting the streets, looking for a job." It was an excuse, a thin one. He knew it, and it sounded in his voice, but she didn't argue with him, only nodded briefly.

They reached the landing and she hesitated. "I…I wanted to say again that I'm sorry if what I said—that I was falling in love with you—made things uncomfortable between us. It wasn't my intention."

She looked up at him with those guileless eyes and her expressive features and he could see the depth of her emotion.

"It isn't that, Erin," he said, voice low. "I'm not… I can't… I want to but I can't—"

He bowed his head and squeezed his eyes tightly closed; his hands formed fists unconsciously. Walking away now was hard, too hard. If he waited until the morning, had one more night of hope, it would only hurt that much more in the morning.

"It's all right." She was there, facing him, fingers lightly touching his fisted hands. "I wasn't asking you for anything, Jesse. I only wanted you to know. Everything happened so fast, with you going out in the blizzard, but then when you'd returned I just… It sort of just popped out. But I'm not upset I told you. You're a good man."

He shook his head. A denial of her words, a denial of what he had to do—walk away. It was better this way. Better that she thought she'd befriended someone like her, someone good.

"I wish…" *Things could be different.*

"I know God has good things in store for you. I hope you'll open your heart to Him, Jesse."

Then she reached up and bussed his cheek, just a fleeting touch. "Goodbye."

His own goodbye stuck in his throat as he watched her walk away, down the hall, and slip into her room.

He would never see her again. He ached all over just thinking it.

When he stepped into the room he shared with Pete, the boy sat perched on the edge of the bed, an unreadable expression on his face.

"I can't believe you're just giving up," Pete said. "Yer just letting her get away. She wants us to go to Calvin with her. It'd be another day together, at least."

Jesse slumped into a straight-backed chair near the bed, rubbing both hands over his face. He was so tired of fighting his emotions, tired of struggling. "It doesn't matter. You didn't spill the beans on me, so she still doesn't know I've been in prison."

"So tell her."

"She won't feel the same way about me once she knows."

"How d'you know? She seems to have forgave you for letting her think I was your brother."

"It's not the same."

Pete jumped off the bed. "I'll just go tell her."

"No!"

Jesse appreciated that the kid wanted to make it simple, but it wasn't. He wasn't worthy of her. "It's more than just prison."

"You told me about your brother dying. Is that it?"

"No." His responsibility in Daniel's death was all mixed up in it but not the totality of his conflicting emotions. "I don't want her to—" *See me as I really am.* "Think less of me." He wanted her to admire him, didn't want to lose the open emotion on her face when they were together.

"So you're just going to let her go on, thinking she pushed you away?"

What the kid said made sense. Erin did deserve an explanation, deserved to know why he wasn't good enough for her. When she knew about his past, she'd agree that they were mismatched and couldn't be together.

He could agree she deserved to know. The trouble was, he didn't think he had the courage to tell her. His past was ugly, and most likely she wouldn't understand it. No one else had ever known about his past and still loved him.

Telling her would ruin the small kernel of respect she'd gifted him with by the admiration in her eyes. When she hadn't known about his past, she'd judged him for the actions she'd seen, like helping take care of Pete.

But once she knew…all that respect and admiration would be gone.

But…he didn't want her hurting, thinking she'd done something to drive him away.

He jumped up from the chair. "I'm going to talk to her."

"Good," Pete said with a matter-of-fact grin.

But Jesse wasn't sure it was good at all.

Chapter Eighteen

A soft knock on her door brought Erin's head up from where she'd collapsed on the hotel bed. She rose, wiping her tears away. When she cracked open the door, she saw the last person she'd expected.

"Jesse."

What was he doing here? Aware that her hair was mussed and her eyes puffy and red from the tears she'd barely held off until she'd reached her room, she mostly hid behind the cracked door.

"Will you take a walk with me?" he asked. His voice was so serious and the look in his eyes told her this—whatever *this* was—was a matter of grave importance to him.

And her own pain didn't matter in the face of his.

She nodded, holding his gaze. "Let me find my coat."

Closing the door momentarily, she scrambled to pin up her hair. She donned her coat and grabbed her scarf, winding it around her neck even as she reopened the door and joined him.

He didn't look any happier. In fact, his expression showed enough apprehension that she might've thought he was going to the gallows instead of going for a walk with her.

He remained silent as they went down the stairs, although his hand came beneath her elbow to steady her. At the outer door, he took a moment to turn up the collar of his coat before he held the door for her.

They walked out into a world of white. Snow covered the ground and gently fell straight down. It was hours past supper, dark and quiet with no one else visible on the streets. Only the two of them. Jesse's hand supported her elbow again and Erin allowed him to assist her off the boardwalk into the street.

"Should be less slick than those planks covered with ice and snow," he explained.

With no wind blowing, and a layer of snow on the ground and still falling softly from the sky, every sound seemed muted. Lamplight shone out of windows in business establishments and upper rooms which were probably the homes of their proprietors, lighting the way for Erin and Jesse.

They were in no hurry. Erin was content just to be with Jesse. She wanted to know what was causing such a heavy burden on his heart, but she had no desire to rush him. She wanted him to trust her enough to tell her, but he seemed hesitant to begin speaking.

They reached the end of the block, crossed the silent street, and kept walking. And still she waited.

Jesse couldn't figure out how to start. The words hovered at the tip of his tongue, waiting to be said, but he couldn't say them.

He loved her more every moment. In the hallway

upstairs when they'd said their first goodbye, she'd offered him comfort with her touch. Even though he knew she'd been hurting.

And when he'd asked her to walk with him, she hadn't hesitated, only responded to his need.

Oh, how he loved her.

But would her love for him stand the test?

When they'd passed another block and he remained tongue-tied, she turned to face him and clasped both his gloved hands in hers.

"Whatever you have to say, I'm listening." Those blue eyes that he could fall into were open and curious.

"You think I'm good, and kind, and noble, but I'm not," he blurted. "When I bumped into you at the train station in Boston, I was looking for a lemon—a target." He could see by her puzzled expression she didn't understand the vernacular. "Someone I could swindle. I'm a… I was a confidence man."

He took a deep breath, and looked away, over her shoulder, though he didn't relinquish his hold on her gloved hands.

"When we met, I had been out of prison for two days."

He heard her soft intake of air, felt the grip of her hands tighten minutely on his. He couldn't bear to look in her eyes again, but he also couldn't resist. She searched his face as if asking whether he was telling the truth.

He closed his eyes, everything inside him freezing and shriveling.

"Maybe you'd better start at the beginning," she said softly.

"You know about my stepfather, and about Daniel. For a long while after Daniel died, I didn't care about anything. Didn't eat regularly, nearly froze to death a couple of times. Then I met a boy a bit older than me, maybe nineteen, dressed real nice.

"He started telling me that I could have fine things and get off the streets and it was easy money. He taught me to run a con about a lost wallet and I had a full belly for the first time in months.

"The next night I had a roof over my head. Then some new clothes. And as I got better at it, I set my sights higher.

"I was a good liar. People believed me easily. I told myself they were giving me their money. I told myself they were wealthy enough to afford it. I thought if they were gullible enough to fall for one of my tricks, then they deserved it. Let's keep walking, all right? I don't want you to get chilled."

He didn't particularly want her to see his face, to see his shame. If they walked side-by-side, she'd only get a profile view and perhaps the shadows and darkness would hide the rest.

"How did you come to be incarcerated?" She allowed him to pull her along, taking a right turn with the intention of looping back to their hotel.

"I met a girl," he said simply. "She was a friend of the man I thought of as a friend—the same one who'd taught me how to gain someone's trust in the first place. She was just like me, shortly off the streets and wanted a better life for herself.

"Turned out she was using me—she betrayed me. Talked me into running a con that required partners, only we got caught. When the dust settled, I took the blame and she got off scot-free. I was in prison five years."

"Prison." She wasn't looking at him and the word was quiet.

"Yes."

She inhaled again, sharply this time, and Jesse knew that the way she saw him was changing. How could she help seeing him differently? And he wasn't even close to finished yet.

"Prison was where I met Jim Kenner. We were cell mates."

This earned him a turn of her head; she gazed at him questioningly.

"I didn't particularly like him," Jesse went on. "He'd had a conversion experience before we met and he preached at me all the time. I admire a person with convictions—like you—but Jim never let it rest. He knew I didn't want to hear what he had to say, but he was stubborn, thought I'd come around to his way of thinking eventually.

"And I started to, but then… I'd made an enemy of one of the other inmates. Mostly I tried to stay away from trouble, but he held a grudge from when I'd first arrived in prison. Three days before I was going to be released, he came after me with a knife. And Jim threw himself in between me and the knife. He died because of his wounds."

"And you felt guilty," she surmised correctly.

"I still feel guilty. He died, I didn't. And I don't understand why he did it." Maybe he would never understand.

"After I got out of prison, I went to check on Jim's family. I found his mother real sick and his sister ill-equipped to deal with it and I promised them I'd find his brother if I could. So I needed a way to get to Chicago.

"And I ended up at the train station. And bumped into you."

He took a deep breath. He was getting to the part of the story that he didn't particularly want to tell.

"The moment we met on the platform, I started to feel something for you."

She looked down, and in the darkness he couldn't see her expression well enough to decipher it. "I felt it, too," she said softly.

This was it. This last thing he had to tell her would destroy any vestiges of feeling she might have left for him.

"Then Pete approached me and we allowed you to think we were brothers. It worked to our advantage..."

Her lips pinched at the reminder of their deception. He stopped walking, as they'd approached the hotel and it was only a few paces off.

He faced Erin again, counting on being able to read her open expression in the faint light given off by the hotel. He had to know if there was any chance of her love surviving this confession.

"Erin, once you'd changed your clothes and I knew you came from a wealthy family, I planned to trick you into giving me your money. All the cash you had on you. I was going to take it from you."

She heard the words, had been listening intently, but it took a moment for their meaning to sink in.

When she realized that he meant he'd planned to make her the victim of a swindle, she felt as if she'd received a physical blow, and drew away from him.

His face crumpled, but he didn't reach for her, didn't do anything other than let his hands drop to his sides. His jaw was tight and that muscle that she hadn't seen ticking at all yesterday or today had gone wild, jumping in his cheek.

But it was his eyes that affected her most. They seemed bottomless with pain. Pain that matched hers.

"You—you were going to steal from me?"

"Erin—" Her name sounded ripped from his lips, but she had no excuse for his behavior. She was shaking.

"Answer me," she demanded.

"Yes," he said in a strangled voice. "But you have to realize—I thought I had no other choice. Being a con man is all I've known since I was a teenager. I thought I needed cash to have a fresh start, but I changed my mind when I'd gotten to know you. When I saw how you were with Pete, taking care of him in that hotel in Chicago—and you didn't even know him. You were taking care of this little boy who was a stranger to you. I've never known anybody—not one person who would do that."

She shook her head, his words and explanations whirling in her brain like the violent snowstorm they'd witnessed last night.

She'd known Jesse had been holding something back, but this? Lies, and manipulations…just like her father.

She couldn't abide the deception.

Jesse watched the life leach out of her eyes, powerless to stop it and wishing he'd done anything but what he'd done—lie and try to trick her.

But if she'd known about his time in prison from the get-go, she'd never have shared her friendship with him.

His arms ached to hold her as hurt filled her expression, but when he finally got the courage to reach for her, she stepped back from him, and his hands fell back to his sides, empty.

"May-maybe it's better that we part ways now," she said quietly, eyes downcast.

He swallowed the last of his pride. So be it. He could beg. He just couldn't leave things as they were now, not if there was a chance, however small. "I'd changed my mind—thought Pete and I should accompany you to Calvin in the morning. It will only take part of the day and I'll still be able to look for a job when we get back."

"I'm not sure if that's a good idea," she said, again in that subdued voice. She still wouldn't look at him.

Her gloved hands shook where she clasped them in front of her.

"Erin, c'mere. You're trembling." He didn't want her to go inside, didn't want this moment to end, afraid he'd never see her again.

She shook her head, refusing his embrace, the comfort he offered her. "I'm just— I'm cold."

He recognized in her words that she only wanted away from him, and didn't argue with her as she backed farther away, turning for the door.

He caught up to her, steadied her with a hand on her elbow when her slender boot slipped on the wooden plank. She jerked away as though his touch burned her.

The irony stung. Now he'd won Pete's trust and the boy allowed a hand on his shoulder or his hair to be ruffled, Erin could no longer stand his touch.

Heart in his throat, he followed a step behind as she climbed the stairs to their hallway. She veered toward her door; this was it, his last moment with her unless he could convince her to give him another chance.

"Please," he begged, voice hoarse. "Let the two of us ride along with you. I won't even say anything to you if that's what you want."

Just being with her for those last precious hours would be enough. It would have to be, if that was all she could give him.

"Fine," she said shortly. "Good night."

And she closed the door behind her with a final-sounding *snick.*

Jesse ran one hand down his face, and found that it was shaking. It had been just as he'd thought. He'd lost everything—her regard, her admiration. He'd seen the light in her eyes dim.

He didn't know what he hoped to gain on the train tomorrow, only knew that he couldn't leave things as they were, not if he had any choice about it.

Chapter Nineteen

The morning dawned overcast and dreary, the same way Erin felt. A glimpse out the window in her hotel room revealed that snow still fell, but this time it wasn't the gentle downfall it had been last night; instead, it blew in from all sides. Sort of like how her heart felt bombarded and battered.

She resolved to make it through the last leg of the journey as best she could, without saying much to Jesse.

It was her own fault for letting her heart become involved with a total stranger. She'd known even as she'd fallen for him that he'd been keeping something back from her.

She just hadn't expected it to be the revelation that the only reason he'd approached her, and stayed with her, was because he'd been planning to steal from her.

Jesse's betrayal was worse than her father's. Possibly because it seemed to validate her father's view that she wasn't mature enough to make her own decisions. She'd wanted to take a trip, make it to her brother's for the holiday on her own to prove she was an adult and could take care of herself. Instead, she'd proved that she allowed the wrong kind of person into her life and had become far more involved than she should've.

Perhaps her father was right and she should allow him to dictate her schedule and decide who she should be involved with.

"Morning, Miss Erin." Pete strode out of the dining room, wiping across his mouth with one sleeve.

"Good morning. I see you've found your breakfast."

"Of course," Jesse said, exiting the dining room and joining them, laying a hand on Pete's shoulder. For once, the boy didn't shake off his touch. She witnessed the progress between the two and was glad Pete had found someone to be his family.

And she never would have met Pete if she hadn't taken this trip. What if he'd gotten sick with the food poisoning and hadn't had anyone to care for him? Possibly he could've died. She couldn't regret meeting Pete, even if it resulted in hurt for herself.

"Now that he's found a cash cow, I doubt this young man will be missing many more meals," Jesse teased. When their eyes met, she could see the strain it was for him to keep things light. The pain in the depths of his eyes mirrored the rend in her heart.

She nodded a greeting to Jesse and watched his smile fade.

"I'll understand if you've changed your mind about accompanying me to Calvin." She looked down, unable to keep meeting his gaze, and fiddled with one of the ties on her satchel.

Jesse cleared his throat. "We'd like to go with you, but we won't force our company on you. I'd understand—"

He broke off and looked away. Beneath the brim of his Stetson, he squinted at something distant. To hide his emotions? He swallowed and his Adam's apple bobbed.

As much as she was hurt by his actions and what he'd told her last night, she didn't want him to feel it, too. They didn't belong together, it was obvious now, but how did one convince their heart to break the connection it had made?

"How can I turn down the escort of two handsome gentlemen? Especially when it means I don't have to carry my luggage to the depot."

She pushed her satchel into Pete's arms, causing him to grunt, but he took it from her. Jesse cleared his throat again as she passed through the door ahead of him.

She braced herself for him to speak, but he remained silent, following at her side without further comment.

This last leg of the journey would be the most painful, but she would make it through. Somehow.

She's leaving. She's leaving. Jesse's heart seemed to surge the words with each *clack* of the train's wheels on the tracks.

He'd taken the seat across from Erin and Pete, because he didn't want to make her uncomfortable by sitting next to her, but being across was proving more difficult. His gaze kept straying to her, and seeing the tight lines around her mouth and how she couldn't quite meet his eye just twisted his gut into a tighter and tighter knot.

Everyone around them seemed to be celebrating the holiday, with festive wrapped parcels, and he'd even seen one man carting a cut tree. Only their little group seemed to be mired in sadness.

Because he'd messed everything up. From the very beginning, but he'd never planned on hurting her this much. He'd told her the truth in an effort to keep her from thinking it was her fault for putting a wedge between them, but he hadn't wanted this deep chasm between them, either.

Was he destined to heap guilt after guilt upon himself throughout his life? Would he never find freedom, only keep disappointing those who cared about him?

All throughout his sleepless night he'd heard his stepfather's voice, berating him and telling him he would never be good for anything. And then he would remember Erin's joy falling away when he'd told her the truth about himself. He hadn't wanted his stepfather to be right, had promised himself he wouldn't end up like the man's predictions.

Unfortunately, he'd only proven the difficult man right, not himself.

And yesterday, Jesse had lost the best thing he'd ever had.

He stared out the window into the iron-gray sky and swirling snow, wishing he'd never been born, wishing he knew what he could've done differently to have prevented this hurt for both of them.

Just after the last stop before Calvin, Jesse excused himself to the washroom.

Pete leaned close to Erin before he'd even gone out of sight. "You gotta forgive him, Miss Erin. He's torn up, can't you see it?"

The boy was intuitive, compassionate. He would make a fine man one day. She tried to smile and failed as misery swept over her. "I don't know if I can, Pete. He lied to me."

He opened his mouth, probably to remind her that they'd both lied about being brothers.

"Worse than when you both let me think you were brothers."

Was there really a worse or better kind of lie? A lie was a lie. She'd wanted to escape her father's machinations, and only found herself in a situation just as false.

"How come you can forgive me, then?"

"Because—" *You didn't know any better,* she started to say but bit down on the words without saying them aloud.

Based on what she had discovered about Jesse's childhood and his stormy growing-up years, she knew he hadn't believed he'd had a choice.

Even with such a flimsy excuse, she couldn't erase the betrayal she felt. How could she trust a man who admitted he'd only approached her in order to steal from her?

She couldn't.

The conductor came through, announcing the last stop, and Jesse returned to his seat, his eyes suspiciously red-rimmed.

She realized he was upset. Had been upset since last night, even before they'd talked, felt much more than he was showing.

But she couldn't deny the way she felt now. She couldn't risk getting hurt even more by allowing the relationship to go on.

The train slowed and pulled into the small rail station. Through the window, Erin could see it was completely different from the large depot she'd left in Boston, with only a small outdoor platform and a shack at one end where she assumed the ticket agent was located. A few people waited on the platform and she strained her eyes trying to locate her brother, but the blowing snow prevented her.

Pete proudly carried her satchel in front, and Jesse followed her down the aisle. Only a few people got off the train, and only two appeared to be waiting to get on. Erin stepped onto the platform and gazed around at this place her brother claimed to have fallen in love with.

There wasn't much to it. It was much smaller than Cheyenne, where the train station had been surrounded by businesses—the train station in Calvin was at the very edge of town. And the town itself was one main street with business on it and a couple of smaller side streets with homes on them.

The surrounding area was flat, probably good for cattle, until she caught sight of the mountain range in the far distance.

It was somewhat like she expected, but in some ways there was no imagining the reality of such a small town when she'd never been out of Boston.

Pete and Jesse seemed to share some of the same sentiments as they stared around them.

"Ain't much to it, is there?" asked Pete.

The train whistle blew and it began chugging forward out of the station.

"Erin?"

A shout from the far edge of the station turned all

three of them. Chas stood tall in the swirling snow, another figure—a deputy?—half a step behind him.

She rushed forward, and Chas opened his arms and she threw herself into his embrace.

"You came to meet the train," she cried.

He hugged her tight and then set her on her feet and leaned back to look at her. "I've come every day since Tuesday, when you were supposed to arrive. Father—"

"—wired you," she finished along with him, with a roll of her eyes. "I suppose I should be thankful you had enough faith in me that I would arrive in one piece."

"Hmm. It seems you finally did," he said, staring with narrowed eyes behind her. "And who is this?"

"A friend," came Jesse's voice. "Jesse Baker. And my… Well, this is Pete."

The two men shook hands and sized each other up. Pete returned her satchel, and she took a moment to hug him.

"We're going to catch a return train to Cheyenne," Jesse explained, still speaking to Chas. "Just wanted to see Erin safely to her family."

"There might not be another train through today," said the person behind Chas and, to Erin's surprise, it wasn't a male voice.

"Danna?" she asked.

The other person stepped forward and tipped their Stetson back, and it was Erin's sister-in-law, wearing trousers and a men's coat with her tin star pinned on the lapel.

"It *is* you," Erin exclaimed, reaching to embrace her sister-in-law.

"Chas wouldn't let me wear the trousers in Boston—

said it would cause too many heads to turn—but this is my standard attire here," the taller woman said with a chuckle. "We're glad you came."

"He was probably right—you would've caused a stir. Where's my niece?"

"At home," Chas put in. "Katy, the teen girl we've taken in, is watching her. We weren't sure if the train would be delayed and we didn't want Minnie out in the cold for too long. Do you have a trunk?"

"Yes, that's it there." She pointed to where the baggage handler had deposited her trunk moments ago.

"I'm Danna O'Grady. Marshal in these parts," Erin's sister-in-law said, stepping forward and reaching out to shake Jesse's hand and then Pete's.

"You're…really a lawman?" the boy asked, eyes wide.

"Yes, I really am."

"Excuse me a moment," Jesse said, making tracks for the shack across the platform.

"You can shoot guns and chase outlaws?" Pete practically vibrated with excitement.

"Better than me," came Chas's voice again, strained a little this time as he trudged past them, lugging Erin's trunk toward a waiting wagon on the street. "She chased down a band of bank robbers almost on her own," he called over his shoulder.

Erin watched Danna's cheeks fill with color even as her eyes lit with happiness. She mashed her hat farther down on her head. "He's a little biased."

Erin grinned. "He's proud of you. Even back in Boston he walked around telling everyone about your exploits. Our aunt nearly had a conniption when he described some of your shoot-outs."

"Well, I'm behind the desk a lot more now that Minnie has arrived. Chas and the other deputies are able to handle most disputes and such these days."

"The marshal was right," Jesse said, rejoining their group as Chas approached from the opposite direction. "Next train back to Cheyenne's not until tomorrow morning."

"We'd offer to let you stay the night," Danna started, and Erin's heart thudded uncomfortably in her chest. "But we've just built the three rooms, and with both Erin and Katy there we'll be full-up as it is. Maybe the barn? It's plenty warm with the horses in there."

Pete glanced from one adult to another. It was clear to see he was keen on the idea.

Erin half turned her head and her eyes met Jesse's, all that was left unsaid passing between them. She could see he recognized her discomfort with the idea. He half smiled sadly. "That won't be necessary. Is there a hotel…?"

The marshal shook her head. "I'm afraid not. There's been some interest from the town council in attracting someone to build one, but…" She shook her head. "But that's neither here nor there. We do have a boardinghouse, two blocks over and turn on First Street. It's a two-story white house."

"C'mon, kid," Jesse said gruffly. He cuffed Pete's shoulder and they turned together toward the street. "Goodbye, Erin O'Grady."

"Bye, Miss Erin," Pete called over his shoulder, giving her one last morose look.

She clutched her satchel to her middle, hesitating. She couldn't ignore Jesse's betrayal, but neither could she let things end this way, with only a paltry goodbye passed between her and the man she'd come to care about.

"I'm sure you want to get in out of the cold," Chas was saying, but she waved him off.

"Will you— I just need one more moment," she blurted and then raced after Jesse and Pete. "Jesse—wait!"

Jesse whirled at Erin's cry, heart thundering in his ears in anticipation and renewed hope. Had she reconsidered?

"I'll go on ahead," Pete murmured and faded away as Jesse's vision filled with the woman he felt so much for.

As she drew near, he saw that her usually open expression was still conflicted, and his heart dropped to the pit of his stomach. She wasn't coming to him to forgive what he'd done.

A glance over her shoulder revealed her brother and his lawman wife standing at the foot of the train platform, watching with interest.

"I can't—" She shook her head, and when she looked back up at him, her eyes were filled with tears.

His own chest felt painfully tight, as if he couldn't draw a full breath.

"I'm sorry," she said. "I can't forget what happened between us—"

It was killing him, watching her hurting. "Don't be sorry," he choked out. "It's my fault. All of it. I wanted—" Now it was his turn to shake his head, swallowing hard to keep his own tears at bay. He didn't want to compound her pain.

Over her shoulder, he saw the brother attempting to come toward them, but his wife stalled him with a hand on his arm. Jesse stuffed his hands in his pockets to keep from reaching for Erin.

"It'll be better if you can forget me."

She bowed her head, struggling for composure, squeezing her eyes tightly closed. "I don't know if I can do that, either," she whispered. "You've touched my heart..."

Did that mean she still felt something...anything for him? An invisible fist squeezed his heart. He wasn't above begging. "Erin, please..."

Tears rained down her cheeks. "Jesse..."

Not caring if the brother came over and arrested him, he reached for her and she came willingly into his arms, wetting his shirt with her tears for the very last time.

"Erin," he breathed into her hair, his own eyes suspiciously wet. "I wish I could take it back—all of it. I wish we could've met in some other situation, some other life, where we might've had a chance."

She pushed on his chest and he released her, though his hands wanted to linger, he stuffed them in his pockets again.

"I can't give you my heart, but I want you to have this." She pushed a book—her Bible—at him and he fumbled to get his hands out of his pockets to take it from her.

"Erin, I can't take this—"

"It's the only Christmas gift I have to give you." She swiped her eyes, then looked up at him and he knew this was the last chance he would have to look in her crystal-blue eyes.

"There is so much more in here than the story I read on the train," she said, eyes beseeching him. "Truths that will set you free."

Free.

He'd thought he'd be free when he'd got out of prison, but the guilt of Jim's death had weighed on him. Same as Daniel's death still weighed heavily.

He would never be free.

He reached forward with one hand and touched her jaw, thumb brushing her cheek. *I love you.* He wanted to say it so desperately, but clenched his teeth against the desire to speak the words.

Instead, he said, "Goodbye." And turned to follow Pete.

Chapter Twenty

Christmas morning, shortly after dawn, Erin stood in the bedroom doorway of Chas and Danna's little cabin, looking out on the kitchen and main living area. She didn't know where her sister-in-law was, but Chas stood in his sock feet in the kitchen, holding the baby close to his chest and talking to her. Or maybe he was talking to the gangly mutt of a dog that seemed to follow him around everywhere and was currently lying across the kitchen rug at his feet.

She'd never imagined her brother as a tender father, cooing soft nothings at his little girl. Seeing it brought tears to her eyes.

It seemed like everything made her cry these last two days.

She felt torn open inside, like she'd lost a huge piece of herself when she'd said goodbye to Jesse.

Seeing Chas and Danna so happy with their growing family made her think about what it would've been like to be married to Jesse and eventually have a family with him.

But she kept coming back to the conclusion that she

wouldn't be able to trust him. How could she, when he'd done the same thing to her that her father had done?

As she watched, Danna came in through the outside door and went to Chas and the baby.

"Say 'hullo, Mama,'" Chas said in a baby voice, waving Minnie's hand. Danna stepped closer and they embraced for a moment, the baby between them.

Erin had to look away.

"Kinda makes ya sick, don't it?" a female voice from behind propelled Erin into the living area.

Katy followed her out of the small bedroom they'd been sharing, and Danna and Chas jumped away from each other, looking a bit embarrassed.

When they'd brought Erin back from the train station she'd had met Katy, the young woman Danna and Chas had discovered was orphaned during their whirlwind marriage and accepted as part of their family. Katy reminded her of Pete, a little rough around the edges, but sweet in spirit.

"They're so lovey-dovey sometimes ya want to knock 'em on the head," the girl said, moving into the kitchen and finding the cutlery. She began to set the table.

Danna took the baby from Chas, and he stepped to the stove to lift the coffeepot. He moved a cast-iron skillet to the stove and then retrieved eggs and a slab of salt pork.

Erin had been delighted and amazed when she'd first arrived to find that her brother did most of the cooking for the family because Danna couldn't cook at all. She supposed a lot of men who lived on their own cooked for themselves, and her brother didn't seem to mind.

"It seems jolly Saint Nick visited us in the night, and

brought rather more than I expected," said Chas, gesturing to the small pile of wrapped gifts in the corner of the front room near the sofa. He raised an eyebrow toward Erin.

She forced a wan smile. "Hmm," she hummed noncommittally.

After the house had quieted last night she'd snuck into the living room and set out the things she'd brought for her brother and his family from Boston. The very packages she'd been juggling that had brought Jesse into her sphere.

She blinked. She must find a way to stop thinking of him every moment. It hurt too much.

"Here," Danna said, handing the baby to Erin. She settled her niece on her shoulder with a gentle pat on her rump. The sleepy baby snuggled its face into Erin's neck and, with a sigh, fell asleep.

"Katy, come outside and help me with the milk cow and feeding the horses," Danna murmured, turning toward the door.

Katy made a face but shrugged into a coat and put on the boots next to the outer door and obediently followed.

Leaving Chas and Erin alone as he fried up the salt pork and eggs.

Not turning from the stove, his back to her, he asked, "You want to talk about it? Him?"

"What do you mean?" She hoped he wasn't referring to what he thought she was referring to.

He was. He gave her a pointed look over his shoulder even as he flipped something in the skillet. "You've been moping since you got off the train. I assume it has something to do with that Jesse character. You two seemed awful friendly at the station—more than just acquaintances."

She kept her eyes on the tabletop. "Nothing untoward happened."

"I didn't think it had," he said matter-of-factly. "I'm guessing Father doesn't know about him?"

"No. We only met when I was getting on the train in Boston. It's not— He doesn't mean anything to me." Even as she said the words, she knew they weren't true. She shook her head gently so as not to wake the baby. "He shouldn't mean anything to me," she amended. "I found out he'd only approached me to— Well, his purpose wasn't pure, that's for sure and certain."

"Did he steal from you? Did he hurt you?" Her brother whirled, leaving the fork he'd been cooking with to clank against the pan. The sound startled Minnie, who squawked but then settled back to sleep as Erin rubbed her back.

"No! No, he didn't do anything like that. He said he intended to in the beginning, but he'd changed his mind. He delivered me here and we parted company and that's all."

Chas gave her a long look as he went back to the cooking pan. "That's not all," he said, with rare brotherly insight.

She hesitated. "No, I suppose not."

"If you don't want to talk about that, perhaps we can discuss why you left home for a surprise Christmas visit in the first place. Not that I'm complaining, mind you. Danna and I are ecstatic to have you here."

Erin gave a chagrined grin. "I'm sorry to have imposed. No, really—I know you weren't expecting company. But I had to get away from Boston—had to have some distance from Father."

"I can certainly understand that impulse." He grinned over his shoulder. She knew he'd had his own falling out with their overbearing father, though she didn't know all the details behind it. "May I ask why?"

She focused on the table again. "Now that I've come so far—" and met Jesse and Pete, who'd taught her much "—it seems a little silly and a little…selfish."

He poured a cup of coffee and set it on the table before her. "I'd like to hear it anyway."

"Papa…well, he didn't particularly like that I was volunteering at a hospital—St. Michael's—for poor children. We'd talked about it once, fought about it, but I kept going to the hospital even though I knew he disapproved. I'd fallen in love with those children, and—" just like she'd fallen in love with Jesse "—they needed me. Not as a doctor, just as someone who could identify with what they were going through."

He shoved the pan back farther on the stove and joined her at the table, a steaming cup of coffee in his own hand. "You all right with her?" He nodded to the baby still slumbering on Erin's shoulder.

"Yes, we're fine."

He rolled his cup slowly between his hands, being careful not to slosh any of the liquid out. Even though he'd been away from home for years, she remembered how he was so full of energy it was hard for him to be still. "I can only imagine what our dear father did when he found out you'd still been volunteering. Did he forbid you from leaving the house? Pay to have the hospital closed?"

A reluctant chuckle bubbled from her lips, then emotion overcame her and she squeezed her eyes closed. "No. He started inventing society engagements for me to attend. Teas and parties and such. And then he encouraged the suit of a young man—really, they were in cahoots together—to keep me…ah, *occupied* was the word father used. As if I would be able to forget about the children simply because I was having too much fun doing other things."

He was silent for a moment, a sympathetic frown on his face. "Ah. I see the rub. So when you found out your young man from the train hadn't the purest of intentions when he befriended you, it was like what happened with Father all over again."

She sipped her coffee, nearly scalding her tongue on the steaming liquid. "Your intuitiveness must be a good thing for your job."

He raised one brow at her, letting her know he didn't intend to let the subject drop.

"Yes," she admitted, fiddling with the handle of the coffee mug. "It felt like a betrayal to find out Jesse had only wanted to be with me for my money."

"Did he…make any inappropriate advanced toward you? I'm certain I can still track him down."

"No," she said crossly. "He didn't."

Although they'd shared those kisses…but she was pretty sure she had initiated at least one of them. "He was a perfect gentleman. Along the way, he helped a young boy, an orphan just like your Katy, and I believe they're going to start their own family. And anyway, he only wanted the money to get a fresh start. He'd had some troubles in his life and is starting over again with nothing. He has no home, no family to speak of, and he's overcome so much already."

"Sounds like you made the right choice to part ways. A man who can't support a wife or a family wouldn't be a good choice for a beau anyway."

Her ire rose. "He's certainly intelligent enough to find a job and make a decent living. And besides that, physical wealth isn't everything."

She punctuated her statement by thumping her mug onto the table, slopping coffee over the rim but managing not to burn her hand.

He grinned, and she realized he'd steered her right into a declaration that revealed her feelings for Jesse just as clearly as if she'd said *I love Jesse* aloud.

He reached behind him and snatched a dish towel from the counter and tossed it onto the table before her. Then his smile faded.

"I guess the real question is, can you forgive him? Both Jesse and our father?"

Danna and Katy banged in the back door, interrupting their conversation and waking the baby, who began demanding her breakfast. Danna went to wash up before taking the baby and Chas set about getting the fried eggs and salt pork on the table, and Erin's moment of contemplation was gone.

But the question remained with her through breakfast and after they'd opened the brown-wrapped gifts.

"It's—it's too much," said a teary-eyed Katy as she caressed the brand-new leather bridle and saddle that Chas had lugged inside from the barn. "You shouldn't have got me something so nice—you should take them back."

Danna knelt and put her arms around Katy while Chas bounced the baby on his knee and Erin watched the interchange from the sofa. "It's a gift, honey. Freely given, and we won't take it back."

Erin gasped softly. Her eyes bounced off Chas's too-knowing gaze. She got up and went outside, forgetting to put on her coat. She didn't go far, just closed the door behind her and stood on the step, arms crossed over her suddenly-aching middle. Danna's words to Katy had cut her to the quick. Wasn't that what Erin had done with Jesse? Given him her heart, even said the words *I'm falling in love with you,* and then taking it back when he'd told her the truth about himself. A truth he'd kept secret only to protect himself.

Tears filled her eyes and she couldn't hold back the soft sob that erupted quickly after them. She'd seen the pain on his face when they'd parted, had felt its echo in her own heart. Some part of her knew that she'd done just as he'd expected—he'd expected her rejection, but given her the truth about himself anyway, when he couldn't let her leave without knowing it.

Had he expected her rejection, but hoped for a different result?

Cold wind sliced through her and she knew she couldn't stay outdoors for long. She struggled for composure, striking the tears from her face. She didn't want to ruin the Christmas celebration for her brother and his family with her distress.

What could she do now?

Jesse had planned to take Pete back to Cheyenne on yesterday's train. Possibly they were still in Cheyenne, but perhaps they had gone back to Chicago. Even if she left Calvin to try to find him today, there was a chance he wouldn't be found.

She hadn't given him her parents' address in Boston, and there was little chance of him returning to Boston with everything he'd gone through there.

She'd sent him away, but now when she wanted a further resolution, she had no idea if that was even possible.

The door creaked open behind her.

"You all right?" Chas asked, holding her coat in one hand. "It's awful cold out here."

"I don't know…"

She didn't know if she'd ever be all right again.

"You two look pretty down in the mouth," said a male voice that brought Jesse's head up from the bowl of beef stew before him. "Mind if I join you?"

The man's dark suit, string tie, and the Bible he thumped onto the table next to his plate made Jesse's first instinct a resounding no, but he shrugged and went back to his soup.

At his side, Pete watched the man warily. "You a preacher?"

"Yep. What're you having?"

"Lamb. It's good."

Jesse had ordered the stew because he didn't feel much like eating. Didn't much feel like getting out of bed in the morning, either, but with Pete to take care of, he'd forced himself up the last two mornings. Pete had been remarkably closemouthed about the situation, which had made things a bit easier.

They were about the only people in the hotel dining room in Cheyenne, so it was strange that the preacher had approached them, but maybe the man was as lonely as Jesse was—he felt like a hole had been blown through his midsection, leaving him hollowed and empty. He missed Erin with an ache like fire in his bones. In the three days since they'd parted ways it hadn't faded, not one iota.

He was starting to wonder if it ever would.

The constant ache made him mostly indifferent to everything else. He couldn't even stir any interest that he was probably going to get preached at for the remainder of his dinner. He remembered Jim's penchant for going on over mealtime about how God provided for His children.

Jesse didn't particularly feel provided for. Not a bit, actually.

"Where you from?" the preacher asked as a server brought him a steaming cup of coffee and took his order for a beefsteak.

"Boston," Jesse said when he realized the kid had a mouth full of grub. He looked down at his soup bowl, purposely not asking the man where he hailed from, hoping to end the conversation and be left alone.

No such luck. "Long way from home," said the preacher.

Jesse shrugged. "Looking for a new start." If he was going to be forced into conversation with the man, he might as well try to get something out of it. "I need work, in fact. You know anyone looking to hire somebody?" Didn't preachers seem to know everyone?

The man leaned one elbow on the table, absently tapping his fingers on its top. "Hmm. What kind of work?"

"Don't care much. Anything I can find." Anything

honest. He'd made that decision when he'd gotten out of prison but in his rush to get to Chicago it had wavered and set him on this path that had led to his broken heart. After knowing Erin, there was no question. He couldn't go back to a life of crime.

"What're your skills?"

Jesse shrugged. "Haven't done honest work in a while," he said. A long while. Might as well be up front about it, if he was going all the way with this honesty thing. "Actually, I just got out of prison. Before that, I was a confidence man."

The preacher didn't show an outward reaction and Jesse was impressed with his control. He could only imagine he'd surprised the man with his confession. "I'm reformed," he added. Again, thanks to Erin and her ideals. She'd changed him. Did she even realize it?

"Might be hard to find somebody willing to take you on with a past like that." The preacher's food arrived and he bowed his head over it silently for a moment before he dug in. He enjoyed his food about as much as Pete did.

"I'm willing to work hard," Jesse said. "I've got another mouth to feed."

He and Pete shared a smile. Jesse knew Pete didn't totally trust him, but the boy had been more open the last two days, talking some about his mother and younger sister.

"It's good you're being up front about your past, though."

Jesse looked down again, this time pushing his half-empty bowl away as thoughts of Erin turned the taste to dust in his mouth. "I've had a…bad experience recently, keeping it a secret."

The preacher kept eating, not really looking at Jesse at all. "Something tells me there was a woman involved."

Jesse sat back, torn between getting up and staying put. He had expected the man to give him unwanted advice, or try to convert him, or at the very least start quoting Scripture at him. But the man hadn't done any of that. It was like he was just a regular guy in a nice suit.

"I didn't tell her about my past up front," Jesse said, the words bursting from him. "I should've."

"And she found out?" the preacher asked, sympathy shining on his face.

"I told her. I had feelings for her and I knew she had feelings for me and I couldn't let things go on without telling her everything. I wanted…I wanted her to know the real me."

"I can't say I know a lot of people who would've done that," the preacher said. "Most of 'em would have tried to hide it. It's admirable."

Jesse shifted in his chair. "Didn't do me a lot of good. She changed her mind about me. She was…she was way above my station anyway."

Pete cleared his throat, reminding him that the kid was sitting there, probably hanging on every word. "Yeah, Miss Erin was pretty amazing. She was the nicest person I ever met. Took care of me when I was sick, even though she didn't know me."

"Hmm," the preacher hummed softly.

"I think…" Jesse spoke softly as the realization

filtered through him, making tears sting the back of his nose. "I think she did care about me, even after she found out. She gave me her Bible and I know she wanted…she wanted me to find peace."

He had to swallow hard.

Erin had been kind to him even after he'd revealed the truth about his past. He couldn't blame her if she couldn't love him anymore, but she'd given him what she could. His heart swelled with deeper love for her, even as he struggled to breathe through the fire in his lungs.

"I just wish I knew how," he said low, almost a groan. "I've got things I've done that I just can't get free from—"

He coughed into his hand, stopped talking, because if he didn't he was going to break down in a public place and he didn't want that.

Pete patted his shoulder awkwardly. He appreciated the boy's sentiment.

"I don't want to step in where I'm not wanted," the preacher said. "But if your gal gave you a Bible, maybe I can point you in the right direction. If you want me to."

And his manner and words were so different from Jim's that Jesse actually considered saying yes.

Two weeks later, Jesse reined in the horse he'd only learned to ride a week ago. Inside the ranch yard, he turned back in his saddle. Pete came to rein in his own mount—a smaller pony—next to Jesse and followed Jesse's gaze to where the sun was setting over the mountains, turning the sky red and purple.

"Pretty," Pete commented, voice showing his awe when his simple word didn't cover it.

"Mmm," Jesse agreed. "Still can't believe we're here, can you?"

"Nope."

Jesse reached over and nudged his adopted brother, grinning when the boy pushed back. Their relationship was growing in leaps and bounds, prompted by the time they were able to spend in the saddle together, thanks to the generous rancher who had hired Jesse and allowed Pete to stay on in the bunkhouse, as well.

"You likin' the honest work?" Pete asked curiously.

"Well enough," Jesse answered honestly. The clear Wyoming air agreed with him.

"Me, too," said Pete, and Jesse was glad to know he didn't mind the chores the rancher gave the boy to do for a small salary—a fraction of what the real cowboys made.

Everything seemed to be agreeing with Jesse these days.

He'd made his peace with God. Thanks to a socialite and a traveling preacher...and partly, he supposed, thanks to Jim. He wouldn't say his former cell mate had laid a foundation, exactly, but certainly Jim's final act had set the course in motion that had brought Jesse away from Boston and to this point.

With the preacher's encouragement, he'd searched the Bible Erin had given him. He read many verses that Jim had quoted at him before, but instead of his cell mate's overbearing voice, in his mind he'd heard Erin's gentle tones, as if she was reading to him herself. Thanks to Erin, he'd found relief from the crushing guilt of Daniel's death, and Jim's death, and his own sins. He'd decided to follow Jesus.

And now he felt free.

But he still felt empty. Something inside him longed for the one person he would likely never see again. Erin.

One of those chickadees like he'd seen in her sketchbook lit on the corral fence. In the saddle, he seemed to see them everywhere.

But instead of feeling despair, the birds made him wonder what God had in store for him. He wondered about going back to Chicago to check in on Jared Kenner and Amelia, and hopefully on Jim's mother.

And sometimes, in the quiet part of night, he wondered about going back to Boston.

Chapter Twenty-One

Seven months later

The late summer sun warming his back, Jesse smacked his Stetson against his leg, shaking free a little dust. He mashed it back on his head as he waited for the departing passengers to disembark the train.

Turned out trail dust clung to a Stetson a lot longer than a body thought it did.

Kinda like the way memories of someone who changed your life clung. He shook away the errant thoughts that being back on a train brought to the forefront of his mind. He was going home for a reason. To see his ma, ask for her forgiveness. Make amends, if that was even possible.

Pete at his elbow, Jesse stepped off the platform and onto the Boston-bound train, ready to leave Chicago behind. It had been a good visit with the Kenners and their growing family. Jim's mother and sister had settled in well with Amelia and her mother. The larger, blended family worked well together, the mothers had become friends and Jared and Amelia were expecting a baby in the spring.

Jesse would've been amazed at how things had worked out for them, except now he knew Who to give the credit to, and had found it was better to be thankful than amazed.

And he knew it because of the changes that had been wrought in his life. Working on the Bar S ranch through the spring and summer, he'd been able to save enough money to take this trip to check on the Kenners in Chicago and try to make things right with his mother in Boston. And he'd have a job when he got back. One that he enjoyed well enough. Most days.

He just figured everything in his life would be slightly lackluster without a certain raven beauty by his side. Maybe eventually he'd find someone, but even after all these months apart, he couldn't imagine it.

He still ached for her like fire in his bones. Especially since he'd seen her brother just outside of Cheyenne a couple of days before that trip East. The man had been distant, offering only the barest information about Erin—that she was fine and had returned to Boston—when Jesse had asked. Jesse felt sure she must have moved on with her life. He had no plans to look her up in Boston, no matter how many times he'd considered it.

He followed Pete to a seat near the center of the passenger car, followed the kid into the row and sat down.

"This all right?" Pete asked, settling the small carpetbag he carried at his feet.

Jesse nodded. The kid had mellowed since they'd agreed to stay together, to be each other's family over Christmas. No longer did he glance around with trepidation or as if looking for someone to pickpocket. He and Jesse had become partners, learned to respect each other.

Jesse settled back in his seat, contemplating letting his Stetson slide down over his face and catching an afternoon nap. It would be a long two days to Boston, aware that he'd be in the same city as Erin once again.

He expected she had reconciled with her father. She was too sweet-hearted not to make up with the man, even if he'd treated her badly.

People were still loading onto the train, but Jesse could hear the conductor from the open door at the end of the car, yelling, "All aboard!"

Before he could get comfortable in his seat, Pete's expression changed, eyes narrowing slightly at something he must've seen over Jesse's shoulder. Or out the window? When Jesse turned to look, he didn't see anything out of the ordinary, only passengers stowing their bags and settling into seats, filing onto the train.

"I've got to use the washroom," Pete said quickly, standing up.

"What're you— Don't cause any trouble!" Jesse called after him, because the boy was already gone.

He craned his neck to spot where the boy had gone, but it was as if Pete had disappeared or even gotten off the train. Before he could start to worry, Pete came back and plopped down in his seat.

Instantly, a hand clapped down on Pete's shoulder.

"I believe this boy took something of mine," a voice complained.

"I'm—" Whatever Jesse had been going to say completely slid out of his mind, because as he turned to face the person behind him, he came face-to-face with the last woman he'd ever expected to see.

Erin O'Grady.

In a dark green traveling suit, a jaunty hat on her upswept curls, gloved hand resting on Pete's shoulder.

"Erin—" He couldn't seem to catch his breath, couldn't seem to get his brain to understand that Erin was here, was standing so close.

"I believe this young man has taken my seat," she said, luminous eyes locked with his.

Pete got up and scampered around their row to the one behind, allowing Erin to switch places with him. Jesse couldn't help noting the kid's pleased grin.

Erin moved past Jesse's knees, skirt swishing lightly against his trousers as she settled into the seat, half facing him so their knees were touching.

Jesse still couldn't seem to get his thoughts to order themselves, could barely get air into his burning lungs to ask, "What are you doing here?"

"Going home to Boston."

"But how did you—?" He didn't even know what to ask, he was so stunned to see her.

"Chas wired me," she said, a soft flush filling her cheeks with roses. "He said he'd run into you outside of Cheyenne—something about taking a prisoner to meet the judge. And he told me you were coming to Chicago. Of course, he had to travel back to Calvin before he was free to send the wire, so I only got it two days ago..."

Her beloved voice—and the familiar rambling—filled the cracks in his heart like nothing else could. He was sure he was grinning like a loon, but he couldn't seem to stop.

"I'd just gotten off the train from Boston when Pete spotted me on the platform—"

"So *that's* where he snuck off to!"

"Mmm-hmm. I'm glad he did. I wasn't sure which hotel you'd be staying in—or if you'd end up staying with Jared and Amelia—"

He nodded. They had, sharing a small bedroom while Jared's sister had given up her room for the two of them.

"So I was planning to come to the depot every day to look for you. But I was going to focus on westbound trains, not east! What are you doing on a train to Boston?"

He smiled as she paused for breath. "I'm going to see my mother."

Her eyes filled with unexpected tears. "Oh, Jesse." She threw her arms around his neck and he rocked back at the contact, but quickly caught her in his embrace. She was warmth, a ray of summer sunshine in his arms, and she smelled better than the sweet wildflowers he'd grown accustomed to on the Bar S.

She sat back with a teary laugh. "I'm sorry. I'm happy to know that you're going to make things up with her—that is your intention, right? Good. You look well," she said finally, sitting back in her seat.

He felt a flush creep up his neck. He hadn't paid particular attention when he'd dressed this morning, not thinking he'd be running into Erin O'Grady on the train today. He'd thrown on a pair of denims and one of his work shirts, a clean one. He still had the duster and Stetson he'd picked up on his way out of Boston last December, only now they showed a few more signs of wear.

"And you smell faintly of horses. Am I to understand you're a real cowboy now?"

"Yep. The kid and me have been riding for an outfit a little ways out of Cheyenne."

"And how do you find it? Do you enjoy it?"

He shrugged. "It's work. Honest work." He tried not to sound too proud of that fact, but he was. And it was hard not to respond to the admiration shining from her bold blue eyes. "What about you? Did you make things up with your father? Are you back to volunteering at your hospital?"

"Yes and yes." Erin's joy overflowed at being with Jesse again. That first moment she'd seen him, all the feelings she'd kept close to her heart for these long months had been renewed, swelling like a bird preening its feathers.

There was a subtle difference in him. Something deep in his eyes that told her…he might be at peace. She desperately wanted to ask him about it, but the months apart, and the way they'd separated when she'd gotten off the train in Calvin, made her hold her tongue.

When she'd first seen him, the back of his head and shoulders sitting tall above the seatback, she'd experienced a thrill of fear—what if his feelings for her had cooled? Or what if he'd never really shared her feelings?

And now, as he sat beside her slightly reserved, that thrill of fear came back, and expanded in her chest until she couldn't ignore it. When she'd rushed onto the train in Boston to find Jesse, she'd planned to confess everything, but now the same reserve that he expressed held her back from saying what she really wanted to say.

"I spent two weeks with Chas and his family," she said instead. "Their daughter Minnie is precious, simply precious. And I traveled back to Boston without incident, I'm sure you're happy to hear."

He chuckled. "I don't doubt you found several people to help along the way."

She wrinkled her nose at him. "When I got back to Boston, my father and I had a long talk. I explained my position on visiting the hospital to him, but unfortunately he was still adamant that I not visit. It's been a struggle," she admitted. "I don't particularly like not getting along with him, but the hospital is dear to my heart. There have been no incidents within the last few months, so I believe he's starting to come around. At least I hope so."

She knew she was rambling, but in her nervousness, she couldn't seem to stop talking. "I also got a chance to sketch some birds that were new to me while in Wyoming and a few of my sketches will soon be published in an ornithology journal."

"That's fantastic," he said. Somehow, they were still connected. And she could tell that he was slightly disappointed.

Forcing herself to be quiet, she took a calming breath. Met his brown eyes. Eyes that showed much more peace than when she'd last seen him. And she wanted to know why.

"Will you tell me why you came to Chicago? To find me?" he asked.

The longer she rambled, the tighter the knot in Jesse's gut became.

When he'd first seen her, he'd thought…he'd thought

impossible thoughts. Like maybe she'd come *for him,* because she still loved him. But as she kept talking, especially about inane things, his heart slowly thudded down to his toes and he began to think she'd come to tell him she forgave him, but that she only wanted to be friends.

And so he'd had to ask why she'd come.

"I will," she said quietly, her eyes soft and serious. "But first, will you tell me what's different about you since we parted ways?"

He couldn't refuse her anything. He breathed in deep. "I guess I should start by stating something pretty obvious. When we met on the train out of Boston, I knew pretty quick that you were someone special. At first, I tried to pretend you were the same as any other rich girl I'd met and spun my stories to. But by the time we hit Chicago, I couldn't deny any longer that you were different."

He paused, gathering his wits, and she smiled tentatively at him.

"But by then I also knew there was no way I could ever be good enough for you. But I couldn't walk away, either. So we got on the train to Wyoming. And when you told me that you loved me, I—"

He shook his head, the back of his throat stinging. The moments surrounding her declarations were pretty fuzzy, but that particular moment was etched into his brain with perfect clarity.

She clasped both his hands in hers.

"I thought there was no way you could really love me, because you didn't know who I really was—

"And—" He rushed on even as she opened her mouth

to speak. "I *was* still the same man I'd been before prison. Even in Cheyenne, I was manipulating things to get my own way. I…expected you to see that in me and leave."

Those lovely eyes were filled with tears again. "I wish we'd had more time, there at the end. So what happened?"

"Pete and I stayed in the same hotel in Cheyenne. Turns out we fell in with a preacher, only he wasn't anything like I expected. Kind of like you turned out to be. He seemed to genuinely care about me, and he showed me where to find some truths in the Bible you'd left me. And I…turned myself over to Jesus. Decided to follow him."

Once again her eyes brimmed with tears but she didn't throw herself at him like he might've expected, she just looked at him with those beautiful blue tear-filled eyes and squeezed his hands tightly in hers.

"I'm so happy for you," she whispered. "I can tell it's made a difference—you're not so loaded down with guilt anymore, are you?"

He shook his head. "I found the freedom you tried to tell me about. Pete and I have been attending this little church in Cheyenne, and I've been learning what I missed out on all these years.

"I have to know… Can you forgive me for deceiving you?"

Heart in her eyes, she nodded.

His spirits soared. She'd forgiven him! And with the way she was looking at him, she might even…love him.

"You seem…happy in your new job," she said softly.

He gathered all his courage in one lump. "I'll never

be completely happy without the woman I love beside me. Without you, Erin. I haven't been able to forget you and I know it's a lot to ask for you to be with someone with my kind of past, but—"

She leaned forward in the crowded rail car, in broad daylight, and brushed a kiss across his lips. Laughing a little while wiping her eyes, she pushed back against his chest and said, "I still feel the same, Jesse. I let my own pride and hurt feelings cloud the moment and I'm sorry for that. That's what I came to tell you."

He gathered her close and pressed his face into her hair, knocking her hat askew. He just held her there, basking in the wonder of the moment.

It hadn't been a declaration of love, exactly, but it was close enough for him.

Pete's head popped up from the seat behind them. Obviously, he'd been eavesdropping the whole time. "Are you two gonna get married?" he asked, his face shining.

Jesse's heart just about burst with the thought of marrying Erin.

"C'mere, you," Erin said, edging a bit out of Jesse's embrace and putting an arm around Pete to bring him into the circle. "There's quite a bit of things still to talk about. And I know Jesse has a lot on his mind right now."

He deflated slightly. He did have a lot to consider with this visit. He didn't know if he could even mend things with his mother but he had to try. And if Erin wanted to take things slowly, then they would.

Except, he had a job waiting for him in Wyoming and her home was in Boston. He didn't have any honest connections in Boston that might get him a job—and he had no intention of renewing his old acquaintances. But he had to remember that Erin was young, too. Six years younger than him, and maybe she didn't want to rush into marriage.

"Will you go with me to see my ma?" he asked, because having her next to him for the most difficult journey of his life was the next best thing.

"Of course." She took his hand again and he was amazed at how well they fit together.

Two days later, Jesse's knees shook as he climbed the stairs to his mother's second-floor tenement, Erin beside him and Pete slightly behind.

He'd insisted they come directly from the rail station, before he lost his nerve. It was a little late to be making a call, but his mother hopefully wouldn't be in bed yet.

His fist trembled as he knocked on the apartment door. Erin touched his lower back, just letting him know she was here.

The last two days with her on the Boston-bound train had been like a dream. They'd talked all night the first night and come close again the second night, catching up on everything they'd missed being apart the last months.

He'd told her about riding the range and driving cattle and setting boundaries with Pete. She'd told him about her children at the hospital and how she'd started drumming up support at all her society parties, which had meant her father couldn't curtail her visits without looking bad himself.

He was proud of her. But he also realized she might

not be happy living in Wyoming away from her hospital children or her friends. And knowing what a lonely childhood she'd had, how could he ask her to leave the nest of friends she'd built for herself?

He wasn't prepared when the door opened and his mother was there. She looked older, much older than the last time he'd seen her, with deeper lines running grooves in her face and hair more gray than brown. Her shoulders seemed to have a permanent slump, and her clothes reflected the state of her finances—most likely empty.

But her eyes were the same deep brown he remembered. As he stood there with a lump blocking his throat, unable to speak, they filled with tears.

"Jesse?" she whispered. She peered over his shoulder, and for a second he wondered if she was looking for Daniel.

"Ma—" His voice broke and he bowed his head. Erin's hand slipped into his and she threaded their fingers together. She gave him the courage to speak. "I'm so sorry—sorry I haven't been here and sorry for letting Daniel die." Though he'd begun to forgive himself for that, at last. "I know I don't deserve it, but I came to beg your forgiveness—"

He'd forgotten the rest of the short speech he'd practiced silently in his bunk in Wyoming, but it didn't seem to matter as his mother moved toward him in slow motion and embraced him.

"You'd better come inside," she said, her words muffled in his collar. She pulled him inside, and he looked back over his shoulder to make sure Erin and Pete followed him. They did, looking curiously around the small apartment.

There wasn't much to see. The furnishings were sparse, though a picture of his family with his biological father held a place of prominence on a shelf on one wall. It was meticulously clean.

His ma led the way into the kitchen and they each took a seat around the table.

"Seeing you is…unexpected, Jesse."

He hung his head. "I know, Ma. I'm really sorry for what happened. I shoulda made Daniel stay at home—"

"Shush, honey. Of course I'm sad about your brother, but I've been asking the Lord to bring you back to me for ages."

He jerked his gaze up to meet hers. "You have?"

She nodded, tears sparkling on her cheeks. "Your stepfather did you wrong. And I was too weak to do anything about it. I'm sorry for that—you'll never know how sorry. But after he died a couple years after you went missing, I started getting my life right. And I started praying you'd come home. And now, here you are."

He clasped his hands together under the table and found he was shaking. His ma still loved him after what he'd done. He doubted she knew about his years as a con man, so likely there were still surprises for her, but he was starting to have faith that things might work out for him.

"Now tell me all about you. Looks like you've got a fine woman here, but I don't see a ring on her finger."

Heat crawled up his spine and into his neck. "Ma," he strangled out, "this is Erin O'Grady."

His ma's eyes widened. "Of the shipping conglomerate?"

"I'm afraid so," Erin said with a sweet smile. "It's nice to meet you, ma'am. This is Jesse's friend, Pete. From what I understand, they've taken up together, a couple of regular ranch hands out in Wyoming."

Jesse sat back in his chair. He'd known Erin's father was wealthy, but he hadn't known his own mother would know the family name. It seemed like another strike against him. What could he give her when all he had was a job that barely supported him and Pete?

A half hour later, they were getting ready to take their leave, with plans to visit tomorrow. He and Pete would escort Erin home and then find somewhere to hole up for the night.

But first he had to escape from his ma, who'd cornered him near the front door, out of Erin's hearing.

"You got a fine girl like that looking at you like you hung the moon, and you haven't settled the deal?" she asked.

"Ma!" he protested, looking over her shoulder to make sure Erin hadn't snuck up on them and heard.

"You love her, don'tcha? So ask her to marry you already," his ma insisted.

He rubbed his palm on the back of his neck. "There's a lot of differences between us. She's from a wealthy family, and I'm barely making ends meet. She's got important work here in Boston—"

"What your son is trying to say—" came Erin's voice from behind him. He started to turn, but she slipped her arm around his waist and joined them. "Is that we love each other, and we're working on those other things."

His ma's face softened. It was obvious she and Erin had hit it off.

"In that case, you'll need a ring." His ma slipped her hand a pocket of her dress and pulled out a simple silver band, one Jesse recognized. "It was mine when I married Jesse's father…"

"Ma, she hasn't agreed to marry me." His face got hot like a fire iron, aware of Erin at his side.

"Well, you haven't asked me," Erin said matter-of-factly.

He froze. Turned toward her slowly, because he was suddenly afraid of saying the wrong thing, of messing up the best thing that had ever happened to him. Erin faced him with her blue eyes serious and steady as they met his.

"I don't have anything to offer you," he said hoarsely. "No home, not much money. Only—" He swallowed. "Only myself."

"It's enough," she said softly, steadily, still meeting his gaze.

"Then, will you—"

"Yes," she interrupted him, standing on tiptoe and throwing her arms around his shoulders.

He caught her tightly to him, shaken, grateful, joy pouring out of every thud of his heart.

"I love you," he whispered into her hair.

"I love you back," she said into his neck.

"Put the ring on." Pete's voice rang out joyfully from somewhere outside Jesse's realm of concentration, but Erin pushed gently on his chest.

His ma handed him the simple silver band and his

hand was shaking when Erin placed her smaller hand in his palm. “If you want something fancier…or…”

She wiggled her fingers, as if in anticipation of him sliding the ring on. “I don’t want anything else.”

And when she looked up at him with her expressive eyes, he knew she really meant his heart.

Chapter Twenty-Two

"You're still here."

Jesse's shoulders tensed at the familiar mix of surprise and disdain in Shamus O'Grady's voice. The tone so similar to his stepfather's that Jesse was momentarily transported back in time nearly every time he encountered Erin's father. Especially when O'Grady surprised him on the job, like now. Erin's father usually reserved his visits for Fridays, but today was Thursday.

After a year of proving himself, Jesse hoped the older man would have accepted his presence in Erin's life by now.

"Still here, sir." Jesse gritted his teeth against what he really wanted to say. He heaved a crate—O'Grady's warehouse was always more full than empty—with help from another worker and placed it carefully atop a growing pile to be moved to the docks for transport later.

The other worker shot Jesse a sympathetic look as they moved toward the next box, but Jesse had no need of his pity.

He was the most blessed man on earth. Erin was going to marry him tomorrow.

And suddenly the reason for Shamus O'Grady's unexpected presence became clear. He was going to try something to make the wedding go away. Would he try to anger Jesse? A bribe?

The older man could try all he wanted but Jesse wasn't walking away from the best thing that had ever happened to him.

Jesse remembered that first night he'd met Erin's parents and how her father had exploded when they'd shared their plans to eventually marry.

Erin had borne her father's tirade in silence, sitting next to Jesse on a fancy brocade sofa. He'd had to force himself to do the same, when he wanted to jump to her defense—not his own. The deep connection they shared had made him aware of how each one of her father's comments hurt her, but he hadn't known whether to intervene or just bear it for her sake.

"I think you should leave, young man," her father had finally come out and said.

Erin's face had crumpled, and that's when Jesse had stood from the couch and put himself between her and her father. "I'll leave when you've apologized to your daughter. You might not like the choice she's making in wanting to marry me, but you've no right to hurt her with your temper."

For a moment he thought he'd seen a glimpse of grudging admiration in the other man's eyes, but it might've been a trick of the flickering lamplight because the man had turned his tirade onto Jesse for an interminable time, while Jesse stood his ground before

Erin, hoping that in some way he was blocking her from her father's hurtful words. O'Grady's anger hadn't been anything compared to what he'd seen in prison from the guards and other prisoners.

When Shamus O'Grady had finally run out of bluster, he'd said a grudging apology to Erin, who had then walked Jesse to the door.

"Are you sure you want to do this—marry me?" he'd whispered in the grand front hall of her grand home, Pete giving them a bit of privacy by standing on the front stoop. "I don't want to cause a rift between your father and you."

She'd had tears in her eyes but to Jesse's surprise they'd been for him, not about her relationship with her father. "I'm sorry for what he said to you," she said with a mighty sniff. Then she'd set her jaw, looking quite a bit like a stubborn Pete. "And I've never been more sure of anything in my life."

Erin had come to him the next day with an offer from her father to work in his shipping business as a warehouse worker. It was a surprise, and had changed his plans to return to the Cheyenne ranch. The pay was about the same, which meant it would take him a while to save enough to get a small apartment in a decent part of town.

But it had kept him close to Erin, and she would be able to continue her work with the hospital. And it would allow him to grow closer to his mother, who'd insisted he and Pete stay with her.

After he'd started working for Erin's father, Shamus O'Grady had made a habit of "checking on" Jesse, often questioning his boss about his behavior and even attempting to goad Jesse into losing his temper. After two months with little response from Jesse, the man had told him he would spend half his time in the warehouse and the other half as a collector for the same business—collecting from customers when they were past due on their payments.

Erin had been elated at the raised pay and additional responsibility, thinking Jesse might be winning her father over, but within days, Jesse understood that the purpose of the job was to try to get him to leave the shipping company on his own accord. Many of the past-due customers were difficult to deal with and often they got irate with him. It wasn't a pleasant job, but Jesse stuck it out, often using his skills at reading people from running cons to get the job done.

He was determined to win O'Grady's respect, no matter how long it took.

But after a year of proving himself, there was no hope of that happening in sight. And with the wedding tomorrow, Jesse wondered if the man wasn't making one last-ditch effort to cause trouble between him and Erin.

"What can I do for you, sir?" Jesse asked breathlessly as he moved another crate. He would be kind to the other man if it killed him. Though this "turning the other cheek" stuff was harder than he'd thought. "About time to wrap up for the day."

O'Grady nodded, smoothing the lapel of his dark suit. "I don't suppose there is anything I can offer you that will make you walk away from my daughter at this point."

Jesse shook his head, so angry it was all he could do to keep his jaw clenched shut.

"And I suppose it doesn't matter to you that she'll live in poverty compared to what she's used to. And to become an instant mother to a brat off the streets?"

Jesse bristled. It bothered him that the man didn't like him, but bringing Pete into the equation was too much.

"If you think I'm going to give you any connections with business or otherwise..."

Jesse's shoulders tightened against the man's threats. Thinking about Erin living in poorer circumstances than she was used to *did* bother him. He wanted Erin's life to be better because he was in it, not the other way around.

But she'd insisted she wouldn't miss out on what she loved—her work at the hospital and visiting with her friends.

"Her mother and I have no intention of supporting the two of you once you are married."

Ignoring O'Grady, Jesse moved to the small satchel he'd brought his lunch in, against one wall close to the other door of the warehouse. He used his sleeve to wipe sweat from his brow and told himself not to react. No doubt O'Grady wanted him to get angry, but he wouldn't.

Besides, he was going to see Erin in a few moments, something that always brightened his day.

He went to the water bucket behind the warehouse and washed off as best he could, aware that the other man watched his every move.

He'd kept a clean shirt in his satchel and he donned

it now, just as he noticed a carriage roll up the street toward the warehouse.

When O'Grady's personal conveyance pulled to a stop near the warehouse, Erin disembarked and ran to Jesse, throwing her arms around him in exuberance.

He was conscious of her father watching, but couldn't resist burying his face in her hair near her ear. He couldn't believe that tomorrow they were getting married!

He felt her stiffen and knew she must've spotted her father in the shadows near the warehouse door.

"Papa, what are you doing here?"

"I came out to check on your young man."

She pushed lightly against his chest and Jesse released her. She looked up at him questioningly. He hadn't told her about her father's workplace visits. He didn't want to cause any more trouble between Erin and Shamus than he already was.

"Your pa's been visiting me at work occasionally." He shrugged as her eyes sharpened and she guessed what the visits had been about.

Her face reddened and he knew her temper was about to spark. Was this what O'Grady wanted? Jesse didn't want Erin to say anything that she might regret later or that might cause dissention right before the wedding.

"Maybe he'd like to come with us to the hospital," Jesse blurted, his focus on Erin but his words mostly for O'Grady's benefit.

"What?" father and daughter echoed.

"You should come and see why St. Michael's matters so much to your daughter."

O'Grady grumbled something Jesse couldn't make out but he sensed the man had agreed.

When Erin questioned him with her eyes, Jesse leaned forward and reassured her softly. "We'll be married in a little more than twenty-four hours. He can't separate us now."

She continued to look doubtful, but Jesse took her hand in his and led her to the carriage, boosting her in and following her, leaving O'Grady to climb in last.

The driver already knew their destination, so they set off without delay. The sun began to wane in the sky, casting shadows between the buildings.

"I'm to understand that you usually accompany my daughter on her trips to this institution?" O'Grady asked, directing his question to Jesse. "Why?"

"Because visiting the children of St. Michael's is important to Erin," said Jesse simply.

O'Grady looked skeptical.

"Erin matters to me and those kids matter to her. Since I've been visiting, I've grown real close to a couple of the little guys."

"I'm glad you're coming, Papa," said his kindhearted Erin. "I believe the kids will win you over. I wish Pete was here. You'd see how good he is with the kids, too. He and your mother are cooking up something for the wedding tomorrow," she explained to Jesse.

They pulled up to the austere brick building. Shamus paused outside the carriage, scrutinizing it. It looked much better than it had on Jesse's first visit. Then, the grounds had been dirty and in need of paint. Some of the roof had been damaged by a previous storm.

It had changed a lot in the ensuing months. Erin had

obtained donations from her wealthy friends and convinced them to spread the word until all the repairs had been completed.

But the real difference was inside.

The front desk attendant greeted Erin and her guests warmly.

She couldn't believe the two men slightly behind her. Jesse for trying to protect her from what she assumed was her father's intimidating behavior. Or her father who couldn't seem to grasp that she and Jesse were a matched pair.

Jesse had sat through many interminable Sunday lunches with her parents and never complained. Why couldn't her parents make a similar effort?

She was surprised her father had agreed to come when he'd made his position clear many times—it made her suspicious of his motives.

But Jesse's words had calmed her. He was right. They'd learned so much about each other and come to love each other so much more these months together—there was no separating them now.

One of the doctors stopped her before she entered the dorm where most of the boys stayed. Jesse must've caught the grave look on his face the same as she had, because he moved closer and put his hand to her back.

"I'm afraid Saul passed late last night," the doctor said softly.

For a moment she couldn't understand his meaning, and then tears filled her eyes.

Jesse embraced her, his arm around her shoulders as proper and as comforting as could be in this public area with her father watching. She leaned into his comfort, clutching the book she'd brought to read to the children to her stomach. They wouldn't read it today.

She could feel the rumble of Jesse's voice as he said something to the doctor and the doctor's answer, but both were muffled as she tried to contain her grief. She knew Saul had battled the cancer valiantly and the doctors hadn't held out much hope for his survival, but he'd come to have a special place in her heart.

Jesse pressed a handkerchief into her hands with the hand not slung around her shoulders. She quickly dabbed at her eyes, working to compose herself.

"You all right?" Jesse asked, voice low.

She nodded, squeezing her eyes against another flow of tears, not because she was all right—her grief would ebb with time—but because the other children needed her. They would probably be scared and have questions.

She straightened her spine and her shoulders and Jesse moved slightly away, removing his arm. She grabbed on to his hand, because she wanted the reassurance of his touch and because she knew he would likely be hurting, too.

Taking a deep breath, she nodded to the doctor. "We'll go in now."

Aware of her father's gaze at her back, she and Jesse pushed through the doors to the dorm room, with its rows of fastidious cots.

The boys looked up, obviously expecting their visit. Each one different, some with dark hair, some light, some curly, some straight. Some with brown eyes, blue eyes, hazel eyes. Many with obvious illnesses or injuries. All eyes dark with shadows and questions this afternoon.

Erin found a tremulous smile for the nearest group of boys. With so many children, even making visits twice a week, there was little time for individual discussion, and she did the best she could by moving into the center of a grouping of six beds. Jesse followed her, stood at her side, while her father hung back.

"The doctor just told me that Saul left us last night," she said, voice cracking. These children were sharp, and if she'd tried to divert their attention to something else, they would've known it.

"I know you all must be missing him terribly." Her voice shook and she swallowed hard.

"I am," Jesse said, and she wasn't surprised at the huskiness in his voice. He laid his hand on the head of the small boy in the bed behind him and gently ruffled his hair, giving comfort.

"Miss Erin," whispered the nearest boy. "Is he…is he really in Heaven, like you said?"

She leaned over and embraced the small body in the bed. "I believe so. I really believe so."

The small boy sniffled against her shoulder. "Am I…am I gonna die, too?"

She knew he had had a spinal injury several years ago and his parents had abandoned him at a nearby orphanage. The doctors at the hospital were working to try to return some functionality to his legs. He deserved more than empty platitudes and, as most of the children in this room, was smart enough to know if she bent the truth.

She hugged him to her. "Alan, no one knows when

their time is up. I have every reason to believe you'll live a long time."

He looked up at her with wide, trusting eyes.

"And you, too, Henry," said Jesse. She saw him rest his hand on the boy's shoulder in the next bed over.

She stayed for a moment, comforting him and his buddies as well as she could, before she moved to the next group of children, murmuring the same reassurances, sharing her touch with children who reminded her of her loneliest days when all she had wanted was a hug from her mother or father.

She was half aware of her father trailing behind, though he didn't speak to the children, only watched.

As Erin neared the end of her rounds, Jesse sidled next to Shamus O'Grady so they stood shoulder to shoulder, watching her interact with the last group of small girls. One particular girl, with dark curls about her shoulders, reminded Jesse of a younger Erin.

His Erin perched on the edge of her bed, in animated conversation with the girl and several others.

Jesse hated to think of her as a child, mostly alone with only a nurse around. She was a person who thrived around others.

And yet she hadn't let those childhood injustices ruin her life.

"Sir, your daughter has an amazing heart," Jesse said softly, so she wouldn't be able to hear them.

O'Grady remained silent, and Jesse went on.

"I know you may not ever come to like me, and that I'm not exactly what you had in mind for a son-in-law, but you should really consider getting behind your daughter's work here. It would mean a lot to her."

O'Grady continued watching Erin's interactions with the small girls. "I didn't know… I didn't realize," he said. "She's comforting these children like she should've been comforted during her childhood."

"She doesn't hold it against you," Jesse told the other man, sensing a softening in him. Erin was full of mercy, full of love, and O'Grady had to know that. It was up to him to choose what to do with it.

Erin joined them a moment later, wiggling her eyebrows. "What are you two up to? I recognize at least one of those mischievous faces."

Jesse shrugged, content to let her father decide how he would react to this visit.

"Your fiancé has been talking me in to a special wedding gift," Shamus O'Grady said. It was the first time he'd acknowledged Jesse as Erin's fiancé.

"Jesse…" She smacked him on the arm playfully.

"Hey—" he said with palms out.

"I thought I might make a donation to the work you're doing here." O'Grady's words drew Erin to him and away from Jesse but he was content to let her go. "Darling, I'm sorry I didn't realize… If Jesse hadn't pushed me to come today I might never have come. Never known what this 'visiting' really means to you."

"Oh, Papa!" she cried, throwing her arms around his neck.

The older man looked at Jesse over her shoulder. "I suppose there are other things I could learn from your young man."

It was a sort of grudging acceptance, until Shamus held out his hand for Jesse to shake, one arm still wrapped around Erin.

Blessing filled Jesse's chest, making it a bit hard to breathe. "Thank you, sir," he said through a full throat.

"We'd better get home. Your brother's train was supposed to arrive this afternoon and I'll bet he and that wild wife of his have arrived."

"Jesse, you'll love getting to know Danna." Erin looped her arm through Jesse's as they made their way to the waiting coach.

And he realized he was in the company of family. At last.

* * * * *

Dear Reader,

Thank you for riding along with Erin and Jesse on their journey to finding true love. I got to do a lot of research about historical travel, but the thing that stuck with me the most was figuring out that the people who traveled back then were just like we are today—they were harried, the moms with small children were tired, people tried to bring way too much luggage. Writing this book brought back memories of Christmas trips to visit my in-laws where my husband and I were those annoying travelers bringing way too many gifts as carry-ons. If you ever have this travel experience, I hope you can find the patience to deal with people like us!

Thanks for reading and please let me know what you thought of the book. You can reach me at lacyjwilliams@gmail.com or care of Love Inspired Books, 233 Broadway, Suite 1001, New York, NY 10279.

Lacy Williams

Questions for Discussion

1. What was your first impression of Jesse Baker? Did you like or dislike him? How did your impressions of him change throughout the book?

2. What does Jesse fear most? What does he do about that fear?

3. Erin makes a rash decision to leave home. Have you ever done something impulsive like this? Did you regret the decision or did it turn out for good?

4. Erin was blessed with material wealth, but tried to always use it to help others. Have you ever been blessed in a financial way by someone else? Tell about the situation.

5. Have you ever traveled over the Christmas holidays? What was your experience like?

6. Jesse had lost someone important to him when his brother died. Have you ever lost someone important to you? How did you cope?

7. Because of similar experiences, Jesse was able to be a mentor of sorts for Pete. Have you ever mentored or been mentored by someone? What was your experience?

8. Erin is angry with her father and runs away to

avoid the situation. Have you ever avoided an uncomfortable situation? How did you resolve it?

9. Do you identify with any of the main characters in this story? In what way?

10. At the beginning of this story, Erin feels trapped by her circumstances and Jesse has just been released from prison. Have you ever been in a situation where you felt stuck? What did you do about it?

11. Jesse and Pete started out the story not being truthful about who they were. How did this affect them later on in the story? How do you think they felt about it when the truth was found out?

12. Erin tried to share the true meaning of Christmas with Jesse and Pete. How do you define Christmas?

13. Was there any part of the story you would change if you could? If so, what was it, and how would you change it?

14. What do you think Jesse and Erin learned about love?

15. What was your favorite part in this story?

COMING NEXT MONTH
from Love Inspired® Historical
AVAILABLE JANUARY 2, 2013

THE COWBOY'S SURPRISE BRIDE
Cowboys of Eden Valley
Linda Ford

Traveling to Canada to escape a dreaded marriage, Linette Edwards eagerly accepts Eddie Gardiner's written proposal. Eddie planned for a well-bred bride, and Linette is not who he expected...can they make a home together before spring?

COLORADO COURTSHIP
Cheryl St.John & Debra Ullrick

In these two heartwarming stories, two women find love in unlikely places. Violet needs a fresh start away from scandal, and Sunny wants a chance to prove herself. Will they both find the courage to trust their hearts?

BEAUTY IN DISGUISE
Mary Moore

Lady Kathryn conceals her beauty since Society will never overlook her scandalous first Season. Lord Dalton begins to fall for the mysterious young woman until he learns of her deception. Can both find hope of forgiveness?

THE MARSHAL MEETS HIS MATCH
Clari Dees

In a world of marriage-minded females, Meri McIsaac is steadfastly single. She's happiest riding horses on her ranch. At least until the town's new marshal startles her and causes her to fall—literally—at his feet.

Look for these and other Love Inspired books wherever books are sold, including most bookstores, supermarkets, discount stores and drugstores.

LIHCNM1212

Brave police officers tackle crime with the help of their canine partners in TEXAS K-9 UNIT, *an exciting new series from Love Inspired® Suspense.*

Read on for a preview of the first book, TRACKING JUSTICE by Shirlee McCoy.

Police detective Austin Black glanced at his dashboard clock as he raced up Oak Drive. Two in the morning. Not a good time to get a call about a missing child.

Then again, there was never a good time for that; never a good time to look in the worried eyes of a parent or to follow a scent trail and know that it might lead to a joyful reunion or a sorrowful goodbye.

If it led anywhere.

Sometimes trails went cold, scents were lost and the missing were never found. Austin wanted to bring them all home safe. Hopefully, this time, he would.

He pulled into the driveway of a small house.

Justice whined. A three-year-old bloodhound, he was trained in search and rescue and knew when it was time to work.

Austin jumped out of the vehicle when a woman darted out the front door. “You called about a missing child?”

“Yes. My son. I heard Brady call for me, and when I walked into his room, he was gone.” She ran back up the porch stairs.

Austin jogged in after her. She waved from a doorway. “This is my son’s room.”

SHLISEXP1212

Austin followed her into the room. "How old is your son, Ms....?"

"Billows. Eva. He's seven."

"Did you argue?"

"We didn't argue about anything, Officer..."

"Detective Austin Black. I'm with Sagebrush Police Department's Special Operation K-9 Unit."

"You have a search dog with you?" Her face brightened. "I can give you something of his. A shirt or—"

"Hold on. I need to get a little more information first."

"How about you start out there?" She gestured to the window.

"Was it open when you came in the room?"

"Yes. It looks like someone carried Brady out the window. But I don't know how anyone could have gotten into his room when all the doors and windows were locked."

"You're sure?"

"Of course." She frowned. "I always double-check. I have ever since..."

"What?"

"Nothing that matters. I just need to find my son."

Hiding something?

"Everything matters when a child is missing, Eva."

To see Justice the bloodhound in action, pick up TRACKING JUSTICE by Shirlee McCoy. Available January 2013 from Love Inspired® Suspense.

SHLISEXP1212